of Special Importance to our American Readers

The Case of the
24 MISSING TITLES ...

Over the years many of our American readers have been distressed that Harlequin Romances were published in Canada three months ahead of the United States release date.

We are pleased to announce that effective April 1972 Harlequin Romances will have simultaneous publication of new titles throughout North America.

To solve the problem of the 24 MISSING TITLES (No. 1553 to No. 1576) arrangements will be made with many Harlequin Romance retailers to have these missing titles available to you before the end of 1972.

Watch for your retailer's special display!

If, however, you have difficulty obtaining any of the missing titles, please write us.

Yours truly,

The Publisher
HARLEQUIN ROMANCES.

WELCOME

TO THE WONDERFUL WORLD

of Harlequin Romances!

Interesting, informative and entertaining,
each Harlequin Romance portrays an appealing
love story. Harlequin Romances take you
to faraway places — places with real people
facing real love situations — and
you become part of their story.

As publishers of Harlequin Romances, we're extremely
proud of our books (we've been publishing
them since 1954). We're proud also that Harlequin
Romances are North America's most-read
paperback romances.

Eight new titles are released every month and are
sold at nearly all book-selling stores across
Canada and the United States.

A free catalogue listing all available Harlequin Romances
can be yours by writing to the

HARLEQUIN READER SERVICE,
M.P.O. Box 707, Niagara Falls, N.Y. 14302.
Canadian address: Stratford, Ontario, Canada.

or use order coupon at back of book.

We sincerely hope you enjoy reading
this Harlequin Romance.

Yours truly,

THE PUBLISHERS
Harlequin Romances

THE GIRL FROM OVER THE SEA

by

VALERIE K. NELSON

HARLEQUIN BOOKS

TORONTO
WINNIPEG

Original hard cover edition published in 1972
by Mills & Boon Limited, 17 - 19 Foley Street,
London W1A 1DR, England

© Valerie K. Nelson 1972

Harlequin edition published May, 1972

SBN 373-01590-9

Printed in Canada

CHAPTER I

'Les, you've got to let me drive. I might never have the chance again . . . in snow.' The boyish voice had a pronounced Australian accent.

Lesley's mouth curved into laughter. 'Darling Rick, if you're going to live in Britain, you'll have ample opportunity of doing that! As far as I understand, it snows here more or less all the time from November to about April.'

'But, Les . . .' This third voice, a girl's, was rather doleful. It came from Richard's twin, crouching in the back seat of the Mini and muffled up to her eyes. 'I thought you said it was warmer down here in Cornwall and they didn't get snow. Didn't you tell us something about the Riviera? That's in the south of France and it's lovely and warm there.'

'Yes, I did read something about the Cornish Riviera where there are palm trees and gums—eucalyptus, they call them here. But this may be a bad spell of weather. After all, we know all about bad spells in Lactatoo, New South Wales, don't we?'

'We do, and we know they get snow in the Australian Alps, but the point is we never got it at Lactatoo,' the boy beside her replied, 'and they might never get it again here this winter. I did some homework, too, Les, and the book said Cornwall had very mild winters. So let me take over, just for kicks, there's a mate.'

'There'll be next winter,' Lesley parried, peering ahead. She could have done without this sort of weather, she was reflecting. Perhaps they should have stayed somewhere over night, but the distance had seemed ridiculously small by Australian standards. What she hadn't anticipated was the amount of traffic on the roads and the fact that this Mini, though it was a nippy little car, wasn't in its first youth, and needed a lot of nursing, especially as it was overloaded and in view of the wicked weather conditions they'd run into after leaving London.

'Better let me keep the wheel, Rick,' she said quietly. 'We're off the main road now and I'm not too sure of the way. The brakes are a bit tricky. I'm used to them now,

5

but you won't be.'

'Listen to Grannie again!' said the girl at the back of the car in a high, scornful voice. 'Rick's as good a driver as you are, Les, and you know it.'

'But he hasn't got a driving licence and I have,' interposed Lesley, peering again through the gloom and the snow driving against the windscreen. If the wipers gave up . . .

'As if having a licence would matter down here in this godforsaken spot! We haven't seen another car for miles.'

Lesley bit her lower lip. She had thought they would reach St Benga Town, the little Cornish seaside spot where they'd booked rooms before it was dark. But it was a murky day, and they'd lost time directly they'd got off the main road. Had she taken a wrong turning somewhere?

Her green eyes were narrowed as she peered again through the windscreen. Rick was supposed to be navigating, but while they had been on the main roads directions had been so clear that he had given up long ago.

She didn't really want to stop to look at the map. The twins were tired and hungry and becoming belligerent. She slowed down on a level bit of road. They weren't likely to meet anyone tonight who would demand to look at driving licences. Rick wasn't quite seventeen, but he had been driving since he was ten in the Outback and he handled cars like a veteran. If she let him drive for a mile or two she could study the map and try to find out how far they were from their destination. The last two signposts hadn't mentioned St Benga Town, but she had noted the names, so she should be able to spot where they now were.

'All right, Rick,' she said crisply, 'stand up and I'll slide over into your seat.' They were both slender and lithe and the manœuvre was accomplished in the minimum of time.

'Take it easy—this sleet stuff is treacherous,' she advised. 'We don't want to go too far on what may be the wrong road. I suppose we'd better put the lights on.'

'Lighting up time isn't till seventeen hours something,' chimed in Rita. 'I noticed it in that newspaper I was looking at when we stopped for lunch.'

Lesley picked up her map. 'Where's the torch? Oh, thanks. . . .' Her voice suddenly rose to sharpened protest. 'Rick, don't be an idiot! You can't go at this speed on a narrow lane. I . . .'

The next words died into a strangled silence as the little car shot on to cross lanes right into the blinding headlights of a big black monster. It seemed as if nothing could prevent their being struck and mangled, but by some miracle the other driver wrenched his car out of their way and it spun into a sickening skid behind them and out of their view. Instinctively Rick braked much too hard on that surface and the Mini too went into a skid which landed them into a gateway which fortunately made a gap in the high bank of the lane into which they had careered.

Lesley wrenched at the door on her side and staggered out, the torch still in her hand. She felt dazed with shock, but the keen biting wind made her take deep breaths and in a moment or two she was all right. To her relief she saw that Rick had moved over to her seat and was now struggling to get out.

'Can't open the door my side—too near the gate,' he gasped.

She helped him out. 'Are you all right?' she asked.

He nodded and Lesley turned to look in the back of the car where Rita, clutching her dog, was blinking in the light of the torch. 'All right, Rita?' Lesley asked.

The girl twin's voice was angry. 'If we are, Dingo and me, it's no thanks to that speed maniac. You *told* him, Les. . . .'

'Shut up!' Lesley spoke between her teeth. 'Remember, *I* was driving. We don't want to find ourselves in jail. Now I'm going to see what's happened to the other car. Remember, though, whatever has happened or what anybody says, *I* was driving.'

Rick said nothing. In the half-light, she could see his young, sensitive face was pale and stricken. Feeling sick with apprehension herself, she flickered the light of the torch forward towards the crossing, her thin shoes squelching in the slush and mud. Why, oh, why had she come to this benighted country? she wondered in despair.

A tall figure, almost giant-like in outline, suddenly loomed up in front of her and a torch played on her face, dazzling her. 'Are you all right?' she asked breathlessly. 'My car skidded. I . . . I just couldn't hold it.'

She had moved out of the torch light, but he flicked it over her again for what seemed a long, long moment. · It was as .if he was imprinting on· his memory her pale face with its wide-set green eyes and its soft and generous mouth.

But he was in no way softened by what he had seen. 'A damned good job it did skid,' he said brutally, 'or you wouldn't be standing here now. You must be crazy to drive over a crossroads at that speed and without lights. You've a passenger, I see. Then there are three of us·who could have been·killed. You stupid, stupid little fool! People like you should never be allowed on the roads!'

'Are you . . . is anyone hurt?' Lesley managed to stammer out the question.

'No, but no thanks to you,' he returned savagely. 'My car doesn't seem to be damaged either, again no thanks to you.'

Lesley took a deep breath that was her expression of thankfulness that things were no worse. She wasn't, she decided, going to eat any more humble pie to this bad-tempered, arrogant man. Maybe he had had a nasty shock, but that was no excuse for bullying her.

She said, in a frosty voice, 'Look, mister, if you're not hurt and your car's not damaged, why don't you get going? Then I·could get out of this wind and snow and do exactly the same. Get me?'

'I ought to report you to the nearest police station for dangerous driving,' he told her, his voice still menacing.

'You were coming at ·a pretty fair speed yourself,' she retorted. 'As *we* don't seem to be damaged, and *you* don't, I suggest we both forget it and get going.'

'Pretty sure of yourself, aren't you, madam?' he commented in a manner that matched the north-easter whistling round their ears.

Lesley gave an exasperated sigh. 'I'm anxious to get on. Take our number if you're so inclined. Our name is Trevendone and our address . . .' she hesitated for a few seconds and then finished grandly, '. . . is Trevendone Manor. And now goodnight.'

'Goodnight,' repeated the tall man in a stunned voice. 'Trevendone Manor!'

And that's put him in his place, thought Lesley on a moment of exhilaration. She turned to go back to the Mini and as she opened the door, she heard him shout, 'If you're making for Trevendone Manor . . . or the village . . . you'll need to reverse and then turn left. But let me get going first. I shall feel safer.'

'Sauce!' Rita who was hanging out of the back window muttered. 'Who does he think he is? These Limeys! I thought they were all such gents.'

'This one's an ill-mannered bully,' Lesley admitted, still feeling ruffled. 'All right, Rick?' She had clambered into the driver's seat via the passenger seat into which the boy now flung himself.

'Of course I'm all right,' he said moodily, but he didn't ask to take the wheel again, for which Lesley was thankful.

'Let me look at the map,' she said now. 'I'm not going to trust that creature's directions.' She settled more comfortably into the driver's seat and reached for the map, staring at it intently. 'I think we must be on this lane. In which case he's right. We go left from here and then we're not so far away from St Benga Town. Thank goodness. The snow seems to be getting thicker.'

Richard and Rita were expressing their opinion of the tall man in no uncertain manner, but Lesley said nothing. She stared in front of her looking worried. Would he report that near accident as he had threatened? Oh well, not to worry, she advised herself. Her dark-faced adversary had got himself out of his ditch all right and was just driving slowly over the crossing, so now she could reverse into the other road and follow him. But not for long, she hoped.

'Did he mention how far it was?' Rita groaned now. 'I'm frozen, and so is Dingo.'

'*He* was born here, so he should be used to the vile weather, or ought to be,' grunted Richard provocatively.

'To think if we'd gone to Sydney with Steve instead of coming here we might this very minute be riding one of the Bondi boomers,' Rita said now.

'You wouldn't ride a Bondi boomer until you're much more experienced in surfing than you are yet,' Ricky scoffed. 'Do you know, on a real boomer, you can be carried twenty yards to the beach. Oh boy!'

'Neither of you would be surfing just at this moment—not at three a.m. Sydney time,' Lesley put in prosaically. 'As to

9

surfing, there are some fine beaches here, or so I've read.'

'But nothing like Bondi or Manly,' said Rita scornfully. 'They'll be mini ones, you can bet, like their cars.'

'How do you know when you haven't even seen them? If members of the Sydney Surfing and Life-Saving Association are coming over here this summer to give exhibitions the beaches can't be so bad. Steve's coming, isn't he, Les?'

'So he said,' Lesley agreed.

The twins now plunged into another noisy argument to which Lesley tried to shut her ears. They were tired and cold and you couldn't blame them for being fractious. Her lips twitched at the thought. Odd how she always thought of these two as if they were babes in arms. For that matter, in many ways so they were.

She drove on steadily, silently thankful that Rick wasn't pestering her again to drive. What could have possessed her to let him do so earlier on? If they had had a real crash she wouldn't have been able to hide the fact that he was behind the wheel. Though they'd probably all have been killed as that man had said. His great juggernaut of a car would have pulped them. He had a car that matched his personality, she reflected.

They were quite high up now, and if it had been light and clear, they perhaps would have been able to see the coast. Lights were visible and they must be those of St Benga Town. In a few minutes they ought to be at the King's Arms where Lesley had booked rooms for two nights. That was the address she ought to have given the dark stranger—not Trevendone Manor—not yet.

The twins had thought it unnecessarily wasteful to book at a hotel, but Lesley had said thoughtfully, 'It will give us time to survey the land and have a look-see. We might be able to pick up some local gossip about the Trevendones and about the Manor.'

They were warmly received by the hotel-keeper and his wife. 'What a night!' Mrs Cleaver exclaimed. 'M'dear souls, you'm be frozen. But the rooms are nice and warm. We had they night storage heaters put in last year and a might of difference they've made. Let me take you up, m'dears, and then when you'm tidied up you can come down for a bite of supper.'

They followed her upstairs. The hotel looked old, but it had been covered in white paint which no doubt was an asset so far as light was concerned but did not give an effect of cosiness. Lesley, who had visualised a Dickensian type of hostelry with oak beams and rafters, was frankly disappointed.

Nor did the supper come up to her expectations. Cold boiled ham and salad was a poor substitute for that huge steaming bowl of soup she had imagined or that sirloin of juicy beef carved by their host, their plates piled high with lovely fresh vegetables.

So much for Mrs Travers who had lived near them at Lacta-too and had once spent a year in Britain. She had told them that one of the places where they would find the real ye olde England, especially out of the holiday season, was Cornwall. She evidently hadn't stayed at the King's Arms in St Benga Town. Still, there was a roaring fire in the hotel lounge and after they had eaten the three sat sleepily watching it. But soon Lesley decided they would all be better for an early night and for once the twins raised no protest. Lesley and Rita were sharing a two-bedded room and Rick had been given a smaller one at the end of the corridor. The rooms were tolerably warm and there were hot water bottles in the three beds. So with very little in the way of conversation they undressed and crept between the brushed nylon sheets where the twins were soon asleep.

But Lesley tossed and turned and slept only fitfully. She was too tired, she supposed, and had too much on her mind. When she finally slept she dreamed about the hot dry country they had left so recently; about the snow which they had seen for the first time today and about that ogre of a man who in her dreams seemed to be pursuing her in a big black monster of a car through narrow lanes. In the end she had to turn, cornered, and he gripped her shoulders and said harshly, 'You're a liar and a cheat, Lesley Arden.'

She woke up cold and shivering, wondering how he knew she was Lesley Arden and not Lesley Trevendone. But she had been dreaming. She clutched her hot water bottle, but it had cooled and gave her very little comfort. Oh, for that warm sunshine back home!

She crept out of bed and went to the window. Sleep seemed very far away now and she wondered how long it would be before she could get up. She wished she hadn't had that stupid dream and that she could forget that near-accident last evening.

One couldn't really blame the man for being angry. Rick had been going much too fast, but *she* was the real culprit for letting him drive at all. After all, he was only sixteen, though he had handled the old Hudson on the station at Lactatoo ever since he was ten. Still, a remote sheep station in Lactatoo New South Wales wasn't England.

The man couldn't have seen who was really driving or he would have confronted Rick. Yet he had made that deliberate pause when he had first looked at her in the light of his torch.

Lesley shivered with something that wasn't the chill of the bedroom. She pushed the curtains aside. There were yellow street lamps making queer topaz flowers in the dark. There was a wind howling rather eerily and the angry roar of a storm-racked sea.

As Rita had said, it was a far cry from Bondi Beach in Australia. Had she been wise in bringing the twins here? But she had promised Margaret Trevendone she would do so, and it was too late to back out now. It was pointless to look back.

But even so, her thoughts *were* going back, at least as far as yesterday. That man! Had he really been so tall and broad, or was it her imagination that was painting him as a giant, the ogre of a fairy tale?

Would he report them to the nearest police station? She had told him their name, given him an address. Again Lesley found herself regretting that last bit of bravado. He didn't seem the sort of man to let anybody get off lightly. He certainly wasn't the courteous kindly Englishman one sometimes read about—the 'gent' of whom Rita had spoken. Far from it. That strong line of jaw revealed in the light of her torch, that hardbitten expression reminded Lesley far more of a forthright Aussie rather than one of those effete Englishmen. But this was Cornwall, and people said the Cornish were different—they were Celts. When you crossed the Tamar you were in a foreign country . . . or so they said.

Lesley shivered and let the curtain drop. She crept back into the bed which now seemed warm after the cold air by the window and the damp sleet outside. She curled up into a tight ball under the thin eiderdown and soon she was asleep.

It was still dark when she woke again. Winter nights were so long in Britain, the days so short. Not that February was winter, surely. She thought again about that neighbour Mrs Travers who had told her about Cornwall. 'Spring comes early down there. You'll find snowdrops and violets there when the rest of the country is covered in snow.' The climate must have changed since Mrs Travers' time, thought Lesley wryly.

She lay brooding on this until she saw that it was getting light. She crept cautiously out of bed and went to the window. There was no sea view, but beyond the grey roofs of the little town she could see smooth green downs, white-walled farms with wind-bent trees around them and further away a valley where there were more trees all in a long line, leaning landwards like men carrying heavy burdens from the coast. The snow had miraculously disappeared and all the land was green, so very very green to Australian Lesley's eyes. The sun coming up over a hill sent out light that glistened on the grass and the trees and the nearby rooftops.

It's going to be a glorious day, thought Lesley, her spirits rising. She found the bathroom, had a quick shower, dried herself vigorously till her body tingled and went back to the bedroom where Rita was just opening sleepy sea-blue eyes. 'Bag the bathroom right now, darling,' Lesley advised. 'Be quick and then I'll give Rick a shout.'

'Are we going to that Manor place first thing?' Rita demanded.

'No. As I've said before we'll take a look round first and see what information we can pick up about the Trevendones. The village and the Manor are three or four miles from here.'

'Oh, it's madly exciting. I can't wait!' Rita squealed in a mocking fashion.

Lesley gave her a quick warning look. 'Pipe down, for pete's sake, Rita,' she expostulated. 'We don't want to get a reputation as loudmouthed brash Aussies before we've been here five minutes.'

'Nobody can tell you're an Aussie,' Rita pointed out. 'It was a pity Ma couldn't afford to send Rick and me to a fancy school in Melbourne instead of letting us be "educated"

Lactatoo style.'

Lesley bit her lip. That reproach had been hurled at her more than once during the past few months and it was hard for her to explain that the money for her education had come from her parents and not theirs. She said now, lamely, 'Neither of you liked school, and if you'd gone away you would have missed Rick and he you.'

'Too right. Even now I keep thinking of dear old Lactatoo and wishing we were back.' Rita shivered. 'Is the snow very deep?'

Lesley pulled back the curtains. 'It's all gone and now it promises to be a marvellous day. Do hurry, Rita. I'm going to wake Rick and then rush down to look at the sea. I'll tell Mrs Cleaver we want breakfast in half an hour.'

She dressed quickly, pulling on a thick skirt and sweater of a green that matched her eyes. A few quick tugs with her comb through her bright, nearly chestnut hair and now her leather coat with a green scarf if she needed it.

Downstairs she asked for breakfast to be served in half an hour and then went out into the narrow high street which ran steeply down to the sea and to the little inner harbour where a few small boats were drawn up above the tide line. St Benga Town wasn't a place for fishing. The coast was too cruel, the seas too stormy. On either side the downs rose green and inviting, and between them was a long stretch of sand ribbed with rocks and pools from which the sea, curling lazily into white wavelets this morning, was receding. When the tide was really out they would be able to walk right along the beach, perhaps beyond that headland that loomed dark against the pale blue sky. Beyond that headland was Trevendone.

Lesley took a deep delighted breath. Above her the gulls mewed as they swooped and soared. This air was wonderful. She could smell the seaweed and with it the real tang of the ocean. That wind that she had heard in the night had gone now and there was scarcely a breeze though St Benga had the reputation of being a windy little town.

First thing they would walk over the downs, or perhaps along the beach to Trevendone Bay and look at the Manor House. The sooner the twins discovered what they could about their future home the sooner she could get them settled.

Neither was down when she arrived back at the little hotel,

pub it was really, but clean, and breakfast promised, if savoury aromas were anything to go by, better than last night's cold offering.

Lesley ran up the steep stairs two at a time and found Rita dressed and fiddling with her long black hair. It was naturally curly, a disadvantage to her mind as she admired the girls with long lank hair that she had seen on television.

'Come on, Rita,' Lesley urged. 'It's marvellous out, and the air is like wine. I'm so hungry I could even eat porridge if . . .'

'Oh, don't!' Rita's face was screwed up in revolted horror. 'I feel terrible. I've scarcely slept at all. I was so cold, cold,' and she shivered theatrically.

'Darling, were you? Why didn't you wake me?' Lesley's green eyes were anxious. She hoped a sleepless night would not bring on one of Rita's migraines. 'Have you a head-ache?'

Rita examined her reflection in the mirror. She had a high colour and wished disconsolately for a skin of the creamy pallor of Lesley's. Red-haired girls had everything, she thought. But still, *she* was supposed to have the Cornish looks of her family, the dark hair and the vivid sea blue eyes and the good, healthy colour.

'It hasn't come on yet,' she admitted, 'but it will if you start talking about porridge.'

'Then I'll talk about bacon and eggs,' Lesley said.

Rita groaned. 'You're a mystery to me, Les. You look —what's the word?—ethereal—with that creamy skin and those enormous eyes. You're as slim as can be and yet you eat like a horse, you're as tough as old boots and you're as full of energy as a spring-mad dingo.'

'Your comparisons aren't very flattering,' Lesley grimaced. 'I must get Richard down or there'll be no breakfast for either of you.'

Rick was still in bed, not asleep but having, as he explained, a nice daydream. Lesley gave him a shake. 'Rick, we've got so much to see and do today. Hurry!'

She was worrying again, this time about the way Richard could, and did, stay up half the night but could never be per-suaded to get up in the morning. It wasn't only these cold winter mornings in Britain. He'd been the same back home.

If he were going to work on the land, learn to manage an estate, he'd have to do better than this. But she mustn't start lecturing him or he'd become resentful and uncooperative, and she'd got to make both Rita and him see that what she was doing was for the best.

'Rick darling, hurry,' she coaxed. 'I told Mrs Cleaver we'd be ready for breakfast five minutes ago. I'll go and placate her.'

Rick gave her his charming, lazy smile. 'Poor old Les! I wonder you bother. Your obligation to the Trevendone family for looking after you when you were an orphan should have finished when Ma died. Now you ought to leave us to follow our own thing and look after yourself. It's time you started thinking seriously about your love life.'

Lesley's green eyes danced. 'We'll get this business of Trevendone Manor settled first. Then there'll be time for me to fall in love.'

'There's not all that time,' he retorted, his brilliant eyes suddenly very shrewd. 'Girls get married very early now. And back in Sydney a certain Steve Wentworth is very popular with the dolly birds.'

'So he is,' Lesley admitted, ruffling his dark hair. 'I wish you'd get some of this cut off, though. I want you and Rita to make a good impression tomorrow.'

'You'll be the one to make the impression, Miss Copper Head,' he said with a grin. 'Do you think there was a redhead among those Camelot people, King Arthur and those knights and dames of his?'

'Queen Guinevere, perhaps,' Lesley laughed. 'But she wasn't a very likeable character, married to Arthur and carrying on with Lancelot. Hurry, darling. I'll go and chat up Mrs Cleaver.'

She ran down the two flights of stairs and saw their hostess carrying in three dishes of tinned grapefruit. 'What a lovely morning, Mrs Cleaver,' she said cheerfully.

'Too bright too early,' the other warned.

'You should know. Have you lived here always, Mrs Cleaver? You're Cornish, of course.'

'Yes, I be,' her hostess replied with natural pride.

'You'll have guessed that er . . . we . . . my . . . brother and sister are Cornish too.'

The other stared at her impassively. '*You* sound like most of they folk who come from London, miss, but the young lady and gentleman I'd have taken for Australians.'

Lesley remembered Richard saying last night that they had come from Australia, so that wasn't even an inspired guess. What she'd been fishing for was a comment on their name and its local connection.

'You'd better start, miss. The bacon and egg will be ready in a minute.'

Lesley sat down, spooning her tinned grapefruit and wrinkling her nose slightly. Perhaps it was stupid to expect as much fresh fruit here as in Australia. And now Mrs Cleaver was back, carrying a plate piled high. 'You did say only one egg, miss. You're welcome to two if you can eat 'un. I know you're used to big breakfasts over there.'

Lesley told her hastily that one egg would be sufficient. She had ordered this cooked breakfast for herself only to encourage the twins to follow her example.

Rita now appeared and began to eat her grapefruit in a lethargic manner. 'Do try to eat most of your egg and bacon, Rita,' Lesley urged. 'In this cold climate we all need more cooked food. Mrs Cleaver seems to think, though, that all Australians eat steak or chops at breakfast time.'

Rita grimaced, but made no remark when Mrs Cleaver came in with two plates which she set down in front of the girl and in the boy's place. 'Could you keep Rick's warm for a few minutes, Mrs Cleaver?' Lesley asked, getting up. 'I'll give him another call.'

'You sit down, m'dear,' advised the stout woman. 'You'm told that young man to come down once. Now let 'un bide. Young men shouldn't be run after by their womenfolk. It makes 'un bad husbands, so it do.'

'Rick is only a boy,' Lesley protested.

'As the twig's bent, so it grows, m'dear. It never pays for a pretty young 'ooman to run after a man, m'dear. Let 'un do the running. I'll keep his plate warm, just for this time.'

She picked up Rick's breakfast and marched out, leaving Lesley rather disconcerted and Rita giggling. 'Do stop it, Rita. She'll hear you.'

Rita, who was a good mimic, raised a finger. 'Just remember that, Lesley Trevendone, m'dear. It never pays a pretty young 'ooman to run after a young man.'

Lesley sat down. 'Rick is the limit,' she sighed.

'Stop worrying about 'un, m'dear.' Rita obviously found the Cornish accent fascinating, and Lesley was pleased. She was desperately anxious for the twins to feel at home in Cornwall.

The sun was still shining when they set off to walk down the High Street, though less brightly than when Lesley had been out before breakfast, and the wind seemed to have got up.

'Let's step out,' she suggested. 'I don't know how far it is to Trevendone and we've got to get back here for lunch.'

Rita and Rick were only too willing. The wind was too cold for any loitering. 'I guess we'll be having some more of that snow,' Rick said as, having reached the harbour, they started up the steep cliff path.

Lesley shook her head. 'Mrs Cleaver says not.'

'Cheers for that,' Rita muttered, shivering. 'I'd never have come if I'd realised the weather was going to be like this.'

'It will improve. February can sometimes be a very mild month down here, Mrs Cleaver says, and you can often find violets and primroses in sheltered spots, just as old Mrs Travers told us. This year, though, they've had a cold rainy winter.'

'You can say that again!' groaned Rita, continuing to shiver.

Lesley gave her a quick anxious look. Suppose the twins weren't able to stand the British climate? Then she advised herself to stop worrying. She had been brought up in Australia and the weather wasn't causing her all that discomfort, so once Rita and Rick became acclimatised they would be all right.

They were on top of the downs now with a view along the coast both ways. From where they stood they could discern only the jutting promontories and the great toothed black rocks, with the sea a dull turquoise colour lashing angrily against them. They moved nearer to the edge of the cliff and a wide stretch of sand became visible broken by great whale-black projections of black and grey slate. White horses were leaping across the heaving mass of turquoise water as far out as the eye could see.

Lesley took a deep breath. 'It's just out of this world,'

she said enthusiastically.

Rick nodded. 'It's got something,' he admitted reluctantly, but his sister shivered again. 'It's cold, cold. Give me Bondi Beach any day,' she muttered.

The wind was certainly colder than Lesley had thought. She turned to look away from the sea. Trevendone village and Manor must be somewhere on their right behind that clump of trees in the far distance. She changed her mind about going there this morning. It was too far.

'Let's go down on the beach,' she suggested now. 'We might get more shelter from this east wind and we can walk quite a distance on the sands now the tide is out.'

'Goodo,' said Rick. 'Anywhere where it's warmer. Rita, your face is blue and your nose is like a little red button.'

'You don't look all that glamorous yourself,' his sister retorted.

'Stop being childish, both of you,' Lesley ordered. 'Come on, there must be a way down, but don't go too near the cliff edge.'

The twins followed her glumly, but she was glad they had stopped quarrelling. The sooner she got them to Trevendone Manor with their own people, the better.

The descent to the beach wasn't easy, but the two were sure-footed, though Lesley, who had no head for heights, followed them more slowly, sighing with relief when she reached the bottom.

'You look pretty green now, Les,' the boy said critically. 'I still have the feeling that the lot of us might have been better staying put in New South Wales.'

'We couldn't. Do I have to remind you?' Lesley asked shortly. 'Where's Dingo?'

'He's in the top class of the climbing school,' Rick chuckled. 'Didn't you see him scooting down that path—if you can call it that. He was down ages before Rita and me.'

'You said it would be warmer down here,' complained Rita. 'Ugh, this wind!'

It was cold, but Lesley wasn't going to admit it. 'Let's have a race along the beach,' she suggested. 'This afternoon, we'll go for a run to Trevendone. I'm disappointed we couldn't see it from the cliffs just now. It must be beyond that headland which the sea is just clearing. Let's go!'

She began to run with quick lithe steps across the sands. The twins might have the edge on her when it came to heights, but not on the level. She threw them a backward glance. 'Come on!' she exhorted, racing towards the sea.

Rick caught the excitement, gave a shout to which his twin responded with a shrill scream and they raced after the older girl. The occasion was too much for the mongrel pup, Dingo. He too took up the chase, barking hysterically as they all ran first to the edge of the waves and then towards the rocky point where a sandy passage had just been uncovered by the retreating tide.

Now Lesley paused to let the twins catch up with her; the dog leaping at each one in turn and still barking. 'Stop it, yellow dog!' Rick commanded, and threw a pebble towards the sea.

'Don't encourage him to get wet,' Lesley warned, 'or we shall have a real performance drying him.'

Dingo, who didn't have a great deal of sense, had enough to pretend to hurl himself after the stone but come to a sudden halt directly his feet began to get wet.

For a few minutes they walked along soberly and then as the wind whipped around them again, Leslie said, 'Look, we'll just run to the point and turn back. I'll give you a start and race you.'

The twins could never resist a challenge and in a second they were away with shouts and screams, the dog Dingo barking madly first at their rear and then well ahead of them as Lesley caught up and passed them.

Now, like the dog, she felt intoxicated with the keen air and her own throbbing vitality. The twins were pounding behind, wasting breath and energy with their screams and shouts, which maddened the excited puppy even more.

And so they arrived at the sandy passage between the rocks and the waves just at the moment when a rider came from the beach at the other side. Fortunately his horse was doing no more than a slow canter and Lesley, who was well ahead of the others, was able to avoid the collision by running into the shallow water receding from the point. She turned, her heart thudding clamorously, to see that the horseman had managed to swerve round the shrieking twins and was reining in. And then Dingo, who had fallen back a few yards to examine a rock pool, suddenly raced forward, barking hysterically and snapping at the horse's hooves.

The animal reared and Lesley clenched her hands, believing the rider unseated. But he held on as the next moment the horse seemed to take further fright and bolted across the beach, Dingo in pursuit.

Lesley's hands were clenched. No, no, no! her thudding heart protested. She was being a fool, seeing what wasn't true. A likeness, perhaps, but nothing more.

CHAPTER II

Ricky, who had at first seemed as shocked as Lesley by the suddenness of the encounter now started to shout encouragement to the puppy. 'Seize him, Dingo! Seize him!'

'Rick, stop that at once!' Lesley called in a horrified voice. 'Are you out of your tiny mind?' She began to run back along the sands, calling and whistling to the puppy. But they had had Dingo too short a time to give him any training and he had chosen Rick as his master and was inclined to ignore Rita and Lesley.

It was perhaps because Rick didn't follow that Dingo suddenly lost interest and came loping back, his tongue hanging out, a silly grin on his face. Lesley scowled at him and managed to grab his collar. 'Don't look as if you've done something clever,' she gasped. 'You bird-brained tyke! You'll stay on the lead after this, see if you don't!'

She dragged him back to the twins and put him securely on the lead. Then almost shrinkingly she looked along the beach to where the horseman had reined in the runaway. Thank goodness he hadn't been thrown!

'You two go right back to the edge of the cliffs and take that silly dog with you,' she ordered crisply. 'I'll have to go and apologise.'

Rather subdued, the twins stared at her and Rick said quietly, 'I'll go. Dingo belongs to Rita and me. *You* said all the time better not to take him when that woman offered him to us.'

Lesley made a gesture. 'Don't let's bother about that now. I'll catch you up.'

With hands that were clenched tightly and thrust deeply into her pockets she hurried along the beach towards the man, who had now dismounted and was walking his animal back. As she drew nearer she realised he was talking to it gently, almost like a lover. It was a beautiful animal, a black mare, obviously highly bred and temperamental.

Even now, she told herself, there was a chance that she was mistaken. After all she had seen him only briefly in the light of her torch and then in the half light of yesterday evening.

His build was similar, but . . .

Lesley stood stock still, an unreasoning panic taking her by the throat. No good trying any longer to think she had been mistaken. He was all too familiar, this tall broad-shouldered figure. He had printed himself indelibly on her memory and last night he had haunted her dreams.

He came towards her, level black brows drawn together, that same formidable expression she remembered so well. It chilled her now far more than the bitter north-easter which was blowing her skirt around her slender body and whipping strands of her burnished hair across a face which had drained of colour.

Her first appalled surmise had been only too right. It was the driver of the car with whom Rick had almost collided last night. And if he had decided to be lenient about that, this second encounter would prejudice him into action. What hope now that he wouldn't report them to the police? What would happen if it was discovered that Rick had been driving?

The man stared at her without speaking, his dark face impassive, his eyes quite cold. They were grey in colour, dark as thunder over a pewter sea. Because he had said nothing, Lesley rushed into speech, hoping that he hadn't recognised her. After all, last night he hadn't seen Rita or the dog. 'I'm sorry about the puppy,' she said simply. 'We were all running on the sand to get warm and you came so suddenly from behind the rocks. Is your horse all right?'

'As it happens we're both all right. Actually you and your companions are the lucky ones. Are you members of a suicide club?'

Lesley's hope that he hadn't recognised her died a quick death. 'You mean last night and now,' she said stiffly. 'We're strangers here, you see, and we didn't expect riders on the beach.'

'We've no objection to strangers visiting our beaches and countryside,' he said, giving her a hard, expressionless stare, 'just as long as the dogs they bring know how to behave. Here's a warning, young woman. If that dog chases after hares it will also go after sheep and cattle. This is the lambing season and a farmer may shoot a dog not under proper control.'

It was the 'young woman' that touched Lesley on the raw.

23

Her cheeks flamed. 'You might at least have had the decency to accept my apology!' she stormed, her green eyes blazing with indignation. 'After all, I wasn't forced to come after you and say I was sorry.'

'It's too late to be sorry when you've done dam'fool tricks,' he said in angry contempt. 'Twice you've been a real menace to me. I hope I haven't to put up with a third encounter. It makes life too risky.'

'You needn't worry,' Lesley choked. 'If it's left to me there'll certainly be no third encounter. I shall lose no sleep if I never see you again!' With colour flaming in her cheeks and her eyes glittering, she turned and ran quickly across the sands to where the twins were waiting.

'What did he say?' asked Rita curiously.

Lesley's lips set in a straight line. 'He was beastly sarcastic,' she said between her teeth. 'A Limey at his most sardonic, superior worst. You recognised him, I suppose?'

Rick nodded. 'I got a good look at him as he avoided Rita. It was the fellow we nearly knocked for six last night, wasn't it? Did he recognise you?'

Lesley nodded and he went on, 'A pity you went after him.'

She said grimly, 'He called me a menace and several other uncomplimentary things. But, Rick, we'll have to keep Dingo on a lead or we'll be in real trouble.'

'I don't believe in keeping dogs on leads,' the boy said forcefully. 'At home . . .'

'. . . Rick, this isn't "home"—not in your sense of the word. At Lactatoo there were hundreds of miles of open country and dogs brought up in daily contact with sheep. Dingo isn't a sheepdog and until we've more control over him we must keep him close to us. That man warned me about him.'

'Too right, this isn't "home" and never will be for me,' put in Rita impetuously. 'Oh, Les, why did we ever come? It's so cold here.'

'Let's hurry into town and get a coffee,' Lesley urged, giving the girl a sharp, worried look, and shivering herself in the cold February wind which now had a hint of sleet or snow in it.

'We've hit a bad patch of weather just as we've twice hit on the worst inhabitant. Last night I hoped he was only a

24

traveller, but it begins to look as if he's staying round here. He isn't Cornish, I'm sure. Cornish people are much more pleasant.'

'Let's hope those at Trevendone Manor are,' Rick put in gloomily. 'Otherwise I'm off home, quick sharp.'

'Darlings, home now is Trevendone. You've got to accept that. If your father . . .'

Rita gave a theatrical shiver. 'Oh, don't let's start on that again, Les. What about that coffee?'

'Come along, then.' Lesley led the way holding Dingo firmly on the lead, though he pulled and tugged and occasionally sat down. If she left it to them, Rita and Richard would be soft-hearted and set him free, and Lesley didn't want any more 'incidents'.

Her thoughts turned again to the tall, cold-eyed, black-haired stranger and her cheeks burned. That was what so many Aussies had against the Limeys, she thought indignantly. They often looked and acted so darned superior. Though in that riding gear, he hadn't looked her idea of a Limey. In fact there was even something of the Outback about him, though he did come from this effete, demoralised, permissive England—which was how Steve Wentworth had described it when they had quarrelled about her coming here with the twins.

That man! If she were fair, she knew he was justified in his anger both last night and this morning and if he had given vent to some strong language, Australian style, she wouldn't have felt so humiliated. But that cold English voice, those icily indifferent grey eyes!

Men didn't usually look at her with that sort of expression. Not that she wanted anything different from him. But she probably wouldn't see him again.

Forget him, she advised herself.

They wound their way out of the rocky spurs which gaped like giant teeth towards the sea, eager to tear to pieces any unlucky vessel that might venture too close. It was a coastline of incomparable beauty with that silken turquoise sea and that white embroidery of surf across the silk, but underneath you sensed the fierceness and cruelty. With a little shiver, Lesley recalled those bleak eyes of the horseman. How stupid could she get, letting him intrude on her every thought!

'About that coffee,' she said quickly. 'Shall we go back to the hotel or have it in a café?'

'If the coffee at the hotel is anything like it was last night,' grunted Rick, 'I would willingly give it a miss.'

Lesley lingered for another moment to look back at the sea. The sun had disappeared and the snow or hail or sleet was coming in from the north. The turquoise or greeny-blue colour of the water had gone now, and the silken appearance. Beneath the white embroidery there was a pitiless dark grey swell, the colour of . . . a man's eyes.

She swallowed. 'Let's make for the hotel, twins,' she said quickly. 'It will be warm there.'

By lunch time Rick and Rita were obviously so bored that Lesley suggested they ignore the weather, take the Mini and explore Trevendone from the land side. However, when another snow shower came the twins turned shivering from the window.

'I'm not going out in this,' Rita said truculently. 'We could get stuck in one of those lanes and have to walk back. I left my snowboots back home.'

Rita had never possessed a pair of snowboots in her life, so Lesley ignored this pleasantry. Again she gave the younger girl a quick glance, concealing her anxiety behind her long dark lashes. Rita didn't look well and she kept saying that she had never been really warm since they had left London.

It was bad luck that they had come down to Cornwall during this cold spell. It was no good telling the twins that the rest of the country was having even worse weather. It would make them only more discontented and more determined to go back 'home' as quickly as they could. She'd got to convince them that 'home' was here, just three or four miles away. She could only hope that the Trevendones in possession would agree.

She left them in the lounge, watching T.V., deciding to go for another walk on the downs. The puppy Dingo wasn't particularly eager to accompany her, but she put him on the lead and dragged him out. This time she took a steep, stony path leading off the High Street, passing one or two small hotels and some rather lovely private houses with balconies. Hotels and houses had a closed, frowning appearance as if they were shut up for the winter and any inspection would be unwelcome.

However, there was a car outside the one with the blue door and shutters, a long low sports car which had been standing near her Mini in the hotel yard when she had gone out to get a bag from the boot at lunch time.

As she passed the gate leading to the drive, the blue door opened and a man and a girl came out, the girl holding a large white Borzoi dog by the collar. Dingo caught sight of the big dog and immediately gave voice. Evidently the Borzoi was not to his liking;—perhaps in his limited experience it looked too much like a wild animal, for he sprang forward barking furiously and almost jerked the lead out of Lesley's hand. She pulled hard, dragging him away, and flung a glance of apology at the couple in the porch.

The girl was black-haired and black-browed and Lesley gained the lightning impression that she had suggested releasing her big dog to take up Dingo's challenge and that the young man was laughingly restraining her.

Lesley hurried on, and out of sight of the enemy, Dingo's barking faded away and he stopped dragging at the lead. 'You've probably had a narrow escape,' she told him sternly. 'You may not be so lucky next time. It's never very sensible to take on an adversary who's much too strong for you.'

It had been an unpleasant sensation. She might have mistaken the girl's expression and the man's laughing remonstrance, but she couldn't dismiss the incident as easily as she would have liked.

She climbed over the stile at the end of the stony road and ran up the little incline to the downs. There was a magnificent sweep of coastline on her right and ahead the downs with some sheep and lambs clustered in a hollow to her left. Beyond lay a wonderful panorama of the countryside—' the coloured counties, that there before me lie,' she thought, recalling a poem she had read in her schooldays. Her eyes ranged over the many greens of downland and fields and of trees sheltering the scattered farms and houses. But her gaze was drawn back to the coast, the mysterious coastline of the legendary country of Lyonesse, of the mist-shrouded island of Avilion, of King Arthur and Queen Guinevere, of Lancelot with his red-cross shield and their lovely town of Camelot.

Trust someone from down under to go all sentimental about the old country, she jeered at herself, especially one who wasn't going to stay here. It was Rita and Richard who should feel this enchantment.

Her eyes were drawn continually to the magnificent coastline. The tide hadn't turned yet and there were stretches of dark golden sands with the cruel teeth jutting from the cliff towards the breakers. Even now on a relatively calm day those breakers were an awe-inspiring sight, stretching to the horizon over the pewter-coloured water. The blue and green colours would not come back until the heavy clouds rolled away.

It would be a magnificent place for surfing, she reflected, keeping her hand firmly on the lead, for Dingo, though not trying to get away or even just now barking his head off, was eyeing the clustered sheep and lambs with an interested eye. When did surfing start here, she wondered—May, June, July? She needn't think about that. She would be back in Melbourne by then, perhaps even thinking of getting married.

She was wearing thick sheepskin gloves, but her thumb wandered to her third finger. There was no ring. She had given it back to Steve when she had decided to come to England with the twins. How angry he had been. He hadn't been able to understand that her deep sense of gratitude to Margaret Trevendone couldn't just stop at putting them on a liner bound for England and leave it there. She had had to come herself, fight for them if necessary and see them settled in their own home.

She shrugged. No point in thinking about that just now. Her own problems must wait until she had done exactly that.

She walked on, keeping fairly close to the edge of the cliffs and peering down occasionally into some inlet where there were little patches of sand and rock pools. Was it worth while clambering down to explore this part of the beach? Perhaps not as it was so cold. All at once Lesley felt tired and a bit depressed. Even Dingo had lost some of his bounce and was keeping close to her as if to shield himself from the biting wind.

'We'll go back, old fellow,' she told him. 'I'd like to give you a run off the lead, but I daren't risk it with those sheep and lambs so near. We'll turn for home.' Dingo wagged his tail and looked pleased. She ran back along the downs', negotiated the stile and warned him not even to whimper as they passed the house with the blue door.

'If she hears us,' Lesley told him in a solemn whisper, 'she may open the door and send that big brute after us.'

But this time the blue door did not open and the rakish-looking sports car was no longer in the drive. In the hotel lounge, the twins looked more relaxed and happier. They had been viewing all afternoon and were able to tell her that there was thick snow over most of the country and chaotic conditions on roads and railways.

'A good thing we got here last night,' Rick said. 'If we'd waited till today we might not have got through.'

'You make it sound like Siberia!' laughed Lesley.

'Any adventures this afternoon?' Rita enquired sleepily. 'You didn't meet the Enemy again, I suppose.'

'The Enemy?' Lesley raised her eyebrows. 'Oh, you mean that man? Thank goodness, no. I hope we're not going to run into him every time we put a foot out of doors. Actually though, we shall have to do something about that puppy. For one thing we haven't a dog licence, and I'm sure that Mrs Wilkes hadn't one either or she'd have tied it round his neck when she wished him on to us.'

'She didn't really do that,' Rita remarked with a grin at her twin. 'Rick asked her if she wanted to sell him and he offered her a fifty. She said he was worth a lot more but she'd take that as she liked us.'

'Rick, you didn't *buy* him! I thought...' Lesley stared at them in outrage.

The boy grinned back at her. 'Dingo fancied a country life, I'm sure. What sort of existence was it for him, cooped up in that grotty London street? Mrs Wilkes didn't really want him. She'd have turned him out as soon as look at him. And he was—well, a yellow dog and he reminded me a bit of home.'

'Now there's something else for you to remember,' Lesley said, her green eyes glinting with indignation. 'You bought him and he's your responsibility. You've got to get him trained.'

'He *is* trained,' countered Rick, laughing. 'You're the best trained dog in England, aren't you, my faithful hound?' And he dragged Dingo on to his knees so that the dog could lick his face in an ecstasy of devotion.

29

'You should have seen and heard your faithful hound when I went on the downs!' Lesley told him grimly. 'Just as we were passing one of the houses a man and a girl came out. She was holding a big white Borzoi by the collar. It stood as high as a pony. Your well trained dog just went mad, tried to drag himself off the lead, leapt into the drive and began barking his head off.'

'Why didn't you let him have a go at the old Russian?' enquired Rick delightedly. 'I bet he'd have chased the old fellow right through the house.'

'The girl holding the Borzoi seemed to have a similar idea, with her dog doing the chasing,' Lesley said thoughtfully. 'I'm sure she intended letting the Borzoi make a meal of Dingo, but her companion dissuaded her. His car was in the drive—it was that one we were talking about at lunch.'

'Oh, that guy. He came in with a girl just as we went out of the dining room,' said Rita. 'Didn't you notice him, Les?' He was quite fab.'

Lesley shook her head, but Rick took up, 'I saw them. He looked ordinary to me, but the girl was gorgeous. She had long black hair, black eyes and a figure . . .' He made gestures with his hands.

'It sounds like the girl with the Borzoi,' Lesley admitted with a nod and a grimace. 'Quite wild and free, I'd guess from her expression when Dingo started his capers. You'll have quite a problem, Rick, if you meet the girl again. I doubt if she'd take kindly to the request "love me, love my dog."'

'Don't be so beastly sarcastic, Lesley,' Ricky stormed.

'Sorry,' she returned. 'It's just that I didn't take to the girl. And I do wish you hadn't bought the dog. It may not be convenient for you to keep him at Trevendone Manor.'

'Then we'll take him back to Australia,' put in Rita, shivering, 'and I vote we start right now. As far as I'm concerned, I can't get back fast enough.'

Lesley bit her lip, sorry she had precipitated this outburst. The twins hadn't wanted to leave Australia and so far nothing in England had appealed to them sufficiently to make them want to stay.

'What about tea?' she asked brightly, deciding to change the subject. 'Shall we go out to a café or ask Mrs Cleaver for some?'

'Let's have it here,' said Rita. 'I can't bear the thought of going out in the cold air.' And Ricky echoed her remark.

It was left to Lesley to take Dingo out again after dinner. The tide had rolled in since this morning and the sands where 'the Enemy' had talked soothingly to his runaway mare were covered now with long lines of curdled surf. There was a last hint of sun behind a big cloud raying out over the sky and down to the horizon. And where the sea, back now to its lovely green blue colour, met the sky there was a band of silver, gleaming like a shining pathway.

It was a wild scene, with the waves curling white as far as Lesley could see across the turquoise waters, here and there the jagged teeth of the rocks appearing and then disappearing as the curdled waves lashed against them.

Something wild and elemental in Lesley leapt to meet this scene. She had even in this one short day become entranced, bewitched perhaps with the brutality, the wild loveliness that lay before her. She loved it, she told herself and then came the reminder. *She* wasn't going to make her home here. She was going back to Melbourne to Steve . . . if he still wanted her. It was the twins whom she must involve in the mystery and romance of the land of Lyonesse.

The wild call of the gulls echoed and re-echoed over her head and she knew she would never forget this passionate lovely coast as long as she lived. But it wasn't for her. It was for Rita and Ricky who had not wanted to come and who up to now were uninterested, even hostile to the idea of staying here. Perhaps tomorrow they might feel different.

Tomorrow at least brought better weather. The sunshine was only hazy, it was true, a pitiful travesty of that they had known at home, but the wind had dropped and the air was milder.

'I'm not sure about lunch, Mrs Cleaver,' Lesley told their hostess. 'We may not be back, or we may. It all depends.'

Mrs Cleaver nodded comfortably. 'Not to worry,' she advised Lesley, who worried too much about those twins, in *her* opinion. 'If the steak and kidney is off, there's always plenty of cold roast beef.'

Lesley now took a critical look at Rita who was still complaining about the temperature. She was wearing high boots and her suede sheepskin jacket and a college-type scarf draped round her neck. She hadn't slept well and Lesley, wondering whether she had a temperature, had tried to persuade her to stay in bed. They could put off their visit to Trevendone Manor for another day. But Rita would have none of it. 'If I don't go today, I may never go at all,' she said defiantly. 'And I'm not letting you two go without me. After all, it's Rick and me who . . .'

'Careful,' Ricky warned. 'Remember our pact. The three of us are in this together. Everything is off if any of us breaks the pact. As to putting it off, let's go and get it over. If they throw us out on our ears we can begin making tracks back to London. And the sooner the better so far as I'm concerned.'

Lesley said soothingly, 'You don't really mean that, Rick. You're coming, Rita?'

'Of course,' the girl sniffed. 'Catch me missing the excitement!'

Lesley hoped there would be no excitement. She said, 'Let's go.' She led the way out to the Mini. 'Did you ever think of trying for a modelling job, Les?' Rita queried as, edged by Ricky who was holding the front seat, she folded herself into the back of the car.

Lesley's eyebrows were raised. 'When I was a teenager, but I've had other things to worry about since then.'

'Particularly us,' grunted Rick. 'Anyway, how long is it since *you* left off being a teenager, Les? Not even a year.'

Lesley shrugged. 'It's not so much a matter of time as experience,' she said dryly. 'Remember, you're to leave all the talking to me. And don't either of you dare to say you aren't interested. After all, it's *your* heritage.'

'Well, don't stress too much the *your*, darling. Remember you're in it too. After all, you're supposed to be the eldest.'

Lesley nodded. 'Thanks for reminding me.'

She drove out of the hotel yard down the high street and then turned off on to a high-banked lane which according to her map ran parallel to the coast. Every now and then a gateway or a lowering of the banks revealed the downs and glimpses of the sea.

Lesley had memorised the route, so she drove steadily though remembering the near-catastrophe of two nights ago, she was careful to slow down at each crossroads. Ricky must have been remembering that incident too, for he said suddenly, ' Do you think that fellow took our car number?'

' I shouldn't think so,' Lesley said more positively than she really felt. ' To change the subject. We're not taking that dog into the Manor with us.'

' If we ever as much as get in,' Ricky finished cynically.

' Dingo will howl the place down if we leave him in the car,' put in Rita, hugging the puppy, who was on the back seat with her. Dingo responded enthusiastically by licking her face and then leaping out of her arms to put his paws on Ricky's shoulders.

' Then he must howl,' Lesley replied firmly, ' for we're not taking him in. Rita, pull him back and hold him on the seat. I can't drive properly with him leaping about behind me.'

Rita pulled him again into her arms, murmuring commiserations. But there were no protests and Lesley guessed that the twins were no less anxious than she was for the forthcoming meeting at Trevendone Manor to be as amicable as possible. Her thoughts ran ahead. Would it have been better to have written announcing their arrival? Thank goodness these high-banked lanes weren't snow-covered this morning. Perhaps inevitably her mind wandered to that encounter of the night before last. How angry that man had been, and what bad luck to meet him again, and be in the wrong once more. It hadn't been any use explaining that they had owned Dingo only for two days and were really quite unacquainted with his foibles.

But she had the feeling that even if she *had* been able to explain he wouldn't have had much sympathy. He'd called her ' a menace ' and in turn for the twins and herself he would always be ' the Enemy '.

She concentrated again on the road. There must be a turning soon. ' Here it is, I think,' Lesley said, her voice suddenly tense. ' This place at the entrance must be the Lodge.'

' Do you think we ought to ask here?' Ricky sounded uneasy as he stared at the scrolled iron gates which were set wide open. Lesley shook her head and clenched her teeth.

' We don't want anybody telephoning that we're coming,' she said grimly. ' We might just as well have written.'

' As you say, ma'am.' Ricky made a little bow and

grinned. 'It's up to you.'

Lesley turned the wheel and shot up the drive past the Lodge before anyone could get to the door to ask their business. At first there were trees, beeches with the brown leaves of last year still rustling in their branches, then the drive opened out to a wide courtyard broken by symmetrical patterns of flower beds full of crocuses and snowdrops and spears of daffodils. They would be ready here in time to 'take the winds of March with beauty', thought Lesley, and something twisted in her heart as it had done when she had stood on the cliffs and reminded herself that the magic land of Avilion was not for her. For her was the long journey back to Melbourne where Steve *might* still be waiting for her.

The house was very large, a black and white structure with three wings giving it the traditional E shape of an Elizabethan mansion. Lesley stopped the car right in front of the great oak door, and none of them spoke as they got out and for the moment even Dingo sat quiet with his tongue lolling out. Still without speaking they walked up the three steps and Lesley pulled the bell rope.

A middle-aged woman with a neat hair style, a neat woollen dress and neat shoes opened the door almost immediately. She must have been very near it when Lesley rang the bell.

She said 'Good morning' and looked at Lesley enquiringly.

Lesley returned the greeting with more composure than she felt and said, 'Could I see Mr Trevendone, please?'

'Mr Dominic?' the woman queried. 'I'm afraid he's out somewhere on the estate.'

'Then Mrs Trevendone,' Lesley said now.

The other shook her head. 'I'm afraid not. Mrs Trevendone doesn't see people these days except the family. I can't take the responsibility of letting her be worried by strangers. I'm her companion, so if you care to tell me what your business is . . .'

Lesley stood silently for a moment. Then she said deliberately, 'I think Mrs Trevendone would wish to see us. As a matter of fact we *are* family . . . from Australia.'

The other looked shaken. 'Family?' she repeated faintly. 'From Australia. You'd better come in. It's too cold to have this door open for long.'

It was an ungracious welcome, but perhaps no more than

34

they could have expected. They went through the doorway into a big hall, oak-beamed with two staircases leading from either side up a gallery where Lesley caught a glimpse of pictures. Then her eyes were drawn back to the place where they were standing. The walls were oak-panelled with open shelves at intervals on which stood articles of glass, pottery and china.

The floor was of oak too, dark and shining and covered here and there with rugs that glowed in jewel colours. There were large settees and armchairs with some elegant upright chairs near the walls a few small gate-legged tables and at the far end a big oak desk behind which was a glass door leading into what looked like an office.

'Wait here,' the companion ordered. 'I really don't . . .' Her voice died away querulously as she rushed to the far end of the hall and disappeared.

'Dominic—he must be the fellow who owns the place,' Rick whispered. 'It's much bigger and more magnificent than I bargained for. Let's cut and run, Les.'

She shook her head. 'No, we'll see it through now.'

In a minute or two the woman returned looking smug. 'Now, madam, I suggest you tell me your business, or if you prefer you could write either to Mr Dominic or to Mrs Trevendone.'

Her tone seemed to imply that she was quite indifferent to what they did, and Lesley hesitated. But they weren't going to be chased out just like that, and by a hired hand.

She drew herself up. 'Our business is with the Trevendones here and now,' she said grandly. 'Actually, our name is Trevendone and we have just arrived from Australia to take up our residence here.'

She paused, highly satisfied with the effect her statement had had on the other, for it was obvious that she had been rendered speechless.

And then one of the doors leading from the hall opened and a small frail figure came out. 'Miss Yelland, I gather we have visitors. Please don't leave them on the mat.'

Miss Yelland rushed over to her. 'Mrs Trevendone, you shouldn't be out here. I think these young people are students up to their tricks. They've come with some ridiculous story. I don't know . . .'

35

'Students!' muttered Rita. 'Sauce!'

The three Australians stared interestedly at the small frail figure. She must be the grandmother, Lesley thought rapidly. But she looked incredibly old and ill with her dark glasses and her white hair. Lesley thought in alarm, 'We can't stay upsetting her. I suppose we ought to go.'

But though she might look old and frail, her voice was high and autocratic as she called out, 'Come over here and tell me who you are and what you want.'

Lesley thought: in for a penny, in for a pound, walked across to where Mrs Trevendone was standing and said, 'Our name is Trevendone. We . . . we're the children of Ralph Trevendone for whose whereabouts there were advertisements in Australian papers many years ago.'

The old woman thumped the floor with her stick. 'Those advertisements were sent in against my wishes. My view was that Ralph had taken himself off to Australia when he was nineteen and as he stayed there he must have preferred it to Cornwall. So let him stay. . . .'

Behind her, Lesley heard Rita mutter, 'Of course he preferred Australia to this cold benighted spot. Who wouldn't?' Lesley hoped this rather formidable old person hadn't heard.

She said placatingly, looking anxiously at the tottery old figure around which Miss Yelland was hovering and clucking ineffectually, 'Would it be better for all of us to sit down, Mrs Trevendone? Then I could explain.'

'Come in, then,' the other said ungraciously. 'Yelland, stop fussing and order some coffee. How many are there of you? Another girl and what's this . . . a boy?'

'This is Rita, and here is Richard. I'm told he looks very much like his . . . like Father. Rick.' She turned to the boy and not without a certain grace, Richard sauntered forward. Till now he had remained very much in the background. Lesley, watching, saw Mrs Trevendone's face change, grow rigid as if with shock and then soften into delighted surprise. Obviously she could see through those dark glasses, perhaps more with her mind's eye than with actual vision.

'It isn't Ralph he's like,' she said in tones of scorn. 'It's Jason, my husband. Jason just as he was when we first met and I was attending my first grown-up party.'

Lesley relaxed slightly. If this elderly member of the family

36

accepted Richard then the others would probably follow suit.

'Come in and tell me everything,' Mrs Trevendone went on now, sweepingly. 'Yelland . . . that coffee, *if* you please.'

The three followed her into a small beautifully furnished drawing room with a decor of cream and nile green. From the temperature it was obvious that there was some form of central heating, but a log fire burned in the cream-coloured fireplace. Lesley thought it was much too warm, but Rita, drawing near to the fire, still shivered.

'Sit down,' Mrs Trevendone ordered, 'and I'll tell you about the Trevendones.' She began to talk in a rambling fashion while Lesley with knitted brows listened and tried to piece together what she was saying. She seemed to be the twins' great-grandmother with only one son, their grandfather surviving the First World War. He had had two sons, their father Ralph and his brother David.

'Now they are both dead,' Mrs Trevendone said vaguely, 'and all that are left are you three, Ralph's children, and Dominic and Jennifer, David's children . . . and me, your great-grandmother, an old, old lady who has outlived all her own friends.'

Lesley's hands were clenched as she stared at her. 'We didn't know . . . didn't realise he . . . our . . . Uncle David was dead. It was *he* whom I . . . we . . . were hoping to meet.'

What should be her next move? she was asking herself. The man in possession, that cousin Dominic, might be a different proposition from an uncle who would know he had supplanted his brother.

'Now let me look at my great-grandson Richard. Come and sit here, young man.'

One of Ricky's more endearing qualities was that he was good with old people. It seemed to come perfectly naturally to him and now without embarrassment he went over to the old lady's chair and perched on the arm.

'You're too high there,' she said coquettishly. 'Get a cushion and sit where I can see your face.'

With the same lazy grace he collected a cushion, placed it near her feet and looked up at her with a smile in his sea blue eyes. 'No need to ask whether you're going to be a success with the girls,' she said. 'You're just like my Jason. You

37

even have his smile, for all you were born and bred in that far-away country.'

With tight lips, Miss Yelland brought in a tray of coffee and proceeded to pour out. Richard and Lesley got up to help her, but Rita, crouching in a chair near the fire, remained where she was. Even when a cup and saucer was placed on a small table beside her she did not stir.

'Rita,' Lesley said gently, 'drink your coffee while it's hot.'

She wished she had persuaded the girl to stay in bed, she thought in a troubled manner. Then the sound of footsteps in the courtyard caused her to turn to watch a figure passing by the windows of the elegant drawing room.

For a space of seconds it seemed to Lesley that her heart had stopped beating. Then she pulled herself together. Was she becoming completely *obsessed*? It was bad enough dreaming for two nights in succession about him. She surely wasn't going to be so crazy as to start *day*dreaming as well!

Now she could hear footsteps crossing the great hall and then in the doorway a figure loomed, preternaturally large to Lesley's horrified eyes. It just wasn't any good her defiant mind saying '*Oh no!*' That didn't make the slightest difference. It was the man to whom the twins now always referred as 'the Enemy'. And 'the Enemy' was here, right inside the place which they were hoping to claim as their home.

He was either very good at disguising his expression or he wasn't as surprised as she was. Then in a swift flash, she recalled her grandiose manner at their first meeting when she had given him their address. Trevendone Manor! No wonder he had stared at her so consideringly.

He said, 'So it's you'—and to Lesley's prejudiced ears his tones seemed to convey the deepest disgust. 'You've arrived at Trevendone Manor . . . at last.'

CHAPTER III

Lesley felt beyond speech and she dared not look in the direction of either twin. She sat motionless as he advanced into the room, followed by Miss Yelland looking unbearably smug. 'I sent for you because I thought you were the person to deal with this . . . invasion.'

He sauntered over to the fireplace with an arrogant composure which revealed that he was very much at home, very much the master of the house, pausing only to lean with a smiling good morning towards old Mrs Trevendone, who had again closed her eyes.

Then looking across to Miss Yelland, he said crisply, 'Couldn't you have told these young people that it's not convenient for us to have guests at the Manor just now, Miss Yelland?'

The companion bridled. 'But, Mr Defontaine . . .'

Lesley didn't hear the rest of her explanation. 'Mr Defontaine,' she murmured, and then, staring at him, 'You aren't Dominic Trevendone?'

His black brows went up in a surprised stare. 'No, madam, I'm not Dominic Trevendone. Whatever made you think that I was?'

Lesley could have replied, 'Because you came walking in as if you were the lord and master of all you surveyed.' To her it had seemed he couldn't be anyone else and her brain had already been groping for some way of coping with this final disaster. But if he wasn't Dominic the situation wasn't quite as hopeless as she'd imagined.

From under her long lashes she gave him a swift glance. He was being just that bit too civil, she thought in deep distrust, and some instinct warned her that the best thing she could do was to sweep the twins in front of her out of the room and immediately get in touch with a good lawyer. She didn't know who this man was, or why he was here, but she was determined to have no dealings with him.

All at once old Mrs Trevendone seemed to wake up. Her face glowed. 'Blake, isn't it wonderful! These young people have come all the way from Australia on their own!'

'Have they indeed?' commented Mr Blake Defontaine, his cold glance ranging from Rita, lolling like a sawdust doll on the chair by the fire, through Ricky who had left the cushion at Mrs Trevendone's knees and gone over to stand by Lesley's chair and finally pinned itself on Lesley, who now rose defensively.

'Perhaps they will introduce themselves,' Mr Defontaine went on, his voice like the cold east wind blowing outside. Instead of chilling Lesley, however, it set her temper alight. Her eyes glittered very green and her small chin set very firmly.

'I really see no particular reason for introducing ourselves to *you*. Our business here is with the Trevendone family, Mr Dominic actually, and not with any outsider.'

'Outsider? Mr Defontaine?' This was from Miss Yelland on a gasp of outrage.

Blake Defontaine made a gesture which seemed to order her to be quiet. Then he turned back to Lesley. 'Mr Dominic Trevendone doesn't happen to be here at the moment and his sister, Miss Jennifer Trevendone, is away from home. So perhaps you'll allow me to deputise for them; madam. You spoke of business.'

Perhaps it was his use of the title 'madam' that put Lesley at a disadvantage. She found herself stammering out an explanation, 'W . . . we . . . are Ralph Trevendone's family. . . .'

'Really!' His cold eyes ranged over them again. 'How odd! Ralph Trevendone was killed in a mine accident in Queensland twenty-five years ago, and I would guess that was before any of you—*any* of you,' he repeated, his eyes on Lesley, 'was born.'

Before Lesley could make any answer there was a little sigh just behind her and she turned to see Rita, her slender form bent double, sliding down on to the green carpet.

'Rita darling!' Lesley and Rick rushed forward, grasping the girl's shoulders and trying to raise her from the floor. Blake Defontaine followed them to the other side of the chair and Lesley looking up saw him standing there tall and broad-shouldered, his dark face a mask of suspicion and disgust.

'Is this part of the act?' he enquired unforgivably.

Lesley flashed him one look of incredulity. Then her attention was again on Rita, whose hands when she touched them seemed to be burning, and yet who ever since their arrival at St Benga Town had been complaining of feeling cold.

She thought desperately: what are we going to do? She can't be ill in a hotel. I wonder where the nearest hospital is . . . though she'll hate being away from Ricky and me.

Now Miss Yelland approached rather gingerly as if she was afraid she might catch something. She said, in a thin voice, 'The girl looks really ill. Was she all right when you set out this morning?'

'Help me to get her on to the settee, Ricky,' Lesley muttered, ignoring the question. She was blaming herself bitterly that she hadn't insisted that Rita stay in bed and postponing this visit to the Manor.

Now Defontaine sauntered round the chair. 'I'll lift her,' he said.

With an almost tigerish expression Lesley turned on him, her eyes flashing green. 'Leave her alone. Ricky and I will manage. You thought she was acting.'

'I was mistaken,' he admitted, 'but you've been up to such queer capers on the other two occasions I've encountered you that I thought it was another in the series. Now move over.'

And when Lesley didn't move he pushed her unceremoniously to one side and lifted Rita, putting her down on the settee. He put his thumb on the fainting girl's pulse and turned to Miss Yelland.

'Ring up Doctor Statham and ask him to come over as soon as he can. Then get Mrs Piper to prepare a room. See there's an electric blanket and hot water bottles. This girl has a temperature and needs to be kept warm.'

The companion gulped, looked as if she would like to protest but daren't and rushed from the room. Old Mrs Trevendone began to cry, 'Poor little girl, poor little girl,' while Ricky, his face very pale, asked hoarsely, 'Lesley, is she going to die?'

'Of course not,' Lesley returned robustly, though she had never felt so frightened in her life. 'She's probably got 'flu. We'll take her back to the hotel and get her to bed.'

She looked at Blake Defontaine with hostile eyes. 'We'll go as soon as she comes round. I'll ask the hotel proprietress about a doctor.'

'Don't talk like a fool,' he told her brutally. 'You can't take her out in to this biting wind. Instead of standing there looking self-righteous, come along and get some blankets.'

Lesley stood rigid until she saw Ricky's face, his dark blue eyes wide and imploring. 'All right,' she said shortly. 'Stay with her, Rick. If she comes round, see if she'll drink some coffee.'

'Do nothing of the kind,' interrupted the intolerably interfering Mr Defontaine. 'Wait till the doctor comes and he'll tell us what to give her.'

Lesley took a deep breath but decided against further speech. The main thing was to get Rita warm, so blankets were a first priority. In the hall, Miss Yelland was standing by the big oak desk telephoning and a motherly-looking, middle-aged woman was coming from the other end.

The man said something to her, and the woman turned to Lesley and beckoned her to follow up the further of the oak staircases. 'I'm Mrs Piper, the housekeeper, miss,' she said with a pronounced Cornish accent. 'I'll soon have a room ready for you and the young lady, but I'll give you a couple of blankets to put round her now. When she's warm she'll soon come round, I reckon.'

Lesley followed her down a scarlet-carpeted corridor right to the end where there was a linen store. Mrs Piper picked out two pale pink blankets, beautifully thick and soft, and bound with wide satin ribbon.

'If you can manage the young lady, I'll get the bedroom ready,' she said. 'Now don't you worry, miss. We'll soon have her cosy and warm.'

Lesley thanked her and sped back along the corridor and down the stairs. Miss Yelland and Mr Defontaine were engaged in a conversation by the big desk, but Lesley scarcely saw them. Rita was conscious now, but she was shivering from head to foot. Between them Lesley and Rick wrapped her in the blankets. Almost immediately Defontaine came back into the room, walking with that loose-limbed arrogance that Lesley resented without quite knowing why. Perhaps it was because he seemed so much at home here.

He ignored the little group by the settee and went over to Mrs Trevendone. 'Take it easy, old lady,' he said gently, and pressed her back into her chair. 'Everything is being taken care of. I'm going to carry the girl upstairs and the doctor should be here very soon. Just relax. Miss Yelland will be here in a minute or two.'

He was smiling down at her, arranging the cushions behind her and generally letting Lesley know, or so it seemed to her, that Mrs Trevendone was a very old lady and that their impetuous arrival might have a serious effect on her. After all, she was very old.

Lesley bit her lip. She had been prepared to fight—indeed she still was—but this collapse of Rita's put them in an awkward position. They were under an obligation before they had stated their case. And there *was* going to be a fight. Blake Defontaine had made that clear by ridiculing their claim.

Having settled Mrs Trevendone, the man now approached the settee. 'I'll carry her upstairs,' he said to Lesley. 'You'd better stay with her up there until the doctor comes.'

Lesley hadn't the slightest intention of doing anything else, but she was anxious not to be beholden to this man in any way. Rita was conscious now and with Richard's help she could get her upstairs.

'Please don't bother any more,' she said stiffly. 'Richard and I can manage.'

'I dare say you càn, but all the same, I'll carry her up.'

'Let him, Lesley,' Richard whispered, his face pale with apprehension which he was trying to hide under a show of bravado and impudence. 'He's got plenty of brawn, as you can see, and he can't really help his lack of brains.'

Blake Defontaine gave him a considering stare and suddenly terrified, Lesley rushed into the breach. 'Please carry her up,' she said hurriedly. 'It's just that she might have something contagious and we don't want to risk anyone else . . .' Her voice died away as he transferred his gaze from Richard, which was what she had angled for.

For a few seconds she braved the sword of his grey-eyed concentration. Then she gave him best and looked away, moving so that he could lift Rita. He wrapped the blankets more securely around her and said to Richard, 'You stay here and keep Mrs Trevendone company and you, madam, follow me.'

It was that word 'madam' that again irritated Lesley

beyond endurance. If she had had a weapon to hand she was sure she would have used it. Instead all she could do was to shoot him a glance of utter loathing from her big green eyes, a glance that was reciprocated in kind.

Oddly enough that gave her a further feeling of shock. She wasn't used to men looking at her like that. But then she hadn't met anyone like Blake Defontaine.

Mrs Piper was waiting at the head of the further stairway and she indicated that they should follow her into a large twin-bedded room, which breathed an air of comfort and quiet luxury. It had cream brocade curtains, a dark rose-coloured wall-to-wall carpet, cream rugs by the beds, bed covers of patterned brocade in cream and rose pink, the brocade repeated on the chairs and the chaise-longue. Trevendone Manor might be Elizabethan in origin, but it was twentieth-century in the quiet luxury of its appointments.

'There's a really thick blanket underneath the sheet and the electric blanket to go on top,' Mrs Piper said in her rich west-country accent. 'A maid will be up soon with hot water bottles. There, put her down, poor little body. Oh, my dear life, she do be in a way! I'm surprised, miss, you let 'un come out on a cold morning like this be. Real unseasonable it be for our part of world. Bright and sunny it may be, but there's a wind that would cut you in two.'

Defontaine lowered Rita still in her cocoon of blankets. 'Just take her boots and her coat off, but nothing else until the doctor comes,' he ordered.

Lesley swallowed. She had no intention of getting Rita properly to bed until the doctor had seen her. If he could arrange it she wanted to get the three of them back to St Benga Town or even back to Australia. Lesley's enthusiasm for the Trevendone inheritance had suffered an eclipse. She was beginning to wish she had never heard of Cornwall and the legends of King Arthur and his Knights, of Camelot, the romance of Tristan and Yseult which in her mind had twined around Ralph Trevendone's ancestral home of Trevendone Manor.

To her relief Defontaine now took his departure and between them Mrs Piper and Lesley made Rita as comfortable as they could. With the thick blankets and the hot water bottles the girl was soon much warmer, though she kept complaining

44

about her sore throat.

'Doctor will be here soon,' Mrs Piper comforted, and then to Lesley, 'You'm come all the way from Australy, Miss Yelland was saying. It's mortal hot there, isn't it? I expect the poor little thing has caught a chill coming to these cold parts.'

Doctor Statham proved to be fairly young and very thorough. 'She has a virus infection. It may be influenza. Her throat is very inflamed and she has a temperature.'

'We're staying in a hotel, the King's Arms at St Benga Town,' Lesley said, looking at him in a worried fashion. 'If we wrap her up well do you think we could take her back? Or is there a hospital or nursing home that would admit her?'

The doctor shook his head very decidedly. 'We can't move her with that temperature. There's plenty of room here and you'll be able to do the simple nursing which is all that will be required. If there are complications we may have to think again, but I'm not anticipating any.'

Lesley said, rather desperately, 'We can't stay here now Rita is ill. We're strangers.'

'But you're Trevendones, cousins from Australia, I understood. Of course you'll stay here. Why not?'

Lesley could think of several reasons why not, among them the fact that so far the only Trevendone she had met had been that old lady of nearly ninety.

The doctor scribbled a couple of prescriptions. 'Somebody will go into St Benga Town for them.' Lesley left Mrs Piper helping Rita to undress while she followed the doctor out of the room.

'I'd like her to start on the tablets as soon as possible,' he said, going down the shallow oak treads with Lesley beside him. 'Could your brother take your car and go into St Benga Town straight away?'

Lesley swallowed. Blake Defontaine was at the foot of the stairs, looking up at them. 'I'll take the car,' she said hurriedly. 'Rick isn't seventeen yet and has no licence.'

The doctor said, as he approached Defontaine, 'This young woman has been talking of taking her sister back to St Benga Town to that dump of a hotel. Utter nonsense, isn't it! Of course they can all stay here, can't they?'

Ironically then, it was from 'the Enemy' that the twins

45

and Lesley from Australia were invited to stay in the ancestral home of the Trevendones. For in response to the doctor's remark, he said curtly, 'If you think your patient should be kept in bed, doctor, then she must certainly stay here until she has recovered. And naturally her sister and brother must stay too.'

'And Blake,' the doctor went on affably, 'could you get someone to fetch these prescriptions? I want my patient on the tablets as soon as possible.'

Defontaine held out his hand. 'I'll send someone immediately. Is there anything else she requires, doctor?'

'No, the tablets should do the trick—and keeping her in bed warm and with plenty of hot drinks. I'll be in again tomorrow, Miss Trevendone, so stop looking so anxious. Goodbye for now.' He turned from Lesley. 'By the way, Blake, I wanted to ask you . . .'

Lesley murmured goodbye and sped in the direction of the small drawing room. Mrs Trevendone was lying back in her chair having another catnap and her companion Miss Yelland was enjoying another cup of coffee.

'Where is my brother?' Lesley asked, looking round, a sudden unreasoning panic tearing her heart.

'Mr Defontaine sent him out to quieten your dog,' the other replied repressively. 'Really, it's very worrying for everybody.'

It was. Lesley couldn't have agreed more. She bit her lip. She'd forgotten all about Dingo. He must have gone mad, having to wait alone in the Mini all this time. And what a problem *he* was going to be. Everything that could go wrong seemed to be doing so.

Lesley heaved a sigh, and went back into the hall, hesitating slightly in the doorway because she did not want to meet the doctor, or rather his companion, again. But actually they had both gone. She despised herself for being so feeble. She didn't know who Blake Defontaine was and she didn't really care. To Rita, Richard and herself, he would always be 'the Enemy'. All the same it was the foulest piece of luck to run into him again here, of all places.

She pulled open the great door and saw Richard, still pale and pinched with cold walking round the courtyard with Dingo on the lead. As soon as Lesley approached, the puppy began to bark a welcoming 'Hello, hello' and to bound towards her, almost dragging Ricky with him.

'Pipe down, Dingo, and keep down, for pete's sake!' Lesley exhorted, but of course he took not the slightest notice and continued to leap towards her, yelping vociferously.

Ricky glanced round nervously. 'Can't you stop him making this row?' he enquired, unreasonably in Lesley's opinion, for Dingo was the twins' dog, not hers, and right from the beginning she had set her face against adopting him.

'That fellow, "the Enemy." You should have heard what he said when he came in and told me to come out and stop our dog raising hell. He's a Limey at his worst, isn't he? Superior, sarcastic and "don't-come-within-a-yard-of-me, I-might-catch-something-from-you," sort of devil.'

Lesley frowned. 'You have to give the devil his due,' she pointed out. 'He's sending someone for Rita's prescriptions to the chemist in St Benga Town and he's said we're all to stay here till she's better. And Ricky, don't you think it might be a good thing to drop those words "Limey" and "Pommie" now we're in England? We don't want to be offensive just for the sake of it.'

'I shall never mind being offensive to "the Enemy",' said Ricky stubbornly. 'As to that prescription of Rita's, he isn't in any great hurry to send anyone. Here he comes . . . and I'm off. Come on, Dingo old fellow.'

With a great deal of ostentation on his part, and a great deal of noise and movement on Dingo's, they turned and went to the opposite side of the courtyard. Lesley looked round and saw Blake Defontaine making a leisurely approach from the great doorway. His attention was concentrated on the boy and the dog.

'Has that puppy received training of any kind?' he enquired sharply.

'He's house-trained,' Lesley replied defensively. 'As to any other sort of training, we've had him only a short time and don't know him very well.'

A mocking gleam came into his dark grey eyes. 'So you didn't bring him from Australia and smuggle him in! No, perhaps not. He isn't a likely candidate for that sort of episode. He's much too disobedient and too vociferous to lie doggo under a lady's coat.'

'And much too large,' Lesley added sharply, knowing exactly what Ricky had meant in his bitter description of 'the Enemy.'

There was more to come. ' I've been wondering why your brother couldn't go into St Benga Town for that prescription?'

Lesley went very tense until she saw that he was staring meditatively at her clenched hands. She shrugged and put them behind her. ' Ricky hasn't a driving licence.'

' Hasn't he now? And he doesn't drive?' He was still eyeing her speculatively and Lesley looked away. He *knew* Rick had been driving that night, and now he was baiting her, waiting for her to say something that would reveal the truth. She clenched her teeth, determined not to speak, and he went on, ' If *he* can't go into St Benga Town then *I* must. It's a nuisance, but. . . .'

Colour swept across Lesley's face. Blake Defontaine had a subtle air of distinction, and yet within the borders of courtesy he succeeded in being more completely ungracious than any man she had ever met.

' Please don't bother. I'll go myself.'

He shook his head. ' Don't take offence so easily, Miss . . . er . . . Trevendone. I thought you Australians appreciated plain speaking and that the last thing you could tolerate is what I think you refer to as the hypocrisy of the Old World.'

' Some of us appreciate good manners,' Lesley returned bluntly.

' I wonder what the difference is,' he asked laconically. ' I've merely told you what's true—that it was a most inconvenient moment for me to be called from my work to confront uninvited guests and then to have to drive into St Benga Town. I should be a hypocrite if I pretended otherwise.'

Lesley shrugged. ' Quite frankly I still don't understand why you have been brought into what is a family matter. But we're wasting time. Will you give me the prescriptions and then I need not keep you any longer from your own affairs.'

She tried to snatch the papers which he was holding in one hand, but he moved quickly and the next moment he had her by one wrist and swung her round. ' Go back to your sister, Miss Trevendone. I'll see that you get the tablets in a short time.'

With black anger in her heart, Lesley watched him walk away.

Rita proved to be a difficult patient. For four days she was really ill and after that so weak that the doctor would not allow her to get up.

To all intents and purposes for those first few days Lesley remained a prisoner in the luxurious room she was sharing with Rita, seeing only the doctor, Mrs Piper and Ricky. The boy twin had been given a room in the same corridor and had his meals with Lesley, carrying their trays up and downstairs. Ricky was Lesley's only link with the rest of the world, and he seemed oddly out of touch too, though he was remarkably cheerful. He spent his time going for long walks with Dingo and sometimes sitting with old Mrs Trevendone listening to her reminiscences of seventy and more years ago.

On the first afternoon of their arrival, Lesley had drawn the boy to one of the windows of the big bedroom, speaking quietly so as not to disturb Rita. ' Rick, just refuse to discuss our . . . your claim to Trevendone Manor with anyone till we're all together. The two people who matter are Dominic and Jennifer. She is over at Torquay staying with friends, Mrs Piper says, and Dominic is living at the Home Farm while his sister is away. Apparently it's the late lambing season and they're all very busy. I haven't asked her about " the Enemy ". I just couldn't bring myself to do it.'

' Nor I,' said Richard in a heartfelt voice. ' I'm just going to ignore him. And by the way, Les, there's a marvellous piano in one of the rooms off the great hall. Do you think I could get some practice?'

' I should think so if you keep the door closed and play properly—not that theatrical vamping you started doing back home. But get permission from Mrs Trevendone first.'

' I'll do that,' Rick promised.

' And remember, no talk of any kind about your . . . our claim . . . until Rita is better and we have a united front.'

The boy laughed and threw a careless arm around her neck. ' You're like a mother hen with us, aren't you, Les? Too right you are!'

' Too right I am,' agreed Lesley. ' One more thing, Rick. Keep an eye on Dingo all the time. We don't want him chewing up anything in the house. And don't let him off the lead when you go out in case he chases someone's cat . . . or something. . . .'

'. . . or snaps at someone's horse's fetlocks,' grinned Ricky unrepentantly. 'I'd let him do that any time, except that I've too much respect for the horse.'

Leslie's brows were knitted. 'Rick darling, avoid that man whenever possible. Actually, though I didn't ask for the information Mrs Piper *did* say that he lives at the Lodge—that pretty little house just where we turned in at the entrance to the drive. Do you remember? I expect he rents it, and that's why he was walking round as if he owns even the Manor, and that silly Miss Yelland sending for him made him feel all the more important. I shouldn't be surprised if he gets the Lodge at a peppercorn rent too. But we'll look into that later.'

'. . . and hand him his notice to quit,' grinned Ricky wickedly. 'I shall enjoy that, and I'm sure you will too.'

Lesley looked thoughtful. She wasn't at all sure they would be able to dismiss Mr Blake Defontaine quite so easily. For one thing he hadn't accepted that they were Ralph Trevendone's children. Where had the story that Ralph had been killed in a mine disaster in Queensland twenty-five years ago come from? She decided not to remind Ricky of that remark, but it continued to worry her. Just now she merely said again, 'Avoid him whenever you can, Rick, and especially when you're with Dingo.'

'Okey doke,' returned Ricky cheerfully.

Later, when she came to think back on it, that continued cheerfulness of Ricky's should have roused her suspicions. He hadn't wanted to come to England and once they were in London he most certainly hadn't wanted to come down to Cornwall.

London was his scene, he had assured Lesley. There he would be able to get somebody interested in his musical talents. He could play the piano quite well, was an accomplished guitarist and had a good voice. Once he got into a group, he had said hopefully. . . .

All the way down to Cornwall he had been gloomy and depressed, so that to find he wasn't moping here at Trevendone Manor under these trying conditions was one of the bright spots for Lesley while she nursed Rita.

The others were those moments when she was able to stand by the bedroom windows, or occasionally in the doorway of the great hall while she waited for a tray to be brought from the kitchen and was able to look out at the masses of snow-drops and crocuses which painted the brown earth of the flower beds, or the flowering shrubs some with pretty little red flowers, other purple. And always there was the brilliant green of the grass, its smooth sward filling her with admiration and wonder.

That would be her lasting impression of England, the green-ness. As to Cornwall! Through the conifers which grew far down beyond the lawn, she could get glimpses of the sea and the creaming surf, the sea of that pewter colour which always made her think of 'the Enemy' and his penetrating cold impartial grey eyes. Yes, so far as Cornwall was concerned, it would always be the sea . . . and those eyes.

She found the lack of sunshine this spring surprising, and it was that which filled her patient with the deepest gloom.

'I shall never get used to it,' Rita said wearily. 'Why did we ever come here, leaving our friends and everybody we knew, leaving a country that is sparkling and alive for this place which is . . . dead?'

'It's a bad period, darling,' Lesley told her. 'When spring really comes there'll be lots of sunshine. They say an English spring is like nothing else in the world.'

'Then let it come quickly,' Rita sighed.

It was that afternoon that Ricky said rather sheepishly, 'Les, you haven't been out for nearly a week. If you like I'll stay with Rita this afternoon. I'll get the transistor from my room and find a programme to cheer her up.'

Lesley was touched. 'All right, Rick. I'll slip out, just for half an hour, perhaps, on the beach. I take it you can get down.'

'I expect so,' he muttered, 'but I haven't explored down there.'

Lesley, shrugging into her leather coat, turned to give him a puzzled look. That was odd. Then where *had* he been? Some days he hadn't come in for lunch, saying he had asked for a sandwich and an apple from the kitchen. It hadn't been like Rick to be so fond of the fresh air, but Lesley with her mind on Rita hadn't given it much thought till now.

'I'll take Dingo,' she said.

Ricky said carelessly, 'Oh, I shouldn't. He's worn out with racing about on the beach all morning. I've got him tied up in a shed at the back. He's too exhausted even to howl, but I'll go and get him later on and bring him up here.'

Lesley looked at the boy with apprehensive green eyes. Something was wrong, she was sure, but she didn't want Rita upset. Ricky was being devious. She went downstairs and as she opened the great door she saw that a rather watery sun had come out and was glinting on the sea. But as she walked across the courtyard to the smooth green lawn her brow was pleated with worry. Ricky didn't know the way down to the beach, yet the puppy was supposed to have been there all morning.

Perhaps the beach he was referring to was somewhere else, at St Benga Town, for instance. But would Ricky walk those three miles into the windy little town and back? Something like terror clutched at her heart. He hadn't been fool enough to take the Mini. He wouldn't, surely.

She bit her lip. She wasn't going in the direction of the trees after all. Instinctively her steps were carrying her towards that shed where Ricky had put Dingo. She couldn't see it, but now she could hear pathetic whines from a lonely puppy.

She followed the sound, along a yew hedge, through a formal Italianate type of garden and so to a part of the estate which was planted with rows of vegetables, with glasshouses and cloches.

She could see the hut now, and the whines had increased, as if by some sixth dog sense the puppy knew that a rescuer was close at hand. Dingo wasn't so exhausted that he was quietly sleeping. She walked round the hut, pushed open the door and was greeted by an ecstatic yelp as he leaped forward, almost strangling himself in the effort.

'Dingo, stop being a noisy fool,' she said. 'Why are you tied with rope? Stop it, silly! I don't want my face washing, nor my hands.'

As she was talking to him she was busy trying to untie the rope which was secured to a stout post in the middle of the hut. Then there came a soft Cornish voice from the doorway.

'I shouldn't be doing that, missie. Not if I was you.'

Lesley swung round. For a moment she wasn't quite sure whether she had understood. The accent was difficult to follow until your ear got attuned.

'I beg your pardon,' she said, staring at the heavy, amiable face peering at her from the doorway.

'I said I shouldn't be undoing that there dog, missie, not if I was you. Orders is orders. I was told to tie 'un up and keep 'un here. He don't like it, natural like, 'un being only a pup, and a bit of a mixture in the bargain if you ax me. No offence meant, ma'am, of course.'

This time, Lesley got the gist of what he was saying. She smiled, 'Oh, that's all right. It was Ricky, my . . . my brother who asked you to tie him up, I expect. But I'll take him now. I'm going for a walk on the beach.'

The man pushed his woollen cap up and scratched his forehead. 'I'm sorry, ma'am, but it weren't anybody belonging to you who telt me to fasten up the dog and keep 'un fastened. T'were the maister, Mr Defontaine, I mean. Said it was a menace, he did. Seems 'un was snapping at horses down on beach when Mr Defontaine was riding with his lady.'

His lady! Even in the middle of her dismay, Lesley noted that phrase. So he was married! Then back to the important thing. She wished she could tell herself she hadn't really followed properly what this old man was saying in his rich west-country burr, but she couldn't pretend. Dingo, poor wretch, had fallen foul of 'the Enemy' once again. What had Ricky been doing to allow it? She had warned him so often. And why hadn't he told her the truth just now? He was really the limit.

'I'm sorry,' she said through stiff lips. 'I'll see he doesn't get loose again. Will you untie him for me now, please.'

'I'm sorry, ma'am.' The man's voice was apologetic. 'But I just dusn't disobey orders. Mr Defontaine isn't the man to stand fer it. "Wonnacott," he says to me, "tie that craythur up and don't let 'un get away or I'll never believe again you was once in the Royal Navy." It's the rope, ma'am,' he explained. 'You won't get that knot untied not this side of Kingdom Come.'

Lesley said heatedly, 'I don't care whether you were in the Royal Navy or the Grenadier Guards. This is my . . . our dog and I'm not moving from here till I take him with me.'

The gardener scratched his forehead and looked more apologetic than ever. 'You'll be staying here a long time, then, ma'am.' His heavy face suddenly brightened. 'Would you think of going down to the Lodge, ma'am, and seeing Mr Defontaine? He wouldn't be saying no to a pretty young lady like you.'

'Saying no to my taking my own dog?' ejaculated Lesley, her eyes sparkling with fight. 'I should like to see him try!'

All the time she was speaking she was pulling at the formidable knots. She hadn't brought her handbag out with her, which was a pity because in it she had a pair of nail scissors which might have made an impression on that thick rope.

She raised big, and for a moment, guileless green eyes to the gardener's. If he'd been a sailor he surely wouldn't be disobliging to a woman. Sailors had a reputation for chivalry.

'Couldn't you say he'd just got away?' she asked.

The man shook his head. 'I'm sorry, ma'am, but I couldn't for shame tell Mr Defontaine that. He's got a tongue that bites and I'd feel real oncomfortable, that I would. I couldn't look 'un in the eye and say that a little old dog had got away when I'd tied 'un up. Mr Defontaine now, 'un . . .'

'Oh, be damned to Mr Defontaine! Who does he think he is?' ejaculated Lesley in exasperation. 'The Lord High Admiral of your Royal Navy?' She was hurting her fingers badly, pulling at these wretched knots.

She was suddenly conscious of a silence behind her, the sort of silence that can be felt. She saw that the gardener's heavy face was wearing a look of consternation while Dingo, flat on his stomach, was crawling forward, wagging his tail ingratiatingly. Naturally, it was Mr Blake Defontaine himself. He'd probably heard her last remark, hence the gardener's embarrassment. For Dingo's peculiar behaviour she had no explanation at all.

'Will you tell this man to release my dog,' she said in a curt clear voice as she got up from where she had been crouching.

'Right, Wonnacott, I'll deal with this. You get on with your own work,' said Defontaine, ignoring Lesley and the dog —obviously both unimportant. 'And don't forget,' he went on coolly, 'I want those tomato seedlings brought to the lab

54

first thing in the morning.'

Lesley was seething with fury. He had turned away, deliberately ignoring her remark and causing the gardener to ignore her too. Yet this estate was theirs . . . well, Ricky's.

'Will you be so good as to do as I ask? Get this man to release my dog,' she said now in a voice that she tried hard to make cold and calm. Raging at him would have no effect, she knew that.

He made a gesture to the gardener who went lumbering down the path. Then he turned back to Lesley, eyeing her with a hard, expressionless stare. 'You were saying?' he queried.

'I was asking you to release my dog,' she said in a voice that she strove to keep very small.

'So he's *your* dog. I've tried to establish his ownership, but that young brother of yours didn't seem very certain. Well, now we can get down to brass tacks. First of all, have you a licence for him?'

'A licence?' Lesley blanched and looked up quickly, noting the irony in his bleak eyes. She couldn't help feeling that he had Ricky in mind for more than one thing. Ricky, who hadn't a licence for his dog and hadn't a driving licence.

She forced her voice into nonchalance. 'A licence?' she repeated. 'I don't really know.'

'What do you mean by saying you don't know? Either you have or you haven't.' His eyes were cold now, that same cold pewter colour of the February sea, and his voice had a contemptuous edge to it. As if in his own mind he was branding her as a liar and a cheat . . . over more than the licence for Dingo.

She thrust her hands deeply into her pockets. 'Look, I don't see what business it is of yours whether we have a dog licence or not.'

'I suppose that means you haven't one,' he said now, propping himself by the lintel of the open door. He looked consideringly at Dingo. That renegade was again wagging his tail ingratiatingly and looking up at his captor an adoring grin on his silly face—the sort of look he had never given any of them, thought Lesley indignantly.

'If you're going to keep him, you'd better get a licence for him,' Blake Defontaine went on, making no attempt to

55

meet Dingo's friendly overtures half or even a quarter of the way. 'And while you stay here,' he continued, 'he must be tied up except when you take him out for exercise. He needs training to come to heel when he's called.'

Who does he think he is, giving out orders like this? Lesley asked herself in a fury. She would have left him standing, but he was between the door and herself and she had still got to free Dingo.

'If you think I'm going to have him tied up all the time you've made a mistake. I wouldn't be so cruel. In Australia . . .'

'You're not in Australia now,' he pointed out irritatingly. 'But even there, one supposes dogs obey their owners and are trained to leave sheep and lambs alone.'

'What proof have you that Dingo would chase lambs?' she asked frigidly.

'None, and I'm not proposing to risk finding out. We're breeding pedigree stock at the Home Farm—animals that are too valuable to be chased over the cliffs.'

We! That word again, as if he identified himself with every aspect of life at Trevendone. What bad luck that Dingo had run foul of him again before Ricky's claim had been established! Once it was . . .

'Do you know anything about training a dog?' The question came suddenly and Lesley, wrapped in her own gloomy thoughts, jumped. 'No, I don't,' she admitted.

'Then why did you buy the dog?'

'I didn't buy him. He was to all intents and purposes a stray, and the twins couldn't bear his being turned out, which is what our landlady in London was going to do. So . . .'

He pounced on that. 'So it isn't really your dog. Those children!'

'They aren't children,' she flung back. 'They both look much younger than they are because they're so small and slight.'

Her face suddenly went very stubborn. Why was he spending so much time here . . . as if he was trying to find out every single thing about her, looking at her with his cold intent eyes?

'Blake darling, so *this* is where you are. I waited . . .'

The speaker wasn't where Lesley could see her yet, but she

stiffened, disliking instinctively that smooth—and what Lesley considered affected—drawl. Dingo evidently agreed with her. He set up his vociferous barking until a cuff from Defontaine sent him down on his stomach wagging his tail ingratiatingly.

In a leisurely manner, Defontaine now turned, presumably smiling a greeting, for Lesley did not hear him speak. She was bending down again struggling with the knots, determined not to give up.

Now that penetrating voice came again. 'Surely that dog isn't still there? I thought we'd decided it had better be put down.'

Incredulous amazement and a kind of tearing rage shot through Lesley. She got up and almost leapt across the space towards the door. She gained a swift impression of a tall young woman with long black hair dressed in an expensive suede coat with a sheepskin collar and high -suede boots which matched exactly the colour of her coat. There was something vaguely familiar about her, but Lesley didn't pause to sort that out. She just thought, so this is his wife—his lady, as the gardener had put it.

She said hotly, 'If anybody injures my dog in any way they'll be sorry for it, believe me!'

'What have we here? Blake, don't tell me you've tied the girl up as well as the mongrel!' The dark young woman's face was a picture of amused contempt.

As she saw that smile for Lesley the picture fell into place. But of course, this was the girl who had stood in the doorway of the house on the cliffs at St Benga Town and had seemed inclined to let her Borzoi take up Dingo's pathetic challenge.

'Sorrel, go on ahead. I'll join you in a minute or two,' Defontaine said, standing between the two girls.

The one he had spoken to laughed again. 'Take my advice, Blake, tie her up with the dog. These wild and woolly savages from over the sea need to be disciplined.'

Lesley decided to ignore that. Her private opinion was that the person who should be tied up was Madame Sorrel Defontaine herself. Two unpleasant types seemed to have found each other in these two, and no doubt theirs was a very successful match.

The girl's smile to her husband was a very special one and then she turned and sauntered away. Now Blake Defontaine let his arm drop from across the door. Had he thought she would fly at his wife's throat? Lesley wondered.

'Don't do anything stupid like releasing that dog,' he advised. 'You're nursing your sister, so you can't keep an eye on the puppy as well. Your brother is evidently not sufficiently responsible to do so. If you have any thought at all for the puppy leave him where he is so that he doesn't get into further trouble.'

Lesley bit her lip. She hated the idea of giving him best, but she had no alternative till Rita was able to go out. If only Ricky . . . Where *had* he been this morning?

She bent to Dingo and gave him a hug. 'All right, old boy,' she whispered, 'I'll have you out as soon as I can.' She turned back to Blake Defontaine. 'I'll be responsible for him as soon as my sister is well and I'll ask my brother again to take him out only on a lead.'

'That's very sensible of you,' he said with a nod, and Lesley could have struck him for his condescension. Seething with fury, she passed him without a glance. One thing was quite certain in her mind. As soon as Ricky had established his claim to the Trevendone estate Mr and Mrs Blake Defontaine must receive notice to quit the Lodge. *She* was unspeakable and he was too large, domineering and arrogant to have on the premises a moment longer than necessary.

CHAPTER IV

Lesley's first instinct was to rush back to the Manor and demand to know what Ricky had been doing since they arrived here, but second and wiser thoughts prevailed. The last thing she must do was to upset Rita, and having a blazing row with Ricky would do that quicker than anything else. So far as he was concerned too, that would get her nowhere. He would just become stubborn and withdrawn or begin to talk of leaving Cornwall. It wasn't as if he had ever wanted to come.

No, the best thing she could do in her present mood of anger, frustration and general feeling of depression and despair was to walk it off and get herself sorted out.

She hurried through the neat vegetable garden, and came to a rougher piece of land, mainly pasture with a few apple trees standing in the hollow. The path led upwards to a wall in which was a gate and soon she was on the cliff top with a magnificent view of the coastline beyond St Benga Town to some distant headland jutting into the lovely turquoise sea. It was rolling out but there were still white-headed breakers churning to foam on the cruel toothed rocks.

As Lesley turned to look in the other direction she saw that there was a path winding down the cliffs, broken here and there by steps which led to a sheltered, sandy cove. It looked like a private bathing beach and probably was, but she had no intention of going down there. This afternoon it was probably going to be private to Mr and Mrs Blake Defontaine and their horses.

She turned in the direction of St Benga Town, walking quickly along the springy downs for a time, her nerves so tense that she couldn't even think coherently.

But the cold wind blowing in her face and the exercise for which she had been pining gradually had their effect and after a while she slackened her speed, having worked off at least the surface of her worries.

She had got to get this matter of Ricky settled without bringing Rita into it. The girl twin would always spring to her brother's defence no matter what the problem. They might bicker and even quarrel between themselves, but to the

59

world they always presented a united front.

Lesley thought despondently, everything had gone wrong. I had the biggest difficulty in persuading them to come and since we arrived here nothing has gone smoothly. It had seemed to start when they were confronted by the ogre-like figure of Blake Defontaine looming up in the half light of that late afternoon a week ago. He had seen who was driving, Lesley felt sure, and he was holding the knowledge over her head until it suited him to pounce. Wild thoughts of blackmail came fleetingly and went just as quickly in Lesley's brain.

Another piece of bad luck had been the twins' insistence on adopting the puppy. He had been a source of trouble since they came down here, and the twins *were* irresponsible about him. Lesley had to agree there with ' the Enemy's ' judgment. She would have to do something herself about getting a licence and try to train him. It would be no good leaving it to the other two.

It had also been unfortunate that the two Trevendones who were in possession had both been away from the Manor when they had arrived and the only people they had been able to see had been the very old lady whose mind was fixed now only on the happy days of her youth and of course . . . Blake Defontaine.

Lesley began to walk quickly again, her hands thrust deeply into the pockets of her coat, her copper-coloured hair whipping across her face. He made her feel like this, tense and strung up in a suffocating excited way every time she met him or even thought of him.

It had got to stop being like that. She must take a hold on herself, treat him with coldness and reserve, refuse to be drawn into battle, where possible, avoid him.

He and his wife, that hateful Sorrel girl, must be renting the stables here as well as the Lodge, and being the types they were, they had calmly taken possession of the rest of the estate. It was a situation that would have to be changed.

Lesley swallowed suddenly, unnerved by the wave of depression which flooded over her. They seemed so formidable, those two together. Separately she felt she could have fought them, but as a couple, married and obviously very much in love—at least Sorrel was. No mistaking the look she had given him when he had asked her to go on and leave him to deal quickly with this upstart intruder from over the sea.

Lesley's hands went deeper into her coat pockets and she found that now she was almost running over the smooth turf. At this rate she would soon be at St Benga Town and then there would be all the way to walk back. What was she going at this pace for? Running away from something or just from herself?

She stood for a few moments looking down at the cluster of grey roofs that made up St Benga Town and the little harbour with its few boats rocking at anchor. And there among the houses winding up the hill was the one with blue shutters where she had first seen Sorrel.

Her eyes went to the cruel coastline with the rocks like sharks' teeth stretching out across the sands, eager to smash to atoms any luckless ship or sailor who should venture too near. For the moment the magic charm of the land of Lyonesse had vanished from her heart. This wasn't a land of courtly knights and fair ladies. It was the wreckers' coast.

She thought again of Blake Defontaine with his dark face and his cold eyes and the black-haired Cornish girl who loved him. In this land of the Celt, Lesley suddenly felt an alien, a foreigner. She wasn't even English, and to the Cornish, even they were 'foreigners'. She was an Australian, a girl from over the sea, and to those two at least she was a hostile stranger.

She thought miserably: if only I could turn back the clock. If only I'd never come here.

And then Lesley shook her head vigorously, pushing back the strands of her hair from her face. How faint-hearted and feeble could she get? Once again her eyes were on the lovely scene before her eyes. Was she going to shrink away from it because its beauty had an element of savagery and cruelty? She had come to Cornwall to fight for the twins' inheritance and was she going to lose her spirit because the fight was going to be tougher than she'd expected?

Now it was her own self-contempt that drove her on. Again she was almost running as she made her way back to the Manor, the cold easterly driving behind her. By the time she reached the wall where the Manor gardens began she was really weary. If instead of going back through the orchard and kitchen garden she went a bit further on, she might find a shorter cut to the house.

She came upon the seat unexpectedly, set back in the wall and fashioned out of half a boat upturned with a board across sufficiently wide for two people to sit. Lesley sank down into it. It was too cold to sit for long, but at the moment she felt she couldn't take another step, and the sides of the boat gave shelter from the bitter wind. Behind were two trees bent in two directions by the wind so that their upper branches met but leaving an elongated oval of sky above the seat.

Lesley closed her eyes. Gosh, she *was* tired, and that wasn't going to help when she tackled Rick.

On the smooth springy turf there was no sound of footsteps. The first Lesley knew that someone else was about was when a hand came on to her shoulder and a man's lips were on her cheek. She had turned just a fraction of a second in time or the kiss would have been on her lips.

She sprang up, looking into the dark face of a young man with sea blue eyes that reminded her of the twins'.

'What . . . what do you think you're doing?' she questioned.

He straightened up, laughter on his handsome mouth. 'Kissing you, of course, or trying to,' he said unrepentantly. 'If you sit in the Kissing Seat that's what you expect, surely.'

'The Kissing Seat?' Lesley faltered, turning to stare at it. 'Is that what it's called?'

He was just a bit taller than she and his blue eyes twinkled down at her. 'Yes, that's the Kissing Seat, and those,' indicating the two trees, 'are the Kissing Trees. Look how they've bent together over the years and are now in an embrace that neither of them can ever evade. It's quite a thought, isn't it?'

Lesley looked at him from under her sweeping lashes. 'Isn't this private property?' she questioned. 'Ought you to be here?' She moved away from him and from the seat, walking towards the cliffs and staring downwards. Yes, they were there, as she had expected—a man and a girl exercising their horses.

'It's not really private, though we try to keep it so,' he admitted.

We! Then she'd guessed right. From the beginning she

had been fairly sure that this young man with his dark romantic looks was a Trevendone. He must be Dominic.

She was on the verge of asking him and then she changed her mind. She would wait to see what *he* said. But he seemed to be waiting for her, so now she smiled, 'I've seen you before. You were lunching one day at the King's Arms in St Benga Town and then you were at the door of a lovely house on the cliff. There was a dog, a huge Russian wolf-hound.'

'Oh, that's Boris. A beauty, isn't he?'

Lesley made a tiny grimace, and her eyes wandered again to the rider below, her black hair streaming in the wind. 'I'm not so sure. I was afraid he was going to make mincemeat of my dog who had dared to bark at him.'

He slapped his booted leg with the riding crop he was carrying. 'Of course, I remember. Sorrel—Mrs Lang—was half inclined to let Boris have a go.'

'I thought so,' Lesley replied, nodding. 'Sorrel! She's the girl down there, isn't she?' and she indicated the two riders now on the far distant beach. Her eyes wandered to the sea, turquoise and dark blue all at once under these changing skies.

The young man's expression changed. 'Yes, they're putting in some intensive practice for a race meeting that's coming up very soon. And now I must be off. I promised . . .'

Lesley's own expression was puzzled. 'You called her . . . Mrs Lang, but I thought—I mean, doesn't she live at the Lodge?'

'Good God, no, why should she?' His voice was suddenly harsh and his dark face half angry, half surprised. 'She lives at Treida, the house where you saw the dog. The man down there, Blake Defontaine, lives at the Lodge. The long low building next to it is his lab. He writes books and lectures at universities all over the world and is an agricultural economist, rather famous in his own sphere, as a matter of fact.'

'Oh,' said Lesley blankly, and then, 'I should imagine she rides well. She's a beautiful girl. Does her husband ride too?'

Dominic made a gesture. 'Lang? He's dead. He was a racing motorist. She's been a widow since October.'

'How sad for her. She's so young.' Beneath her lashes,

Lesley's green eyes were curious. She sensed a certain reserve in his manner, perhaps even conflict. It's Sorrel, she thought. He's jealous of Defontaine. He hates her being down there with him.

The young man said abruptly, ' I must go. I promised I'd join them. See you.' He gave her a quick smile, a half salute and left her. Lesley's eyes followed him thoughtfully as he went down the cliff path. She would make a guess that he hadn't been invited to join the two on the beach.

So he was Dominic Trevendone. Lesley decided that she liked him. He was young and gay and attractive. A pity—for him—that he was so interested in Sorrel Lang. But one couldn't be surprised. The Cornish girl was so vital, so vivid, like a dark red rose, that Lesley couldn't imagine any man not being attracted. But it was Blake Defontaine whom Sorrel loved. Lesley, remembering the look she had given him, felt pretty sure of that.

There didn't seem any way into the garden here, so she retraced her steps and went through the gate following the path which led through the orchard and the kitchen garden to the courtyard at the front of the house. To her relief she couldn't hear Dingo whining. If she had she couldn't have borne to pass by and leave him. Perhaps he was asleep.

Had Dominic Trevendone guessed who she was? She felt almost sure he had. Perhaps if their conversation hadn't turned to Sorrel and Blake Defontaine he might have decided to give her his name and challenge her about hers. But once Sorrel had been mentioned, once he had seen the two riders on the beach, he hadn't had a thought for anyone else.

Lesley went into the great hall, pausing to smooth her hair. As she did so, Mrs Piper came through from the kitchen carrying a tea tray for Mrs Trevendone and her companion. ' Your tray is ready, miss, if you'll wait to carry it up,' she said pleasantly. She came out of the small drawing room a minute or two later and smiled when she saw Lesley standing in front of a lovely Venetian mirror still smoothing her hair.

' I'm real glad you'm been able to get out for a bit of fresh air, miss,' she said, staring admiringly at the girl. ' You'm got a nice bit of colour in your face. You'm been real good to that little sister, nursed her well, you have. But perhaps you'm been a nurse, miss, in that Australy you'm come from.'

Lesley laughed. 'No, in Australia I worked in an office.'

'You'm were one òf they secretaries, I expect.'

Again Lesley laughed, turning her glowing face to the Cornish woman. 'No, I worked in a very small office. I was a clerk doing general duties, receptionist, book-keeper, shorthand-typist.'

'Were you really?' Mrs Piper exclaimed admiringly. She bustled away and returned with the tea tray. 'That walk *has* put a nice colour in your cheeks. Did you go on the beach?'

'No, I walked on the cliffs,' Lesley replied.

'I expect Mr Defontaine and young Mrs Lang would be down along training for they Cumballick Point to Point steeplechases. We're all real set on them keeping the cups they won last year.'

'Mrs Lang?' Lesley's voice was a query.

'Young Miss Sorrel that was. Married and a widow within the year, poor young thing. Not but what she's got over it nicely, I will say. Young Lang was killed motor racing last October, but with no money worries. She be very well off that way. I expect she's waiting for biggest part of year to be out before she weds again.'

'Yes!' Lesley turned away, forcing her voice to an un-interested drawl. 'I met Mr Dominic Trevendone this after-noon.'

'Did you now, m'dear soul? Un's usually around when they'm training. I don't know whether un's riding at Cumballick or not,' she added in a voice that sounded as dis-interested as Lesley's had. The girl gave her a quick look and Mrs Piper spread her hands and shrugged. Lesley could think what she liked, her expression said.

Lesley went slowly up the shallow treads of the oak stair-case. Blake Defontaine and Sorrel weren't married, but the old gardener had said 'his lady' and that told the tale.

She paused half way to look down at the great hall with its lovely and, she felt sure, valuable furniture, glass and pottery. All along the wide corridor on which their rooms were situated were cabinets and open shelves with silver and porcelain, beautiful pictures. The carpets beneath her feet was thick and soft to her tread and not worn. The whole atmosphere was one of luxury and quiet comfort. No doubt most of these things had been collected in bygone years, but they were being preserved here in an elegant setting. And it all belonged to Ricky.

She set the tray down on a table and opened the door. The twins were laughing and she could see that Rita was sitting up and looking much brighter than she had done for some time.

'Tea,' she said cheerfully. 'Rita darling, you look heaps better. I can see Rick has been entertaining you.'

'I'll say he has!' Rita returned with a quick, secretive look at her twin. And then in a changed voice, 'Where's Dingo?'

Lesley put the tray on the table by Rita's bed and looked across at Ricky. 'He's tied up,' she said briefly.

'Tied up!' Rita's voice rose excitably till it was almost a shriek, and Lesley frowned. 'Where?'

'In the gardener's shed,' Lesley replied shortly, her eyes still on Ricky. Under her accusing stare, he began to bluster.

'I *told* you he was tied up, Les, before you went out, but I thought you'd have the gumption to get him untied.'

'I might have done just that—if I'd wanted to risk his getting into further trouble,' she said dryly, and then in a reproachful voice, 'Ricky, why did you let him go off on his own this morning? I expect you know he was down on the beach, snapping at that man's horse's feet again. It was *he* who had him tied up.'

'I guessed you'd been talking to that grotty old Enemy,' sneered Rick. 'Don't tell me, Les, that he's managed to *frighten* you.'

'No, I'm not frightened of him,' said Lesley slowly, and wondered if that were really true, 'but, Ricky, he is exactly that—our enemy.'

'Our best plan is to tell him to get out of that Lodge place where he's living,' Rita put in. 'After all, if we own everything around here we must own the Lodge.'

Lesley began pouring the tea. 'I doubt if it will be as simple as that.'

'Why not?' the twins asked, speaking together.

Lesley shrugged. 'He seems to be very deeply entrenched. There's a lab attached to the Lodge, I gather, and he does experiments there. Incidentally, Rick, he said that if you'll go down to the Lodge tomorrow morning he'll give you a few tips about training Dingo to come to heel.'

'Will I heck!' returned Rick furiously. 'I've no desire for Dingo to be trained. He suits me fine the way he is.'

Lesley sighed, having expected no other reply. 'Maybe he does,' she replied dryly, 'but this is farming country and Dingo will have to fit in or be destroyed.'

'Les darling, you *do* exaggerate. The Enemy has certainly got you on the run,' taunted Rita.

The older girl heaved another sigh. When the twins were in this mood there was no reasoning with them. But even so she'd got to find out what Ricky had been doing all this week.

'Rick, where were you this morning when Dingo was on the rampage?' she asked, handing him his cup of tea.

The boy turned away and walked over to the window, holding his cup and saucer. Lesley's eyes followed him and then she turned to Rita who was beginning to look tired. 'Drink your tea and then lie back, darling,' she said gently.

Rita shrugged, 'I'm all right,' and then in a louder voice, 'You'd better tell her the whole story, Rick. She'll have to know.'

Rick came back and sat down on the brocaded chair beside the bed. 'If you want the truth, Les,' he said with apparent nonchalance, 'I've got a job.'

This was the last thing that Lesley had expected. Her green eyes widened. 'Where? What sort of job?' she demanded.

'Vocalist with a group at a discothèque in a place called Penpethic Harbour about two miles further down the coast.'

Something between indignation and despair shook Lesley, but she willed herself to silence. She had hoped so much when he came to Cornwall and found himself with a family with long traditions that he would forget this craze of his. He played the guitar well and had a good and, for his build, a remarkably powerful voice. But as Lesley had tried to point out before they left Australia, so had countless other young men.

How stupid she had been not to guess that something like this was happening. His good temper and gaiety at a time when he might have been forgiven for being bored and frustrated, sent out each day on his own because his twin was too ill to sit up and Lesley too anxious to get her well again.

She ought to have remembered, Lesley told herself bitterly, how keen, once they got to England, he had been to stay in London. That was his 'scene' as he had kept saying, the place where he might develop his talents. He had been depressed and uncooperative all the way down to Cornwall and while they were at the King's Arms in St Benga Town. Then all at once he had changed and she had been too dim to suspect anything.

Lesley sought for words, knowing both of them were eyeing her closely. 'What about this place . . . and your inheritance here?' she asked, and even to herself the question seemed absurd.

Ricky shrugged and took the sandwich she was offering him. 'You know I've never been dead keen on this,' he replied.

Lesley looked around the room, taking in all its elegant comfort and luxury. What was the use of arguing, at least at this stage? 'How . . . how did it happen?'

'Why don't you start from the beginning?' Rita put in languidly. 'Les will see then how in . . . inevitable it all seems.'

'Go on, Rick,' Lesley prompted, starting to eat her own sandwich.

'I'd have told you before, Les,' the boy said contritely, 'but I didn't want to worry you. You'd got enough on with looking after Rita. Actually it was that same day when she collapsed. I'd got Dingo in the courtyard when he slipped the lead and dashed off down the drive. I went after him as far as the Lodge gates, but I couldn't see him anywhere. As I was standing looking about, this van drew up and this fellow asked me if I wanted a lift. He said he was going only as far as Penpethic Harbour, so I asked him how far that was. He said about two miles, so I thought I'd go with him, looking out for Dingo on the way, and hop off if I saw him. I guessed I could easily walk back.

'Well, we got talking and I found out he was the drummer in a group that worked in this disused cinema in Penpethic. There's a coffee bar and at first they had sessions at the week-ends just for free, but they had such crowds they're charging now. In the season they'll be on every night non-stop, and that means forming another group of which I'm one.

'Tim Drage is the man who runs it. He's a great guy, Les, and he's sure going places and I'm going with him. He's giving himself this coming season down here, and then he's going to be London based. They're getting loads of publicity down here now. There was a bus-load of kids from the other end of the county last Saturday night.'

'Isn't it madly exciting, Les?' Rita broke in, her blue eyes blazing like her brother's. 'Imagine a discothèque down here. Les, as soon as I'm up we must go.'

'We'd better wait till you *are* up,' Lesley warned, and for the moment added nothing else. They were no different from most of their age in being obsessed with the pop music scene. She'd had a phase herself, but it had passed. But Ricky especially seemed more obsessed than most. How often she had tried to talk him out of it, warning him he would be courting disappointment and even heartbreak if he went on dreaming that once he was in England fame might be round the corner.

'You've been going down to this discothèque place every day?' she asked.

'Yes, I've always managed to thumb a lift from somebody,' he replied. 'It's only properly open on Fridays, Saturdays and Sundays just now, but the boys are always there, some practising, some lounging around, because of course there are hangers-on. They drink coffee and talk about the way success has come overnight to some groups.'

Lesley bit her lip. She could see the attraction only too well. The discothèque seemed like an exciting new world to the boy from the Outback and far more interesting than what he had already called 'stuffy old Trevendone Manor and this dreary old inheritance.'

What was it like, this place? She shivered, imagining the sleazy atmosphere of a would-be night spot.

'I'm almost dazed by my sensational luck,' said Ricky. 'All that I've been looking for is here, right on the doorstep of Trevendone Manor.'

Lesley thought, it's no good my saying much at this stage. I've just got to meet these Trevendones as soon as possible and get Rick's future settled here. He'll see it differently when it's established that he owns this place.

'Look,' she said, 'I've had quite an afternoon while you two have been making plans for Rick to win fame and fortune as a pop star. Not only did I run into the Enemy—that was when I was trying to untie poor old Dingo—but also his girl-friend.'

'His girl-friend?' The two spoke together in tones of disbelief.

'And a bit later,' Lesley swept on, 'surprise, surprise, surprise, I met that pin-up boy with the sports car. Remember, Rita, he was at the King's Arms.'

'I'll say I do,' Rita replied enthusiastically. 'He was quite something. How come you met him, Les? Did you speak to him?'

'As a matter of fact I did. Also his girl-friend, that sultry-looking brunette who owned the Borzoi. Remember?'

'I'll say I do,' Rick put in with a mischievous grin, echoing his sister's remark. 'She was quite something, too.'

'She's quite gypsyish on nearer view,' Lesley went on. 'Very handsome, but *my* first impression was the right one. She's not at all nice. She wasn't with the dark young man this time but with her *real* boy-friend, the Enemy.'

'No!' This came in a chorus from the twins. 'Lesley, you're making it up,' added Rita.

Lesley shook her head. 'No, she was with Blake Defontaine this morning when Dingo went for their horses and she came this afternoon when I was trying to untie him. It was she who said he ought to be put down.'

'She didn't!' Rita didn't speak, but her shocked white face and blazing eyes were reflected in Ricky's and in his startled exclamation.

Then Rita turned on her twin. 'Rick, you beast! Every day you said you were taking Dingo with you.'

Lesley looked silently from one to the other. So Rita, even though she had been lying here really ill, had known what Ricky was up to.

'I did take him most times and he loved it,' Rick answered. 'But this morning he just disappeared and I hadn't time to look for him. I'd been promised this lift.'

'It's no good bothering about that now,' Lesley broke in. 'We've just got to keep an eye on him all the time from now on. That girl is as much our enemy as Blake Defontaine is.

'Now one more thing. He didn't tell me so himself, but I'm pretty sure, Rita, that your pin-up boy is also your cousin Dominic.'

That startled them, and there were further exclamations and remarks. Lesley began to put the cups back on to the tray. 'We've had enough excitement for one day,' she said briskly. 'Rita, I think you'd better lie down now. Rick, take this tray down and then go and get Dingo. Take a knife to cut the rope. We'll keep him close to us from now on.'

Much later, Lesley stood by the window in the darkened bedroom. Behind her Rita was sleeping peacefully, but to-night Lesley felt wakeful and depressed. She stared absently out of the window at the glittering stars and the clouds scudding across a cold moon. She shivered, though the room itself was warm enough.

She had problems enough with the twins and that meeting with the Trevendones, but she could tackle those. She wasn't the sort to be cowed by difficulties. It was something else. Surely though her depression had nothing to do with Blake Defontaine and the girl whom old Wonnacott had called 'his lady'. It was stupid to be like this. The sooner she went back to bed the better.

On a bright morning two days later, Lesley hurried into the great hall. She had just taken Dingo for a run and was smuggling him upstairs to Rita's room while she helped the girl to dress. Rita was getting up now, but so far she had not been out of doors.

Just as Lesley crossed to the second staircase the door of the small drawing room where old Mrs Trevendone usually sat with her companion opened and Dominic Trevendone came out.

He stared at Lesley and she smiled back. He made a gesture. 'We're both caught out, I think,' he said easily. 'I'm Dominic Trevendone and you're one of our visitors from "down under". I guessed who you were the other day, but I don't know your name.'

'I'm Lesley . . . Trevendone,' she added as if on an after-thought, 'and I guessed who you were too. This is an un-conventional situation, isn't it? I'm more than grateful for your hospitality while my sister Rita has been ill.'

'How is she, by the way?' he queried, his sea-blue eyes telling her that he found her most attractive with her flushed cheeks and her windswept hair. 'Bad luck that she went down with 'flu as soon as you arrived,' he went on smoothly.

'She's almost better,' Lesley replied. 'Which brings me to the question as to when we can talk to you and your sister. I don't want to say anything now, because Rita and Richard and I are all together in this. . . .'

She felt she was putting it badly, but he skimmed lightly and expertly over the awkwardness. 'Are you now?' he said, and his lips still smiled, but Lesley was all at once conscious of his dark reserve.

She said impatiently, 'Oh, be quiet, Dingo!' The puppy had begun to bark and jump up and she looked round distractedly.

'Let's get him outside,' Dominic suggested, and when they were out in the courtyard, Lesley asked, 'When do you expect your sister home?'

'She came back last night,' he said briefly. He made a gesture towards the house. 'She's in there right now, sitting with Great-grandma while Miss Yelland changes some library books.'

'I think perhaps we ought to go back to the King's Arms tomorrow,' Lesley said slowly. 'Perhaps you and your sister could meet us there.'

'Why do that?' he demanded. Again his eyes were full of admiration as they wandered over her face. 'This cold weather seems to suit you, though it's no great advertisement to Cornwall. Often we get a mild February, though I suppose it's stupid talking to you in terms of "mild".'

'At least you aren't short of water,' Lesley said with a little shrug. 'That's our problem, particularly in the Outback. But tell me, Mr Trevendone . . .'

'Oh, come off it,' he entreated with a grin. 'You can't be as formal as that . . . Lesley. Aren't we claiming each other as cousins?'

Lesley smiled back at him, warming again to his charm and his friendly manner. 'I ought to get back to my sister. She hates being left alone. Rick is . . . out.'

'Rick? He's the boy twin, isn't he? The one who's been spending a lot of time down at the coffee bar place at Penpethic Harbour, or so Defontaine was saying this morning.'

Defontaine! Lesley scowled but did not put her thoughts into words.

'There are some very odd types getting down on our Cornish coast these days, Lesley. I'd warn him to be careful.'

Lesley nodded but said nothing. She wasn't prepared to discuss Richard and his doings with Dominic or anyone else. Trust that Blake Defontaine, though, to put the visitors from over the sea in as bad a light as he could.

They were crossing the old orchard now, avoiding the leaves and spears of the daffodils which clustered around the trees. Later, it should be a pretty scene here, Lesley reflected; first the spring flowers and then the blossom. She smiled up at the young man.

'I love your county, Dominic.'

'It's yours too, if you're a Trevendone, isn't it?' he questioned. 'Once a Celt, always a Celt.'

Lesley started and gave him a quick glance. But she wasn't a Celt, though even in these few days the part of Cornwall she had seen had seized on her imagination and captured her thoughts. The place or . . . She shook her head, dismissing the word which had occurred to her. People! No, that was absurd. It was the place. What people could have captured her thoughts? She loved the soft west-country accent, the old-world politeness, but as to people, she didn't really know any of them. Not yet. Or perhaps one.

But he wasn't Cornish, or she never thought of him as such. He had no soft west-country accent. His voice, at least whenever he was addressing her, was curt, clipped and commanding and his manners were abominable. She had received not even the minimum of politeness from him.

But he had no real place here. He was merely a visitor, renting a property for a season. Soon he would be gone, and it couldn't be too soon for her.

'You're looking quite fierce,' Dominic teased, laughing down at her. 'Just like an Australian Boadicea, determined to take and hold her own.'

Lesley tried to skate over the implication of his remark. 'Surely she belonged to the other side of the country? I saw her statue in London. No, you must think of some other character for me. Some Cornish lady. But it can't be Yseult

73

of the White Hands, I'm afraid.'

And she looked ruefully down at her small, square capable paws, still tanned by Australian sunshine.

He put his own long-fingered hands on hers. 'Not to worry, little girl from over the sea,' he told her gaily. 'I like you as you are, little brown hands and all. But I shall call you Yseult.' And he dropped a light kiss on the top of her burnished hair.

'And now it's quite time I went back,' she told him, pausing as they came to the gate in the sea wall.

'When you get back to the house, have a word with my sister Jenifer. We both want you to tell us about yourselves and why you decided to come over here. Between you, fix a time for our meeting and I'll fit in.'

'Yes, we'll do that,' Lesley replied.

He gave her a smiling salute and went through the door on to the cliffs while Lesley turned back. She decided to take Dingo upstairs first and then after a word with Rita who was already dressed she ran down again into the great hall, pausing for a moment by the door of the small drawing room. Then she braced her shoulders, pushed it open and stood in the doorway.

Old Mrs Trevendone was nodding beside the log fire and at the writing desk was a girl with smooth dark hair cut short, dressed conventionally in a two-piece of kingfisher blue wool. Her eyes narrowed as she looked up and saw Lesley.

'Great-grandma is having a nap,' she said repressively.

'Yes, I see,' Lesley whispered, her first impulse to retreat. Then she changed her mind. Jennifer must have guessed who she was and Lesley was determined to put their own presence here on a correct footing.

So she came further into the room, closed the door quietly and walked over to the writing desk where the older girl remained seated, a hostile look on her dark face. You could tell she was Dominic's sister. Their colouring was similar, though her eyes were of a lighter blue. She was a plainer edition of Dominic with heavier features and a more serious expression. Lesley guessed she would be far more formidable than her brother.

'I'm Lesley . . . Trevendone,' she said quietly. 'I want to thank you and your brother for allowing us to stay while my sister was ill.'

'I don't see what else could have been done under the circumstances,' Jennifer answered ungraciously. 'I understand from Mrs Piper that your sister is practically better now.'

Lesley went pale reading the implication that they had now outstayed what welcome they had ever had. 'I've just been talking to your brother, Miss Trevendone. He . . . he suggested that you and I fix a time when we could all meet to . . . talk things over.'

Jennifer gave her a frozen stare. 'If you think it necessary.'

Lesley went very tense. All right, she thought recklessly. 'I do. Will it be convenient for us all to meet tonight?' Rita must rest this afternoon and then she would be able to sit up tonight.

Jennifer nodded. 'I'll send you a note by Mrs Piper about times. Now if you'll excuse me I've letters to write.'

'Of course.' Lesley did not smile. In a way Jennifer's hostility was easier than Dominic's charm. She retreated quietly, anxious not to disturb the old lady. But suddenly Mrs Trevendone sat up, her old eyes fixed on Lesley.

'You know, what Blake Defontaine wants, Jennifer, he gets,' she said solemnly. Lesley stared first at her and then at the girl by the writing desk.

'It's all right,' Jennifer said with a nod. 'It's just the tail end of a conversation we were having before she nodded off.'

Lesley smiled and said good morning to the old lady, who was showing signs of nodding off again. Her face was thoughtful as she walked slowly up the easy treads of the old staircase.

Ricky was out all day down at Penpethic Harbour, but as soon as he came in Lesley said abruptly, 'I saw Dominic and his sister this morning. They've sent a message by Mrs Piper a few minutes ago that they'll meet us in the small drawing room tonight at eight.'

Rick was obviously in a cock-a-hoop mood after a day at the discothèque. 'They'll meet us?' he echoed in a lordly voice. 'Surely it's we who should be calling the meeting. However, I'm all for a friendly settlement. If Cousin Dominic cares to buy me out I'm all for it. With some cash, Tim Drage and I can make for London much sooner than we'd planned.'

Lesley's eyes were troubled. That was the last thing likely

to happen or that she would want to happen. The only reason for her bringing the twins to Cornwall was to secure for them a home and a background, and the inheritance that was theirs by right.

'Look, Rick, I know you've got a good opinion of this Tim Drage and you're enjoying this discothèque place, but . . . but . . . is it all right? So many of these night spots are just dives . . . there are drugs, and—well,' she finished in a rush, 'if you want the truth Dominic told me to warn you.'

'And how does he know anything about my movements, I'd like to know?' Rick challenged, and the hostility on his face reminded Lesley of Jennifer this morning. 'Did you tell him?'

Lesley shook her head. 'No. As a matter of fact.. . .'

'Don't tell me. Let me guess,' he burst out. 'It was that trouble-shooter Defontaine. What does he mean by sticking his nose in my business?'

Lesley shrugged. 'Don't ask me. You know as much about him as I do. Perhaps it was because of Dingo ranging around on his own. Maybe he wondered where you were.'

'But how did he find out? Has he got spies all round the district?'

Lesley shrugged again. 'I expect everybody knows everybody else around here just as they do in the Outback. Dominic mentioned it only in passing, but he did look—er—well, serious.'

Richard turned away. 'I don't intend my cousin Dominic to dictate to me,' he said loftily. 'If there's any dictating to be done, I'm the one to do it.'

Lesley said nothing further, though her expression remained troubled. Neither of the twins seemed to realise the tight-rope on which they were walking. They had so little in the way of paper evidence to support their claim. Had she made the biggest mistake of her life in bringing them here? But she had sworn a solemn promise to their mother. If only Richard and Rita had been a bit older and a bit more cooperative!

CHAPTER V

The twins were very quiet that night when they sat with Lesley in the small drawing room waiting for their cousins to put in an appearance. It was now well past eight o'clock and Lesley was puzzled. Where *were* Dominic and Jennifer? Since this morning there had been no sign of them in the house. Was Dominic still staying at the Home Farm which was where he had been when they first arrived? But what about Jennifer?

Lesley thought, we've been here over a week now and we know no more than we did when we first arrived. Rita has never been out, I've been practically a prisoner with her and Rick has just opened the big door and gone rushing down the drive to get to that discothèque place.

Mrs Piper had said when she came up with Jennifer's note, 'The mistress is a bit on the tired side, so she's gone to bed early and Miss Yelland is going to stay in her room with her.'

Lesley realised that though Mrs Trevendone had accepted them, particularly Ricky, she was too old to be brought into the discussion. Perhaps too Dominic and Jennifer had heard of the unreasoning fancy she had taken to the boy because of his supposed resemblance to her husband.

'They're taking their time about coming,' Rita muttered. 'I wonder how much longer we've got to hang about.'

'I wonder,' Ricky agreed darkly.

But all three were shocked at first beyond any words when Jennifer and Dominic eventually came into the room, accompanied by Blake Defontaine and his girl-friend Mrs Lang.

It was Dominic who started the conversation, apparently quite self-possessed and easy in his manner. 'Well, here we are. Lesley, you and I have met and I think you know Jennifer, Sorrel and Blake. Will you introduce your brother and sister?'

Now Lesley found her voice. She jumped from the settee on which she had been sitting with Rita and Ricky on either side. Her eyes were a wide and hostile green as she stared at him. 'These are Rita and Richard, my twin sister and brother. But I thought this was to be a *family* discussion.'

It was Jennifer who replied. 'Sorrel, Mrs Lang is our cousin and has a right to be in any family discussion. Mr Defontaine is here . . . well, you'll understand *why* he's here in a few minutes.'

Lesley was far from satisfied. Four to one, she thought bitterly. For after all the twins were children, under age. She said angrily, 'I'd hoped we could settle this matter amicably just with a family discussion. I'm sorry any outsiders,' and she shot a hostile glance at Blake Defontaine, 'had to be called in.'

'Blake can scarcely be called an outsider,' Jennifer replied flatly, and Sorrel Lang, with a sidelong look at the dark face of the man beside her, added in a creamy voice, 'Far from it.'

'Suppose we all sit down.' It was Defontaine who spoke now for the first time. Earlier someone had moved a table from the side of the room to the centre and had placed chairs around it—seven chairs. I ought to have guessed, Lesley thought wrathfully. She and the twins took the chairs at one side of the table. Dominic was opposite her with Jennifer and Sorrel on each side and at the head or foot of the table sat Blake Defontaine, dominating the proceedings, with Sorrel on his right. At what point, Lesley wondered angrily was she going to get up, shepherd the twins in front of her and walk out?

Defontaine spoke as soon as they were all seated. His voice was quiet, almost impersonal, very different from his usual arrogance. 'Shall we all stop beating about the bush? As I understand it, Miss . . . er . . . Trevendone, you and your brother and sister have come from Australia. May we hear *why* you have . . . er . . . descended on Trevendone Manor . . . other than to make a pleasant social call?'

Lesley shot him a glance of green dislike. 'Directly we arrived here I told the people who received us, Mrs Trevendone and Miss Yelland, who we were,' she replied curtly. Quiet and mild his voice might have been until that last crack about 'a social call', but there was something in his attitude, and it had been the same every time she had encountered him, that roused her to angry rebellion.

'I made a claim for Ralph Trevendone's son. I understand that he, Ralph Trevendone, was heir to this estate. He is dead, but Richard is here, his eldest son and heir.

'It isn't,' she went on in a voice that was suddenly trembling with earnestness, 'that we want to dispossess anybody, but . . .'

'I suppose we all get up and bow at that point and thank you for your generosity,' interrupted Sorrel Lang with an ostentatious yawn. 'Look, hasn't this farce gone on long enough? Why don't we . . . ?'

'Just a moment, Sorrel,' Blake Defontaine put in. 'I'd like to hear this young lady out. On a previous occasion I informed her that the Trevendone family had believed Ralph Trevendone dead for the past twenty-five years and if that were true, none of them could be his children. Possibly she has documents which prove this to have been a false report.'

Lesley swallowed. She began to feel that she was getting the worst of this discussion and that the others were just as amused as Sorrel Lang appeared to be. If only she could put a sheaf of papers on the table and say, 'Look, look, look,' they might alter their attitude, but she couldn't.

She said quietly, 'Ralph Trevendone died fifteen years ago, a few months after Richard and Rita were born. That can be proved. As I said, we don't want to make trouble, but the plain fact is that we, or perhaps I should say Richard, is heir to this house and all that goes with it. Richard and his sister are only just sixteen, their mother is dead and Lactatoo which was their home had to be sold. Because of bank loans and dry seasons there was very little money left when everything was finally settled. I'm old enough to fend for myself, but it isn't right that these two should have to lead difficult lives when here in Cornwall there is property and money which rightly belonged to their father.

'That is why I gave up my job in Australia and brought them here as I'd promised their mother I would. She thought they would have a better life here than in Australia.'

'Better than in Australia? But surely that's the boom continent just now—the land of opportunity,' Blake Defontaine murmured with deceptive gentleness.

Lesley's face was still hostile. 'If you're very strong and tough it may be,' she said tersely.

'My dear young lady,' Blake Defontaine's voice was still gentle, 'those are exactly the words, were one so ungallant, with which one could describe *you*.'

79

Her glance flickered away from him. He was deliberately trying to enrage her, perhaps to make her look a fool, perhaps even worse. There was no doubt that he regarded them as adventurers and impostors. But it wasn't with him she had to deal.

She looked across at Dominic Trevendone. 'What I want to suggest, Dominic,' she said in a quiet voice, ' is that Richard and Rita come to live here at least until they are eighteen, possibly until they are twenty-one. Here they would have a home and a secure background. During that time something can be worked out. None of us wishes to turn you and your sister out or anything dramatic like that.'

' My dear cousin-that-would-be, you are really too kind,' purred Jennifer, but her pale blue eyes flashed venom. In her own quiet way she was as hostile as Sorrel. ' Isn't she just too kind, Dominic?'

Colour rose in Lesley's pale face. Also her temper. They weren't making it easy for her, but she supposed one couldn't blame them.

' Well, Dominic, will you give the twins a home?' she demanded.

But Dominic didn't speak. He hadn't done so so far and had sat with his head bent, doodling with his finger on the polished top of the table. Was he really so spineless? Lesley wondered. His sister and Sorrel and that insufferable Defontaine had all had their say, but he just sat without a word.

It was Blake Defontaine who leaned forward and examined her face with satirical grey eyes. ' You keep mentioning your sister and brother, Miss . . . er . . . Trevendone,' he said suavely, ' but there is no entail on this estate. Have you by any chance a will left by your father? If not, then in theory you have a right to a share in your father's estate. Actually as you are the eldest it could be *you* who is . . . or claims to be . . . Mistress of Trevendone.'

Lesley sat silent, but beneath the table her hands were clenched. It was uncanny the way this man was able to discern her every weakness. It almost seemed as if he had guessed that she wasn't Lesley Trevendone but Lesley Arden. Somehow she'd got to convince him that she wasn't wanting anything from the Trevendone estate for herself.

She said, 'I want no claim to anything like that. When I've seen my . . . the twins settled here in Cornwall I shall go back home to Australia where I'm . . . I'm going to be married.'

Rita's voice ripped the air like tearing silk. 'Lesley, you never told us that.' Her face was white and accusing. 'You're going to marry Steve! You . . . he . . . never said, and you're not wearing his ring.'

'Your sister doesn't seem to approve of your matrimonial plans,' Sorrel's voice came purring amusedly across the table.

Lesley put her arm round her sister, but the girl flung her off. 'Rita, we can talk about that later,' she said placatingly. 'I'll explain everything when we're alone.'

'Oh, don't bother. Just leave me out of this.' Rita pushed her chair petulantly from the table and went back to the big settee by the fireplace.

Lesley bit her lip and shot a glance of pure hatred at Blake Defontaine. It was his probing and questioning that had brought about this unpleasantness. Now Rita was hurt and upset, and goodness knew how long it would take her to come round again.

Sorrel Lang was leaning back in her chair, laughing. 'That seems to settle one of our queries,' she said in a silky voice. 'Actually we were wondering whether you'd arrived here with some sort of marriage proposal up your sleeve to set matters right.'

'Marriage proposal?' Lesley echoed now, uncomprehendingly.

'Yes, Miss Australia, we wondered if, having come over the sea to claim your inheritance, you might suggest that you and Dominic should marry and become co-heirs to the old place. The poor boy has been positively trembling in his shoes, haven't you, Dominic darling? Didn't you notice the relief on his face when you mentioned you had other marriage plans?'

'I say, Sorrel,' protested Dominic, speaking for the first time and looking profoundly uncomfortable.

Lesley turned a disdainful face from the dark gypsyish girl. 'I still think it would be more satisfactory, Dominic, for you and me to discuss our affairs without other people being present. The ones who count are Rita and Richard, and as they are not of age I must speak for them.'

For the first time Richard entered the discussion. Till now he had sat looking rather bored by the whole subject. 'If as this . . . fellow says'—he made a gesture towards Blake Defontaine, and his voice was wickedly offensive—'you, Lesley, as the eldest can inherit the estate then you *are* the one to do the discussing. Like Rita, I'm opting out.' And he got up and went to sit by his sister on the big settee.

Lesley shot a glance at the four sitting on the two other sides of the table and her eyes were angry. 'Rick, can't you see,' she said, turning round to the boy, 'they're just trying to cause dissension among us? That man knows quite well that the estate *must* go to you. If there's no entail then the property must have been left to Ralph Trevendone or there wouldn't have been those advertisements in the Australian newspapers. As he left no will his property will be divided among his children. All I wanted to do was to let our cousins know that I needn't be considered, but you and Rita *must* be.'

'Oh, for God's sake, Dominic, why don't you tell them? You can't expect Blake to do it.' This was from Sorrel Lang, her magnificent black eyes blazing at Dominic.

He looked back at her almost pleadingly and Lesley called to mind the afternoon when she had stood with him on the cliff and Dominic had looked down at the two riders on the beach. She hadn't been mistaken. He was desperately in love with Sorrel Lang.

'I just don't know how to put it,' the young man muttered miserably. 'It's such a let-down for them. Look, Blake, suppose we clear out and *you* just explain.'

Sorrel broke in again almost angrily, 'We're not the ones to clear out. Tell them the truth and let them go home to Australia tonight if possible. I for one shall be glad to see the back of them.'

Lesley wondered silently why this dark girl should have so much animosity towards them. They were not going to deprive *her* of anything. She owned that lovely house on the cliff and according to Mrs Piper was a wealthy widow. She had no place at Trevendone. They said she was a cousin, but Lesley was sure she was a remote one.

'No,' Blake Defontaine put in now in a measured voice. 'They've come for their share of the Trevendone inheritance. *Then I suggest they stay . . . and take their share.*'

There was a frozen silence. As Lesley raised her eyes to Blake Defontaine they glinted green while her slender figure tautened. Now what did this mean? He was actually asking them to stay and share the inheritance. Though what it had to do with him she still couldn't think.

'And now you'd better explain, Dominic,' he ordered curtly.

Dominic shrugged and cast him a glance that wasn't exactly friendly. 'It won't take long,' he said. 'What it amounts to, you three, is that there *is* no Trevendone inheritance. At least not for the family. Blake owns absolutely everything around here, and the estate, or the family—put it which way you like—is also in debt to him to the tune of several thousand pounds.'

Lesley realised that she had grown very, very cold. This explained so much. The way he had dominated not only this place but everyone in it. And yet . . . and yet . . .

It just wasn't true, she thought wildly. It couldn't be true. It was a plot—a way of getting rid of the unwelcome visitors from over the sea.

'It can't be true!' she gasped, not daring to look round at the twins. So far they had said nothing, possibly because this had shocked them into silence.

'Not true?' It was Jennifer who stood up now. 'Not true?' she flashed back hotly. 'Why do you think we've turned all this part of the Manor into a hotel? Why do you think we spend all the season slaving in order to pay back some of the debts?'

And now it was Ricky who jumped up. 'We . . . ll,' he drawled. 'Can you beat it? That's what Joe, one of the boys down at Penpethic Harbour, meant when he made some crack about my living in a classy hotel. I didn't get it. I thought it was his way of referring to the Manor. But a hotel! Oh, boy, that should rake in the lolly!'

His listeners received that remark in silence.

Hotel! The word was pounding in Lesley's brain, and yet in a way once the word had been used, she wasn't surprised. She ought to have guessed. All those bedrooms and bathrooms on the one corridor they had seen. The quiet comfort and luxury and yet the impersonal feeling. In its way, she supposed, it must be a super hotel.

Trevendone Manor, to which she had come from the other end of the world to claim for Ricky . . . a hotel . . . owned by a cold and cruel stranger.

She looked across at Dominic. 'I can't believe it,' she whispered.

'It's true,' he said flatly.

Lesley's big green eyes searched the faces opposite her. Sorrel's was triumphant, Dominic's uncomfortable and ashamed, Jennifer's angry and Blake Defontaine's—just impassive.

'Is it true?' she demanded, and for the first time that night she addressed him directly.

'In essentials it's true,' he replied curtly. 'Dominic's inheritance was a mortgaged property and a further debt, both to my family.'

His voice went cold, icier than that north-east wind which was still blowing outside, and his expression was sardonic. 'You three came here to demand your share of Dominic's inheritance, or perhaps to take all of it. Now it's up to you. *Take* your share. Stay and shoulder the responsibility of paying off some of the debt. Dominic and Jennifer are playing their part. *Now it is your turn.*'

Richard laughed in a rather raucous manner. 'If this is true, it's a jolly good thing you and I opted out, Rita, before we heard about it. We're in the clear and Lesley is too, because she said she was off back to Australia to marry Steve.'

Rita interrupted him shrilly. 'But Steve's coming here to Cornwall this summer with a Sydney life-saving and surfing team. He's going to be staying at some place near here. He told me. So Lesley *can't* go back yet.'

The older girl gave an impatient gesture. 'Be quiet, you two,' she said abruptly. 'I just can't take this in. If it's true, then the Trevendone family are . . . *his* . . . slaves,' and she made a motion in the direction of the powerful impassive figure at the head of the table.

'You could put it like that,' said Dominic with a bitter smile.

Lesley's glance roved from his romantic dark face to Blake Defontaine, sitting there with a kind of controlled patience. Were they all putting on an act? she asked herself once more. Was this just a curious, even shabby trick to get rid of the inconvenient strangers from over the sea?

It was Sorrel's turn again. She yawned like a pretty young black cat. 'Well, that's it,' she said creamily. 'As that boy has just reminded us, you've all opted out, so I suggest that you leave first thing tomorrow and pay your hotel bill before you go.'

Lesley's face took on a curiously stubborn look. Why should Sorrel Lang have so much to say, and why did she seem to have so much spite towards them? And how serious had Blake Defontaine been when he had spoken of the three of them playing their part? Was he really challenging her to stay? Lesley wasn't sure, though it was quite evident that his girl-friend wanted them out of Trevendone Manor at the earliest opportunity. Again Lesley wondered why.

She looked down at her hands and her long lashes swept her cheek. Two could play at this game, she thought. She would accept this joke of theirs tonight as if she believed it true. That should confound them.

'Naturally, I shall have to talk over this new situation with my brother and sister,' she said, a glint in her eye as she stared at Blake. 'But how exactly could *we* help in settling this debt to you?'

Sorrel stood up so abruptly that her chair almost over-turned. 'Haven't we had enough drama for one night?' she asked passionately. 'My advice to you three,' and her dark eyes whipped over them, resting longest on Lesley, 'is to clear out here and now, or in the morning at the latest.'

'But not before we've paid our hotel bill,' Lesley said with a white smile.

Defontaine rose too. 'You ask how you could help, Miss Trevendone? I understand that you've worked in an office as a receptionist, typist and book-keeper. In the season we could use you in the hotel, but in the meantime I'm in urgent need of a typist and you could fill in your time with me.'

There was a sudden challenging brilliance in his eyes and Lesley looked at him warily. Although she had tried to convince herself that she and the twins were the victims of either a plot or a joke to get rid of them she was all at once sure that this man would be no party to it. He would always come out with the brutal truth, the whole and nothing but.

If they stayed here at the Manor, it would be on *his* terms, and her heart failed her. They just couldn't stay. Before she could stammer out a shocked refusal, Sorrel broke in impetuously, 'Blake, you can't employ this girl. It would be far wiser to cut your losses and let them go. Maybe they *have* had luxury hotel accommodation for a week, or more, but better to let them go rather than keep them here to pay for it.'

He shrugged. 'As I judge it, they came here with the idea of cashing into an easy life. All I'm asking them to do is to look at the other side of the coin.'

Lesley took a deep breath. How hatefully difficult he was making it for her, as if he guessed how her heart had failed her at the idea of working for such a ruthless man.

Sorrel would not be silenced. 'You'll regret it,' she said darkly. 'They'll all be more trouble to you than they're worth.'

'You can say that again, sister . . . or should I say cousin,' Rita cried. 'If we do stay, and I'm not saying we shall, the more trouble *I* can cause the more I will, especially to you.'

'Why, you impudent little. . . .' Sorrel leaned forward, her face aflame, and Lesley remembered again that day when she had wanted to send her large Borzoi after the hapless Dingo. This was a very dangerous young woman.

Lesley put a restraining hand on Rita's arm. 'Rita, you will cause nobody any trouble,' she said coolly. And then to the four who were now all standing, 'I don't want to say anything more tonight. We three have got to talk things over. Tomorrow I shall be in a position to say what we're going to do. And now, goodnight.'

With Richard and Rita on either side, she went out of the room.

After a night of broken sleep, Lesley got up early, watching the sun come up from a stormy red eastern horizon. Thoughts and ideas churned through her mind to be discarded and then brought back again and re-examined, as possible ways out of their dilemma.

Rita was pale and tired when they got up to the big luxurious bedroom and Lesley had tried to cut short the discussion. 'Let's not commit ourselves tonight. Tomorrow morning we'll make up our minds whether to stay here or leave immediately, go back to London and arrange to sail for home as soon as we can.'

Both twins looked uncertain, even obstinate. 'Steve's coming here in the summer, or near here,' Rita muttered, and Richard kicked the toe of his shoe, saying, 'Penpethic Harbour is my scene, not Sydney Harbour, Les.'

Lesley's fingernails were digging into the palms of her clenched hands. 'Let's leave it till we've slept on it. Tomorrow our brains will be clearer.'

But the trouble was Lesley hadn't slept, at least only in snatches, and now it was morning and she was no nearer a solution than she had been last night. She dreaded the thought of staying here and working for Blake Defontaine, but what real alternative was there? She was trying to let the twins choose . . . or think they were choosing. She must wait to see what they decided.

When Rita woke up, Lesley said softly, 'Stay in bed, darling, and I'll go down and get our breakfast tray. Why, I think . . .' she opened the door, 'Rick's bringing it up now.'

'You *are* bright and early,' Rita jeered as he came in.

'Couldn't sleep,' he answered briefly. 'Could you two?'

Lesley shook her head, but Rita shrugged. 'I'm not losing *my* sleep about a crummy place like this.'

Lesley poured out the tea. 'We might as well get down to our problems,' she said simply. 'Just now we've got to decide whether we leave or we stay. Suppose we leave. The only sensible thing is to go back home. No, don't interrupt. I haven't finished. The truth is there's only enough money to pay for one fare. I might try to get a loan from Australia House. . . .'

'You're spending no more of your money on us, Les,' Rick said now, his face white. 'I'd planned to pay you back directly I got my hands on some Trevendone money, but . . .'

'Pay me back?' Lesley stammered.

'Yes, Jim Travers told me when Lactatoo was sold that it had always belonged to you, not to us. Mother and Father were only managers, caretakers for you after your parents were killed. They brought you up and Rita and I have almost forgotten that you aren't our real sister. Father was a poor sort of manager, I would guess, and after he died it was too much for Mother or for any woman to run the station profitably. No wonder when you came to sell you found you were up to the ears in debt. And then what you *did* salvage, you blued on passages to bring us to Cornwall to claim an inheritance that never was.

'No, Les, you've done enough and more than enough for us and some day I'll pay you back. But now we've got to fend for ourselves.'

Lesley shook her burnished head. 'It doesn't matter about the money. We're in this together. I take it you won't go back. What about you, Rita?'

'I won't go back without Rick,' the girl said sullenly.

'All right, then we'll stay. But where?' Lesley said.

'Les, do you think it's really true that the Enemy owns just about everything round here?'

'I'm afraid I do,' she replied slowly, 'though I'm going to make some further enquiries. All the same, everything points to his being master of all he surveys. It looked like that right from the beginning, you know. He's ruthless. We'd have to work our passage if we stay here.'

'But what on earth could we do?' Rita asked petulantly.

Lesley shook her head. If they stayed she had no intention of the twins doing anything, but she didn't say so at this point.

'As to repaying that debt, if debt there is,' Rita continued, 'it's just ridiculous.'

'I think it's only a kind of token payment he's been expecting from Dominic and Jennifer, and it would be the same for us,' Lesley said thoughtfully.

'Les, you don't want to work for him. Couldn't you get a job in St Benga Town and we'd get a flat or something and. . . .' Rick's voice died away. 'No, I see that wouldn't do.'

'The point is, will you stay on here if I can arrange for us to do so?' Lesley demanded abruptly.

'Yes,' Rick returned decisively.

Rita shrugged apathetically. The poor darling was still depressed after that wretched 'flu, Lesley thought with an anxious look. 'I suppose so,' Rita said. 'But I hope you both realise that what Les said last night will be true. We'll be slaves, and that man will be slave-master.'

'It was a stupid thing for me to say,' Lesley put in hurriedly. 'Right, we'll give it a month's trial here. If it doesn't work, we'll think of something else. Rita, you've eaten nothing.'

'I'm not hungry,' the younger girl said morosely.

Half way through the morning, Lesley walked out of the big main door determined on an outside exploration of the Manor and the immediate grounds. Some time soon she must seek out the Enemy and make their decision—and her conditions—known to him. But when she saw Dominic Trevendone tinkering with his sports car in the courtyard she altered her mind and went over to him.

'Hello, little Yseult,' the young man said, straightening up at her approach and smiling into her eyes. 'I hope you've decided to stay on. It would be a pity to lose you just as we're getting acquainted.'

Lesley resisted the blandishment on his handsome face. 'We haven't quite made up our minds,' she said cautiously.

'Then you'd better hurry, darling. Blake is coming over just before lunch to find out what you're going to do. The hotel correspondence is piling up and I'm not much of a hand at dealing with it, while Jennifer is the world's worst typist. Mrs Thomas who has done that side of the work for the past five years has just remarried and we've got to have somebody in her place. Blake is going mad because his precious book is being held up.'

His handsome eyes were amused, and Lesley saw that he had got over his gloom of the previous night.

'I've still a few questions to ask,' she said, looking at him gravely. 'How does that man come to be the owner of everything round here?'

'Darling, he inherited it from a great-uncle, when he was exactly fifteen years old, and he's been around here more or less all the time ever since.'

'But how . . . how did his great-uncle get the estate?' Lesley asked in a puzzled voice.

Dominic said with a shrug, 'It's a long story, but in essentials it amounts to this. Our grandfather—yours too—was a gambler, a dishonest one too. He mortgaged this place to pay his debts and then borrowed thousands from Blake's great-uncle on the security of a house that wasn't his. He could have been jailed and the family turned out, but instead old Miles Defontaine took over the mortgage, let the family remain in possession and hoped the Trevendones would pay him back one day. They never did, and now they never will.

'When my father died, he made Blake our guardian—Jennifer's and mine. It was ludicrous, for he wasn't old enough to be anyone's guardian. But he takes everything very seriously, so he started on the Home Farm for pedigree sheep and cattle and then when Jennifer and I were old enough to run it, he turned this part of the house into a hotel. So we slave here, the pair of us, throughout the season.'

'So it's really true,' Lesley said, but her wide green eyes rested curiously on his expensive sports car. 'Last night, I half believed you were all joking.'

'Joking!' Dominic gave a hollow laugh. 'It's a joke I've lived with all my life, little Yseult, and I haven't found it very funny.'

'Tell me about the hotel,' she demanded now.

'It's in the new part of the house—the part you've been living in. But if you stay, you've got to move to the Manor proper where Jennifer and Great-grandma and I live. This new part is closed up normally at this time of the year, but we had a big party of Americans for the whole of January and when they left, Great-grandma took the notion that she'd like to stay in that part as well. Jennifer was going to be away, I was at the Home Farm, so we had our housekeeper, Mrs Piper, move over to look after Great-grandma and her companion just when you three put in an appearance. Convenient, wasn't it? But Great-grandma decided last night that she wanted to get back to her own cosy quarters in the old house and off she's gone this morning. She's over ninety, you know, and we like to indulge her little whims.

'You'll like the Manor proper, the Old Manor we call it, tucked cosily at the back of this monstrosity. It's the original house, built of grey Cornish stone.'

'Monstrosity?' echoed Lesley, staring at the Elizabethan black and white front towards which he had gestured.

'Yes, that's the new part.'

'The new part? But—but it's old, Elizabethan, surely,' Lesley said now.

'Pseudo,' he shrugged. 'It was built about a hundred years ago by an ancestor who'd struck lucky, one of our roving ancestors of whom there have been a large number.' And he cocked a brilliant quizzing eye in Lesley's direction.

She refused to take up the challenge of his laughter. 'The hotel . . . Mr Defontaine didn't have any compunction about turning a home . . . *your* home into that?'

He made a gesture. 'To do him justice, he hadn't much choice. You must have heard of the predicament of most of England's stately homes. Not that this is a stately home in a big way and neither Jennifer nor I worry about this part. It's the old Manor we love. But in order to keep even that going, to pay the expenses of rates and upkeep, there's got to be some sort of income.

'As to the sort of hotel it is—well, smallish but very exclusive and fantastically expensive. We're very choosey about our clients and more or less the same people come year after year and, as I said, pay fantastic prices. But it's very well run. Blake sees to that, and sees to it too that Jennifer and I work like galley slaves during the season.'

'I'm sure he does,' she said slowly. 'My sister Rita says if we stay we too will be slaves, and Blake will be the slave-master.'

Dominic laughed discordantly. 'Your little sister has got something there, Yseult. That's what we all are . . . his ruddy slaves.'

Lesley turned away. She had found out what she had wanted to know. There had been no joke last night. Just the stark reality that the Trevendone inheritance was in Blake Defontaine's hands, and for the sake of the twins she had brought from over the sea, she must do her part in discharging the debt.

CHAPTER VI

The first month would end tomorrow and they were still here. Sometimes in her sheer fury against her boss—the slave-master, as Rita persisted in calling him—Lesley asked herself why after the first day she hadn't got up from her typewriter, flung his notes into his face and departed.

But always it was the thought of the twins that restrained her. Here they had a home, comfort and healthy surroundings. Where else could she, on the salary she could earn, provide so much?

That was one of the conditions she had made in her brief interview with Dominic and Blake Defontaine.

'I'll stay,' she said quietly, 'and work to the very best of my ability to earn our keep. But I won't have Rita and Richard tied down to any sort of job. They're too young and their education isn't finished. In the holidays they could perhaps help, but that's all.'

Defontaine looked at her thoughtfully. 'Your anxiety for the welfare of your . . . er . . . brother and sister does you credit, Miss . . . er . . . Trevendone. We'll discuss them later.'

Lesley did not look up, though once again she wondered whether that was something else he had guessed—that she wasn't really a Trevendone? If so, he was just being his usual subtle scheming self, saying nothing outright till it suited him to do so. But it was no good getting angry because he was mocking her. She would have to steel herself to accept his hateful mannerisms if she was going to work for him.

'We'll stay for a trial month,' she went on firmly. 'By then I shall know if I can cope and whether the twins have settled. It will also give you both the chance of judging whether you want me to stay in the post.'

'Posts,' interposed Dominic with a sly look at Blake Defontaine. 'Don't forget you'll be working for the hotel as well as being secretary for Blake. And that's a full-time job, I would imagine.'

'I don't mind how hard I work,' Lesley said between her teeth, driven as she always seemed to be into excesses whenever she was with Defontaine. ' In Australia, the Trevendones paid their way by hard work '—that wasn't strictly true so far as Ralph Trevendone went, but they weren't to know that. ' Now we're here I'll do the same. I'll put in long hours to settle even a small part of the family debt.'

' The sentiments do you credit,' murmured Blake Defontaine, and a faint cynical smile twitched one corner of his mouth.

She turned on him. ' At least I could do something to save Jennifer and Dominic working like slaves,' she flashed. There was a tense little pause. Dominic shuffled uncomfortably. Lesley's green eyes were fixed on Blake. His gaze, ironic, veiled, slid from hers. He cleared his throat. ' Quite,' he said, and then, after a pause, ' Right, you can start tomorrow. Use today to move into the old Manor and get settled there. Tomorrow I'll show you the type of work I want you to do for me, and Dominic can give you an idea of what clerical work needs to be done on the hotel side.'

That had been twenty-seven days ago and tomorrow she must find out whether she was to stay. Nearly a month since she had begun work here and now there were daffodils round the orchard trees and in the ornamental beds lining the courtyard and blue, pink and white hyacinths a glory of colour in the sheltered beds on the south side of the Manor.

Lesley took the last sheet of paper out of the typewriter, covered the machine and turned to look out of the window. For the past month she had worked in this little office at the end of the great hall in the new part of the Manor near to the big reception desk. She went towards the window behind her, revelling in the sunlight and the warmth which came from the sun, though outside there was a blustery March wind and to her it was as cold as it had been in February.

Lesley thought again: A month! We said we'd give it a month's trial and the time is up tomorrow. I wonder. . . .

She hadn't really wanted to start thinking about her employer, but it was something she found difficult not to do. He was so dominating, so strong, so ruthless that he overshadowed everybody else in the Manor. He was, as she had decided that first evening when she had heard of the family debt, he *was* Trevendone.

And the odd thing was that everybody acknowledged it and gave way to him at every turn. Lesley reflected that she had never heard anyone challenge a single statement—at least not to his face. The staff of the Manor obviously held him in the deepest awe and respect—and even more. She had discovered the first suspicion of that 'even more' in her first week of working here.

Blake was away for a couple of days and though he had left her enough work to occupy her during his absence she stayed in the office late in the evenings and completed it well before time. That gave her the opportunity of finding out more about her hotel work which Dominic was supposed to supervise.

Lesley found it was almost impossible to pin the young man down and his knowledge of the job seemed to her scanty in the extreme. His handsome face became more sulky as she persisted. 'Look, Yseult my darling, why don't you relax and stop worrying? I'm an outdoor sort of bloke, not an office clerk. My responsibility around here is really the Home Farm, and that's enough for one ordinary fellow. We're not all supermen like Blake. Mrs Thomas, your predecessor, was efficient—I'll say she was, and even Blake admitted it, which is something—so I never interfered. If you really want to know about the job, sweetheart, I suggest you find Mrs Thomas. She lives in a bungalow in St Benga Town. But, darling, why worry?'

Lesley was coming to the conclusion that Dominic seldom did. That afternoon, however, she took him at his word and drove the Mini to a small bungalow on the outskirts of the town.

She was welcomed by a smiling little person who invited her in. 'Yes, I *was* Mrs Thomas, but I remarried last week and I hardly knew how to write telling Mr Defontaine. He has always been so good to me, so considerate.'

Lesley received this surprising information in silence and looked round the sitting room which showed evidence of packing.

'I'm in the most frightful muddle,' the other confessed. 'It all happened so quickly—Mr Raybold's proposal and his being able to sell his hotel. It's only a small place really, but he had a splendid offer and he's taken it. He's always wanted to travel and so have I.

'Do sit down, Miss Trevendone.' She swept some books from a chair and plumped up the cushion. 'You *did* say Miss Trevendone, didn't you? That's odd really, because I thought I knew all the members of the family—just on nodding terms, as you might say. It's Mr Defontaine who is the mainspring at the Manor, and don't you know it when he's away!'

'I'm a distant relation on a visit from Australia and I've been doing some typing for Mr Defontaine,' Lesley explained. 'Mr Dominic Trevendone suggested I come along here to ask you about your method of book-keeping and accounts.'

Mrs Raybold smiled. 'Mr Dominic—now there's a charmer for you, but no idea about office work. I just used to tell him to run away and let me get on with it. It was easier in the long run.'

Her face took on a worried line. 'That's what has worried me and made me feel really guilty—letting Mr Defontaine down. You know, it was the one thing that made me hesitate when Mr Raybold proposed. You see, I know how difficult it is to get a really efficient receptionist book-keeper for seasonal work. I feel awful.'

Lesley said quietly, 'I've done book-keeping and accounts in an office in Australia, so I have the general idea. Mr Defontaine wondered if I might be able to take over . . . if you could give me a few tips. Have you time?'

Mrs Raybold's face cleared. 'Of course I've got time. I'd do *anything* to help Mr Defontaine. He's a grand person.'

Lesley left her three hours later, her face rather thoughtful. Mrs Raybold had been a great help, had showered Lesley with good advice and even congratulated her on her good fortune. Lesley thought it was all rather odd.

So good! So considerate! The memory of the phrases and Mrs Raybold's glowing face as she had uttered them remained with Lesley as she drove back to the Manor. Hardly the sort of description *she* would have used about the slave-master, she thought wryly.

Another of his great admirers was Sorrel Lang, though that relationship was different, as Lesley was the first to admit. After all, if you are madly in love with a man you are naturally convinced that he is a person set apart, and that was Sorrel's attitude.

She was always at the Manor House. She kept her horse in the Trevendone stables and rode with Blake most days. Even now when he was once again in London on business, she came to ride on the beach and stay for lunch with the family in the dark little dining room of the old manor.

She never bothered to disguise her hostility to Lesley, but she seemed to have started an odd sort of love-hate relationship with Rita, who had always been keen on riding and didn't hide her admiration for the young widow's beauty and her daring if rather slapdash horsemanship.

Lesley couldn't disguise her surprise when, on the day before Blake was expected back, Sorrel strolled into her office and said, casually, ' Rita says you're thinking of driving into Exeter tomorrow to buy some boots.'

Lesley looked at her warily. ' I haven't any really decent ones. I ought to have got a pair in London when Rita bought hers. I thought I'd go in the morning, as I'm quite up to date with my work.'

' Better come with me, then.' Sorrel's voice was still casual. ' I have to go in for a fitting and it seems stupid to take two cars. I know the road and you don't, and my car is bigger and faster.'

Lesley hesitated, wanting to refuse but not quite knowing how. In a way it would be churlish to draw back from the first offer of friendship which the dark girl had made, casual though it had been.

Perhaps it wasn't really a sudden change of attitude. If the rest of the family knew Sorrel was going to Exeter it would look very mean to them if she didn't offer to take Lesley and strange, too, if Lesley refused to accept it. So. . . .

' Thanks, I'll be glad of the lift,' she said briefly.

' Be ready at nine. I want to get back here for one o'clock lunch. That should give us more than two hours in town, long enough for me to have my fitting and do some shopping and for you to buy your boots.'

Sorrel's car was a big Italian model which she drove badly and far too fast. The girls exchanged very few remarks during the journey, for Lesley was watching the road so that she could use her own car next time. Sorrel wasn't in a good mood, it would seem, for she snapped out very brief replies to the few polite remarks Lesley felt constrained to make and in the end Lesley settled for looking at the scenery, marvelling at the greenness of the fields and admiring the trees still standing with their delicate lace outlines against a pale blue sky.

Sorrel parked in the Cathedral close and then said briefly, 'The High Street is just over there and you'll find plenty of shops. Be back here at twelve prompt, not a minute later. And if we do miss each other there's a coach station further up the High Street.'

She turned away and Lesley, feeling that she was dismissed, wandered over to look at the shops in the precincts and then through a narrow street into the main thoroughfare.

She made her purchases within the hour and then browsed round the shops for another half hour, going back to the parking place well before the time Sorrel had mentioned. But there was no car—at least no Italian model.

Lesley wandered around the parking places without success. Then she thought: I didn't wait to see, but she probably drove off to wherever she had her appointment. She'll come back here at twelve and pick me up.

But the Cathedral clock boomed out the hour, then the quarter, then the half, and Lesley guessed that Sorrel wouldn't come now. She'd better go and find where the coach station was. Actually she wasn't particularly upset. Sorrel had been an uncomfortable companion this morning and her driving was erratic and fast—not a safe combination. Lesley told herself comfortably that she would be happier returning on the coach.

She didn't feel quite so contented when she eventually reached the coach station and found she couldn't start the journey back to St Benga Town till ten minutes past five and that it would take all of two hours.

Actually it took about forty minutes longer, for all traffic on the road was held up by a giant transporter moving at a snail's pace. When she finally reached St Benga Town it was dark and the local bus which passed the Manor gates had gone. So there was nothing for it but to walk.

She arrived back in the small panelled hall of the old Manor House to find a reception party awaiting her—and heading it, Blake Defontaine, his eyes the cold colour of dull pewter.

So he was back, a day early, and she supposed that coldness on his face was because she had taken a day off. 'Where the hell have you been till now?' he demanded as he strode up to her.

His unexpected return and his abrupt question plus the fact that she was overwrought put her immediately at a disadvantage. She went very white and began to stammer. 'I walked. I'd been expecting—to come back with Sorrel, but somehow I missed her. I waited for a long time, but eventually I had to get a coach.'

She sat down abruptly on one of the straight-backed chairs. 'And what about the man you picked up . . . or who picked you up . . . in Exeter?'

Jennifer, who had been hovering in the background with the twins, now said rather accusingly, 'Sorrel rang up at lunch time. She said you hadn't come back to where she'd left the car, and after she'd waited and waited she'd concluded you were returning with the man you'd been talking to in the Cathedral precincts.'

Lesley was still trying to recover her breath and Richard, elbowing the rest of them aside, came to bend over her. 'You aren't hurt, are you, Les?' he queried anxiously. His hand was on her arm, and his thin young face a mask of alarm. 'We've been worried stiff, Rita and me. We knew you wouldn't go off with someone else if you'd promised that Sorrel woman you'd meet her. What happened?'

'I told you, she wasn't there,' Lesley said in a faint voice. 'I . . . I . . . waited and waited. The only man who spoke to me in Exeter was that salesman who was staying at the King's Arms when we were there. As I got out of Sorrel's car, he was just passing and he said, "Hello, Miss Australia, so you're still around," and I said "Yes." That was all. So I came home by coach.'

Beside them, Blake was standing listening to every word. 'I phoned and found the coach arrives at seven-ten,' he said, his voice sharp. 'The connecting bus along the coast leaves five minutes later. Look at the time now!'

Lesley got up, her chin tilted. She had recovered her breath and her spirits. 'I'm looking . . . and what time I arrive here is no concern of yours, Mr Defontaine. If you'll excuse me, I'll go to my room.'

She turned and ran up the two flights of stairs to the room which she shared with Rita. Her sister followed more slowly.

'I'm glad you told him where he got off,' Rita said with immense satisfaction. 'He was steamed up about you, though. You might have been his favourite girl-friend the way he was pacing up and down asking Rick and me why you'd gone to Exeter and why you hadn't gone in the Mini. But, Les, what really happened?'

Lesley was, shrugging herself out of her leather coat. 'Exactly what I said,' she remarked. 'The Exeter coach was late because it got behind a huge transporter which took up all the road, and so the other bus had gone.'

'Why didn't you get a taxi or ring up here for someone to fetch you?'

Lesley shrugged and turned as Jennifer Trevendone knocked at the door. 'Are you all right, Lesley?' she asked nervously. 'Mrs Piper is making sandwiches and coffee for you. We aren't really callous, you know. Just . . . just . . . suspicious because we don't know you very well. And though I don't really excuse Blake's high-handed manner he really was anxious.'

'If it's the Trevendone family he's bothered about, then he has no cause to be anxious about Lesley,' Rita said, and with a significant look walked out of the room.

Lesley's expression was worried. 'It was bad luck that you missed Sorrel,' Jennifer went on, preparing to follow Rita.

Lesley shrugged. 'It certainly was,' she remarked dryly. 'Travelling all that round-about way back by coach isn't my idea of an evening's entertainment.'

Jennifer opened the door. 'Here's your supper. Did you want it up here?'

'Yes,' said Lesley shortly as Rick brought in the tray.

As she drank her second cup of coffee, Lesley said thoughtfully, 'Rick, what's wrong with Rita?'

The boy hunched up his shoulders. 'We had a row. I said I bet that Sorrel woman had let you down and Rita got on her high horse and stuck up for Sorrel. She's completely soppy about her because she lets her groom her horse. Rita hangs on her every word. You'd think she's never ridden herself. They may have been rough, tough little Outback ponies, but they're every bit as difficult to manage as these fancy blood stock animals the slave-master goes in for.

'And by the way, Les, he really *was* worried about you.'

'Nice of him,' said Lesley acidly. 'Let's talk about something else.'

She had thought that she would sleep soundly after that exhausting day, but she lay wakeful for a long time, worrying about ·Rita whose quiet even breathing she could hear from the bed on the other side of the room. Rita had so little to say to her these days and when she did speak she was often rude or offhand. And Ricky—would he ever be weaned from this ambition of his to join a group and become a popular singer? Once she had hoped he would become reconciled to life here on the estate, but what opportunity was there for him here now? Sadly she recalled what Rita had said to Jennifer, not in so many words but by implication. That Lesley wasn't a Trevendone!

As to Blake Defontaine, it was just his intolerable habit of interfering in the lives of everybody who was a Trevendone —even the girl from over the sea.

He walked into her office in the New Manor House next morning with his usual loose-limbed arrogance and stood in front of her desk eyeing her with a rapier-like glance.

'I want a promise from you,' he said abruptly. 'That you'll never walk back from St Benga Town again after dark, unescorted.'

Lesley shrugged. 'I don't suppose the occasion will ever arise again, Mr Defontaine.'

'A promise,' he said insistently.

She nodded. 'If you insist.'

'Mrs Lang is very upset,' he went on. 'She can't understand what happened that she missed·you.'

'No,' commented Lesley dryly, and looked at the wad of notes he was carrying. 'Shall I start on those right away, Mr Defontaine?'

'Yes, do that,' he said, gave her downbent head an exasperated look and went out of the room.

As she walked round to the old Manor House for her lunch break, Lesley met Dominic who had been out when she had arrived back on the previous night. He had evidently heard what had happened and spoke about it directly he saw her.

'Look, Lesley,' he said, and for once his face was serious, 'Sorrel wouldn't let you down on purpose. Jen is sure you think she did.'

' I haven't said so.' Lesley's voice was suddenly ragged. Sorrel! Sorrel! How tired she was of this concern for the girl, first from Blake and now from Dominic.

' Look, Dominic, do me a favour, will you?' she asked, and managed to rake up a smile. ' Forget it. I'm sick of the whole subject.'

' As you like,' he returned rather huffily.

But Sorrel never once mentioned the matter to Lesley nor thought fit to make either an explanation or an apology, and Lesley on her part was determined not to speak of it again.

Lesley's primary reason for buying a new pair of boots had been the point-to-point in which Blake and Sorrel and Dominic were competing. Even Jennifer was riding, though not one of the Trevendone horses.

The meeting was held at Cumballick, about twenty miles' drive from Trevendone Manor. It was a bright, gusty day in early March, still within the month of Lesley's time of probation, with a feeling of spring in the air and the daffodils blooming everywhere in the flower beds of the cottages of Cornish stone, lending them a glamour which till now their rather grim greyness had lacked in the eyes of the family from over the sea.

Rita was plainly out of humour because they were going only as spectators.

' But there aren't any spare mounts at Trevendone, Rita, you know that,' Lesley said soothingly. ' You heard Jennifer say she was riding one of the Drews' horses from Tresparret Farm. Besides, you've had no experience in jumping.'

' So much for our coming to a life of luxury in Cornwall,' Rita muttered, scornfully. ' At least there was always an Outback pony to ride when we were at home.'

' You weren't all that keen on riding back home,' Ricky pointed out. ' In fact in the last year or two you'd practically given it up. As to this meeting, you'd only to say the word and we needn't have come. It isn't my idea of an entertaining Saturday watching Cornish high society perform at a steeplechase. I'd much sooner be with the boys at Penpethic Harbour.'

Lesley frowned slightly at the mention of that place. ' It's a good opportunity for you both to meet friends of the Tre-vendones in the county. By now I should imagine that it's got around that we're living at the Manor, and people may be wondering what we're like.'

'As if any of us really cared!' commented Ricky con-temptuously.

There was a bigger crowd at the meeting than Lesley had imagined. She had thought in terms of the riders and just a few spectators, but by the time they arrived a good number of people were milling around and the tote seemed to be doing excellent business.

They found Dominic almost as soon as they had parked the Mini and he took them into the members' enclosure where a buffet lunch was being served.

'Jennifer is with Bob Drew, but Sorrel and Blake are around somewhere. Oh, there they are.' He began pushing his way through the crowd, people around him slapping him on the shoulder and wishing him luck. He was obviously very well known and very popular.

Outside on the course, the rich Cornish accent had been noticeable, but in here what Ricky still referred to as 'Limey talk' was more apparent.

'I'm only an also ran,' Dominic was protesting to one elderly lady. 'Blake has really good mounts and he's favourite in his two events, but in my opinion the really fast race will be the Ladies. Sorrel Lang has a superb horse and so have Carol Williams and Griselda Knowles. It'll be a close finish. Griselda is favourite, but I'm backing Sorrel.'

Lesley smiled rather wistfully. Dominic seldom missed an opportunity of flirting with *her*, but she had guessed at their first meeting that he had no real interest in any girl except Sorrel Lang. But Sorrel . . .

Lesley bit her lip and told herself it was no business of hers.

The twins, having already said they were ravenous, had pressed on towards the buffet and, Lesley, having lost Dominic, tried to force her way through the crush in search of the twins.

'You'd better let me lend you a shoulder,' a voice said above her ear, and she turned to find Blake Defontaine beside her.

'I'm really with Dominic,' Lesley said repressively, 'but now I've lost him and the twins.' She shivered, wondering why she suddenly felt so very cold.

'The twins are tucking in at the buffet,' he said, smiling down at her, and just now his grey eyes were brilliant. Obviously the sweet smell of success was in his nostrils, Lesley thought. She had just heard Dominic say he was the favourite in both the races he had entered. 'They're all right. I was with them a moment ago. Now what would you like? You look cold. You'd better have hot coffee with rum. You're not used to this chilly weather.'

'I'll find the twins. Please don't bother about me, Mr Defontaine,' Lesley said repressively.

But he either didn't hear or didn't choose to, still keeping his hand firmly on her arm as he made his way through the throng.

Soon they were at the counter, but nowhere near the twins who had evidently bought what they wanted and retreated to the back of the marquee.

Lesley was still shivering. She hoped to goodness she wasn't getting the same sort of virus as Rita had had last month. Rita had not seemed her usual self since, though the doctor had pronounced her fit.

Blake tipped some of the rum into the coffee. 'Now drink that. I've put in only half, so it won't make you tipsy. You're not teetotal, are you?'

'I suppose not,' she murmured ungraciously, 'but I don't care for spirits.' Her eyes wandered uneasily. 'Dominic will wonder where I am.'

'Will he?' Blake looked sardonic but made no further comment. He stayed beside her until she had drunk the coffee, laughing at the way she grimaced as she did so. Next he pushed a Cornish pasty in front of it. 'Now eat all of it,' he ordered. Then with a glance at his watch. 'I'll have to go now. I'm riding in the first race. Don't stay to the end if you still feel cold. If the twins don't want to leave, I'll bring them back with the horse box. There'll be plenty of room for them up in front.'

'But won't you have to bring Sorrel—Mrs Lang back?' As soon as it was out, Lesley could have bitten her tongue for asking such a question.

Blake raised an eyebrow. 'Dominic will look after her,' he said.

He left her then and Lesley realised she hadn't wished him luck. Her eyes followed him thoughtfully. What had he been trying to say just now—that Sorrel had no particular claim on him? Lesley thought that Sorrel would have put it differently, and a snatch of conversation she overheard later bore out that view.

'I would have thought young Mrs Lang would be the favourite in the ladies' race.'

'She's more than that in the Defontaine stakes,' the young man grinned down at the girl who had made the first remark. 'She's the winner. They're waiting a decent interval of a few months before announcing it, but they're to be married some time in the summer.'

Lesley moved on. So that was it. They didn't want a formal announcement just yet. Well, they were well matched, both ruthless, unpleasant people. She found them equally hateful and felt even more convinced of the hatefulness of one of them when later in the afternoon Sorrel, who rode with the same reckless abandon as she drove her big car, was thrown at the second fence. Lesley didn't see what had happened, but when she heard that it was one of the Trevendone horses which had fallen she hurried round the course and was in time to see the St John Ambulance men carrying the stretcher into the first aid tent. Even now she wasn't sure whether the rider was Sorrel or Jennifer. By the time she had pushed her way through the crowds several minutes had elapsed, but eventually she reached the first aid tent and pushed back the flap.

It was Sorrel who had fallen, but she was already sitting up pushing her long black hair away from her face. The St John Ambulance attendants had stepped back and beside Sorrel were two men in riding clothes, Blake and Dominic, one on either side.

Lesley stood silently just inside the tent wondering how she could retreat before anyone saw her. Sorrel would welcome no solicitude or offer of help from her, particularly while she had Blake standing beside her and Dominic bending over her.

And then Sorrel's voice rang out in irritation. 'Dominic, for the last time will you stop fussing, and go away. You get on my nerves!'

She pushed the young man from her and then, struggling to her feet, she seemed to melt into the other man's arms. 'Oh,

Blake darling, I'm all right. I really am.'

Lesley shrank back against the canvas as Dominic turned and strode towards the tent flap. She didn't want him to see her, but she really needn't have worried, for he walked like a blind man, his face stricken.

Lesley followed him out silently. Poor Dominic!

Although she had lost all interest in the meeting, Lesley stayed to the end and collected the twins in the Mini when most other people were leaving. Sorrel, apparently none the worse for her fall, was with Blake and presumably would return with him.

Ricky was in high spirits and began recounting his winnings as Lesley put the Mini in gear and turned for home. 'Blake gave us some tips and I'd the gumption to follow them,' he said jubilantly. 'Rita was silly enough to back Sorrel in the Ladies' Plate and that didn't do her much good. How did you make out, Les?'

'Badly,' she said with a wry grin. 'I stuck pins in and the pins didn't seem to know about winners.'

'Didn't you even back Blake?' he asked incredulously. 'He was a cert in both his races.'

'So it would seem!' And then in a surprised voice, 'When did he give you those tips?'

'At the lunch counter. He stood us our lunch—a jolly good one, didn't he, Rita?'

'And it nearly choked me,' Rita said morosely.

Ricky laughed uproariously. 'You gave the best exhibition of choking I've ever seen,' he remarked. 'You didn't leave a crumb.'

Rita's lips twitched into a smile, but she shrugged, 'Well, he's a bighead all the same. Fancy tipping himself to win and saying he'd got two exceptional horses just to tone his conceit down, as it were. And then saying he didn't think Sorrel would pull it off and that we ought to back that Griselda Knowles on Honeycombe.'

'Well, if you'd accepted his advice you'd be a pound or two better off,' Rick pointed out. 'After all, he *did* win, and that Griselda too. She's a far better rider than Sorrel. You could tell that even before Sorrel came off.'

That started a wrangle to which Lesley only half-listened. She was surprised that Blake had approached the twins and she wasn't sure what was behind it. She smiled wryly. One thing seemed almost inevitable. Everybody at the Manor had been anxious for trophies to be brought back and the person who was bringing back two was not one of the Trevendones but Blake Defontaine.

Did he ever lose? she wondered. Tonight he would return with the trophies and the girl, while Dominic who had told someone in her hearing that he would be an 'also ran' had been exactly that. And Sorrel had dismissed him and said that he got on her nerves.

And so on a sunny March morning just a month after she had started work in this small office, Lesley stood by the window looking out but not really seeing the green lawns nor the daffodils that had 'taken the winds of March with beauty'.

She was remembering the weeks that had passed and wondering what Blake would say when he came to tell her whether she was to go or to stay.

She knew perfectly well that when she had started work that day in February he had been suspicious of her motives and sceptical of her ability. He had never once tried to make any task easier for her. The notes she had had to type for him were technical in the extreme and his handwriting was atrocious. Whenever, in the first day or two, she had had to refer to him he had been either curt or sarcastic, but gradually as she became accustomed to the terms and to the writing she had been able to work alone. She was a swift and accurate typist and though he had never given her a word of praise, neither had there been any complaints.

The hotel would not open till Easter, but with the tutoring she had received from little Mrs Thomas she believed she could cope with that. So now it was for the slave-master himself to decide whether she was to stay.

As he came sauntering into the little office she turned, feeling almost guilty that she wasn't working. But she had finished the last batch of notes and the hotel clerical work at the moment was minimal. All rooms were completely booked for the high season, so she had little to do except type the occasional letter accepting a booking for a late season holiday or answer the telephone to say that no accommodation was available.

He was carrying a sheaf of papers which he placed on her desk and then stared at her with his usual craggy expression. 'I can guess what you're going to say,' he remarked in a quiet voice. 'The month of trial is up. Well?'

Lesley faced him, her hands behind her back so that he should not see them trembling. As usual he was forcing her to speak first, make a fool of herself, possibly, and then he would devastate her with a few sarcastic words.

'I'm willing to go on working here,' she stammered, 'at least until the hotel closes at the beginning of October.'

'That's remarkably considerate of you,' he answered, but there was no warmth in his voice and there was a preoccupied look on his face. 'But remember I shall still want part of your time for typing my research notes. For that, you'll have to work down at the Lodge, in the small office adjoining my lab. It's a nuisance, because I like to keep the Lodge completely separate from everything connected with Trevendone Manor, but in the circumstances I can't do anything else.'

Lesley, concluding that the interview was over, walked towards her desk to pick up the notes he had brought in, but he put a hand on her arm as she passed him. She went tense and cold as she had last week when he had touched her in the members' marquee at the point-to-point.

'There's just one point I'd like to clear up,' he said.

'Yes?' With an effort she forced herself to brave his cold eyes.

'This fellow in Australia. Your sister said something about his coming here in the summer. You wouldn't let his arrival interfere with your work here, would you? These surfing exhibitions usually last only a short time. It would be very inconvenient if you left us in the lurch before the end of the season. There was some mention of marriage, wasn't there, though I notice you don't wear a ring.'

Her green eyes, black-fringed, looked back at him with contemptuous antagonism. Was there any limit to his intolerable interference in Trevendone affairs? she wondered in exasperation.

'I'm not in the habit of breaking my word, Mr Defontaine. If I promise to stay till the beginning of October, I shall stay, and if it's of any interest to you I don't wear a ring because I'm not engaged.'

'Oh!' If the information had given him any satisfaction there was no evidence of it on his dark face. 'One other point,' he went on casually, 'if you aren't engaged to that fellow in Australia and not waiting for him to arrive here, what's made you decide to stay on? You're working for no salary and you're working damned hard. How come?'

It was only later that Lesley began to wonder what lay behind that question. At the moment she took it at its face value and answered simply, 'I'm staying because of the twins. I brought them here and I must see them settled. I hope my work here covers the cost of their keep and my own. The Trevendones try to pay their debts, Mr Defontaine.'

'Most admirable,' he returned in a voice of silk as he strolled over to the window.

She watched him, aware of tension in her neck and down her back. In so far as she could ever have any warm feeling for this man she was grateful for what he had done for the twins in getting them both admitted to a local technical institute where Rita was studying commercial subjects and Rick a G.C.E. course which included a study of music.

Rita had been moderately amenable about the arrangement, but it had been touch and go with Rick until Tim Drage down at Penpethic Harbour had weighed in with his approval.

Suddenly Defontaine swung round. 'You worry too much about those twins. You're much too young for so much responsibility. Isn't it time you made some sort of life for yourself?'

She gave him a straight look from her clear green eyes, but she was careful to keep her voice indifferent, even colourless. 'When *are* you too young for responsibility, I wonder? How old were you, Mr Defontaine, when you took over the responsibility of Trevendone?'

A small muscle in his jaw tightened. 'Actually I was fifteen . . . much, much too young. But I'm a man, Miss . . . er . . . Trevendone. I'm tough. Too much responsibility is bad for a woman. It makes her hard.'

Hard, thought Lesley, remembering Sorrel Lang. You should know. 'I'm sure you're a very good judge,' she said politely.

CHAPTER VII

It was later when she was remembering that conversation that Lesley suddenly thought of Dominic. Had Blake's probing questions about her reasons for staying been put to find out whether Dominic was the attraction?

Perhaps she was being kinder to the young man than was altogether wise, though she doubted if Dominic would misunderstand no matter what other people might think. But she had felt really grieved for him after witnessing his curt dismissal by Sorrel in the first aid tent at the point-to-point meeting and the way the girl had quite unashamedly shown she preferred the other man. If any kindness on her part could help him over a bad patch, Lesley was only too willing to show it.

Of course she had liked him right from the start not only for his good looks and charm but also because from the beginning he had accepted them as Trevendone cousins from over the sea, not the unwelcome strangers which they had been to Blake and Sorrel and even to Jennifer. He always had time for the twins, and was interested and indulgent about their ' crazes '—Rita's about horses and Ricky's about his music.

On his side, Dominic flirted with her quite openly and unashamedly as he probably did with any pretty girl, and only gradually did it begin to dawn on Lesley that Blake suspected she had more than a passing interest in the young man.

Was that why he had questioned her about Steve Wentworth, or was his real reasoning for exacting a promise that she would stay to the end of the season a fear that when she realised that there was nothing serious behind Dominic's blandishments she might in a fit of pique decide that ' slavery ' here at Trevendone wasn't leading to anything worth while and she might as well leave?

She began to notice that Blake always looked particularly sardonic when Dominic called her Yseult. One day they even came to the verge of a quarrel on the subject. Lesley was upset, for she could never be sure what Blake really thought behind the mockery that forever tinged his bleak eyes when he looked at her.

'This Tristan and Yseult caper,' he said, stretching his legs indolently. He had been dictating letters to her in the little office off the great hall and Lesley was looking through her notes for any queries before she began to type.

She looked up, her white brow pleating, her eyes wary. 'I beg your pardon.'

'Oh, not at all,' he said with a curl of his lips. 'I merely wondered who was featuring as Tristan and who was the one she came over to marry—Mark, wasn't it? Do I recollect he was rather a dull old stick and Tristan was the handsome young man about town?'

'I really haven't the slightest idea, Mr Defontaine,' Lesley replied repressively. 'I'm not really very familiar with your Cornish legends.'

'Now I *am* surprised to hear you say that,' he mocked. 'The twins have always given me the impression that you were the romantic one of the family, you were the one, as they put it, who was "sold on Cornwall".'

'But in any case I thought all you visitors from the Antipodes and the States were very familiar with our legends, much more so than we are ourselves. King Arthur and Guinevere and Sir Lancelot are the trio in another version, aren't they? One of these days I must take you over Bodmin Moor to Dozmary Pool and you can picture the sword Excalibur glittering with jewels as it was thrown into the lake . . . or the three queens bearing King Arthur to the fabulous Isle of Avilion.'

Lesley said coldly, 'I've read the stories, of course, but I'm not in the least romantic and not really interested.' Which was a lie and he took her up on it immediately, a gleam in his grey eyes.

'You were down at Tintagel with Dominic the other day. Wasn't it the legend of King Arthur and the Knights of the Round Table that took you there—the magic of . . . Tristan . . . Or shall I say Lancelot?'

Lesley's eyes shot green fire and something odd constricted in her throat. What exactly was he getting at? 'What I do in my spare time can be of no interest to you, Mr Defontaine.'

He shrugged. 'You're right about that, of course. I'll be in my lab if there's anything in those letters you want to ask me about. But use your own initiative as far as possible and don't bother me. As I've told you I like to keep the Lodge and my lab completely separate from Trevendone affairs.'

He sauntered out, arrogant as ever, and Lesley watched him go, gritting her teeth. That particular crack was because she had had to seek him out twice yesterday with queries. If he thought she was doing it for the pleasure of seeing him or hearing his voice, he couldn't be more mistaken. He was the most infuriating, hateful man she had ever met. She wished she could have reminded him that she had agreed to stay on here to help the Trevendones—but the truth of the matter was that he *was* Trevendone.

Why this sudden—or perhaps it wasn't so sudden—interest in Dominic and herself? She thought: I must begin to mention Steve more often. It won't be so very long now before he flies over.

For that matter it wouldn't be so very long before visitors in large numbers began to come to Cornwall. And then as Blake had said, the hotel business would keep her occupied and she would have less time for typing his lecture notes and the book on which he was still working.

Then her thoughts were back again to his latest remarks. He mocked at everything, she thought angrily. He knew quite as well as she did that Dominic was laughter-loving and gay, and his pleasant little conceit of calling her Yseult meant nothing very much. But it made her feel happy for the dark romantic-looking young man to pay court to her. It wasn't as if they took each other seriously, but if her smiles assuaged Dominic's pride and helped him to forget his ill-starred love for Sorrel what was the harm?

Later that day she sat idly for a few minutes, her work finished, planning to stroll on the cliffs for a while until it was time for the evening meal. On this lovely evening of early April you could almost be forgiven for thinking that summer was already here.

As so often her thoughts were on the twins. They grumbled far less these days and seemed to be making lives of their own even at Trevendone where Ricky was on excellent terms with Dominic and Jennifer and also with Blake. For Rita, Sorrel came first, though she was also attached to Dominic. But life at Trevendone Manor as Lesley had imagined it and painted it to them in the romantic country of Lyonesse just didn't exist. Perhaps it never had in the way she had pictured it. And not for worlds would she let Blake Defontaine guess how romantic her ideas had really been.

Her life here was completely workaday, she told herself, suddenly feeling lonely and depressed. Perhaps that workaday world was redeemed occasionally by views of the lovely coastline and the burgeoning countryside now spring was really here. She had imagined they would see it when they drove down to Cornwall that early February day of cold sleet, but it had been late in coming. But now it was here giving the country lanes an embroidered pattern of yellow primroses that sent Lesley into raptures of delight as she went out to pick them and arrange them in bowls of glowing sunlight on the dark polished tables and chests in the old Manor House.

Lesley thought of all that loveliness and wondered why she should feel so dissatisfied. Was it because every time she walked on those magnificent cliffs that separated Trevendone Manor from the turquoise and emerald sea she was reminded that sometimes on that beautiful and treacherous coast that same sea was the colour of dark pewter—the colour of a man's eyes; and that when the curling, sparkling foam fell back, there were malignant black rocks jutting brutally out of the water—but no more brutal than a man's tongue could sometimes be.

The Easter weekend in mid-April brought a spell of fine weather and during that busy time Lesley had her first real taste of hotel work. Each night she went to bed so tired that she slept quite dreamlessly the moment her head touched the pillow.

The worst of the rush was over by Wednesday and in the hour during the afternoon when Jennifer had taken over from her at the reception desk, Lesley decided to find a sunny spot at the edge of the garden, close her eyes and just relax.

She walked across the courtyard and the lawn with its gay flower borders and suddenly remembered the spot which Dominic had called the Kissing Seat, the half of an upturned boat with a board across to make a seat, and sheltered between the two trees which leaned together, their branches for ever entwining. There she would find some shelter from the wind that now seemed fresher than it had been over the warm weekend and where she could get a glimpse of the distant sea, this afternoon stretching smoothly like a length of turquoise silk.

She had sat for only a few minutes when she saw Dominic standing above her, a grin on his good-looking face. 'I followed you out, little sweet, and I wondered if I might catch up with you here. Remember what it is—the Kissing Seat? Well, anything to oblige my pretty little Yseult.' He bent over her, obviously intending to kiss her, but as she had done once before, Lesley jerked away. She flirted with Dominic often enough, but he must not get the impression that she was leading him on. With Lesley Arden he would have to learn that it was so far but no further.

He laughed, and his grip on her shoulder tightened as he leaned still further towards her. 'Oh no, Yseult, you pay the forfeit this time. No escape.'

'Dominic, no!' she whispered, and breathed a sigh of relief when he straightened up. 'I'm off,' he said curtly, and strode away.

Lesley, though she had had every intention of repulsing any further attempts at lovemaking, was rather surprised that he had been so easily snubbed. Then the reason for his precipitous departure became all too apparent. She had long suspected that Dominic in spite of the smoothness of their surface relationship disliked Blake Defontaine as much as she did. It appeared he wanted to avoid him just now. She was anxious to do the same, for there had been a scene in the little office this morning between Blake and herself that she didn't want to think about.

All the same, she wasn't going to beat a retreat quite as obviously as Dominic had done. So she remained firmly seated inside the boat, looking steadily ahead of her. Blake advanced, a glitter in his eye.

'So you're taking up the challenge, Miss Trevendone,' he smiled, and it seemed to Lesley that there was in his voice as always when he spoke to her the flicking of a whip against her senses. 'Is this your first time in the Kissing Seat?'

All at once, and quite stupidly, Lesley's heart began to beat at a rapid pace. He wouldn't . . . dare . . . She got up in what she hoped was a leisurely manner.

'Surely you're not going to run away when you've succeeded so quickly and presumably at your first attempt,' he mocked her. 'I gather Dominic is not the man to lose an opportunity. I do apologise for my own inopportune appearance. I'm sure you realise that I'm too old for such nonsense.'

Lesley gave him a swift, startled look. His dark eyebrows were raised, and a faint cynical smile twisted one corner of his mouth. Her face flamed in indignant fury at the implication of his jibes. That she had sat here to encourage Dominic to make a pass at her, and remained here on the chance that he too . . .

'Mr Defontaine, believe me,' she said between her teeth, 'I never bother to have a single thought about you apart from my work. And now if you'll excuse me I'll go. The sun seemed so bright I thought it would be pleasant to sit here, but the wind is treacherous like so much of the English . . . climate. Apparently warm but really bitterly cold.'

'You sound rather disillusioned. Why not, since you feel devastating, call it the Limey climate?' he asked, the mocking inflection still in his voice but something fiery in his usually cold eyes. 'That's a word I used to hear often from your young . . . brother and sister.'

'So far as I understand, Limey is just used for people,' she returned. 'But don't let me detain you, Mr Defontaine. I was just going to move.'

'I'm sure you were going to do nothing of the sort,' he challenged. He seemed to be looming over her, but despite her every inclination, Lesley was determined not to run away.

'You like Dominic? You get on well with him?'

'Of course I like him.' Lesley's voice was light. 'He's a very pleasant young man—good-looking and charming and considerate. No girl could help liking him.'

'And working together as you are doing in the hotel? You find that satisfactory?'

Now what was this in aid of? she wondered. Well, if he thought she was going to venture some criticism about Dominic's easy-going attitude to work, he was mistaken. 'Of course,' she remarked non-committally. 'We get on very well together indeed.'

There came then what to Lesley's stretched nerves seemed a long, long silence. When she ventured to look at him she saw something in his eyes that she had never seen there before, something dangerous which filled her with trembling alarm. In spite of all her resolutions she *was* going to retreat. In fact she was going to run.

She said, chokingly, 'I'm cold,' turned from the Kissing Seat and ran through the nearby gate. Once behind the wall she stood beneath the Kissing Trees, willing herself to still the stupid panic in her heart. She had closed her eyes and so his arms were around her and his lips were on hers before she knew he was there.

For a moment she stood rigid in his hold, and then it seemed as if all her bones had melted. There was just one kiss, hard and swift and merciless.

'We can't let Dominic have all the fun, can we, my love,' he whispered softly. 'But I didn't intend kissing you in the Kissing Seat—only under the Kissing Trees.'

Before she could think of anything to say, he had strode away. By the time Lesley had to some extent recovered her composure, she was alone and a quick glance round showed no one else in view. Trembling, her thoughts completely chaotic, she hurried to the old Manor, walking through the dark panelled hall to the warm, well-appointed kitchen.

She was on good terms with all the staff at the Manor, but she particularly liked the housekeeper, Mrs Piper, who had been so good when Rita was ill. She was a Cornish woman from St Benga Town and with daily domestic help from the village, she ran the old Manor House, cooking for old Mrs Trevendone and her companion and some meals for the rest of the family. She lived in a flat over one of the garages with her son Jeff who drove the hotel Landrover and acted as handyman.

'What you want, m'dear, is a nice hot cup of tea,' she said with a quick glance at Lesley. 'I'll have it in a jiffy, and you just get warm by the stove. A real cold wind there is out. It's turned this afternoon, as I know, having just walked back from the village.' She chuckled. 'No wonder you're all but frozen, m'dear soul. I see'd you there sitting in the Kissing Seat.'

Lesley swallowed hard and put on an innocent expression. Had Mrs Piper seen . . . ? 'The Kissing Seat?' she repeated. 'I was sitting in a sheltered place, a kind of upturned boat to keep out of the wind.'

'That's it, m'dear, the Kissing Seat. I see'd you and I said to myself, "Now I wonder what young man will come along and catch her there. She'm expecting Mr Dominic, forbye, and then I could a'died laughing when I saw Mr Defontaine talking to 'un.'

Lesley stared at her, her heart in her mouth. What next? 'I'm sorry, Mrs Piper, I don't quite follow. I'm all at sea.'

Mrs Piper almost choked with laughter. 'That's just what 'un bain't, me handsome. 'Un were all on land.'

Lesley braved the old woman's merry blue eyes and began to smile. 'What is this all about, Mrs Piper? Mr Defontaine stopped to say it was cold for sitting around and I agreed with him and came in for a cup of tea.' The housekeeper seemed to have missed seeing Dominic, which was all to the good, and what had happened behind the wall was well out of anyone's view. 'My love,' he had said as he held her. Lesley shivered.

'Here's your tea. You'm still real cold,' Mrs Piper said with a look of concern. 'And you be careful, m'dear, about they old Kissing Seat. Hereabouts they say that a maid never marries the one whoe first kisses her there. Not, I'm sure, that Mr Defontaine would be doing any such thing. More reserved like, he be, wouldn't you say, m'dear?'

Lesley avoided answering that question by a pretended eagerness to know more about the local superstition. 'So they say you never marry the boy who first kisses you under the Kissing Trees. That's rather sad, isn't it, Mrs Piper?'

'Now don't get the little old story wrong, Miss Lesley,' the other said, shaking her head. 'It b'aint the Kissing Trees —them's different. It's the Kissing Seat. Un you kiss under the Kissing Trees, un's the one for you, so they say, but what beats me is how you can kiss under the trees and not on the seat. That's what beats me.'

It hadn't beaten Blake Defontaine, though. Behind the wall, you could stand under the Kissing Trees and be forced right against the wall and your mouth bruised with just one kiss. . . . The cup rattled in the saucer she was holding.

'Now don't 'ee get me wrong about Mr Defontaine, Miss Lesley. Reserved un may be, but un's a man, m'dear . . . a real man. I guarantee Miss Sorrel knows that all right.'

Mrs Piper like the rest of the staff had the greatest admiration for 'the Maister'. Lesley turned away. 'I expect she does,' she said dully. 'Thanks for the tea, Mrs Piper.'

'Don't mention it, me handsome,' smiled Mrs Piper.

Still feeling entirely unlike her usual self, Lesley walked back to the New Manor to take over the reception desk duties from Jennifer. If it weren't for Blake Defontaine and his girl-friend, life at Trevendone Manor, despite the hard work, would be tolerable, she thought.

She liked old Mrs Trevendone who though very vague and keeping to her rooms very much now the season had begun was always pleasant and welcoming. She seemed to have accepted Lesley and Rita as her great-grandchildren, though it was Ricky who was her first favourite. Jennifer appeared to have got over her initial hostility. She worked hard in the hotel, much harder than Dominic, and Lesley had grown to respect her.

When she arrived at the big reception desk she saw that in the little office behind it Jennifer was talking to Sorrel Lang. They were very deep in a discussion and Jennifer at least seemed rather embarrassed by Lesley's appearance.

'Oh, there you are, Lesley. I hadn't realised it was time for you to come on again.' She walked towards the door where Lesley was standing. 'I've just been hearing what happened this morning, Lesley. I'm sorry. I'll see Blake and explain that it was my fault.'

'Oh, I shouldn't worry,' Lesley said with a shrug. 'Forget it.'

Jennifer shook her head. 'Oh no. Coming, Sorrel?'

'Not for a moment,' Mrs Lang called out carelessly. She was in riding kit and Lesley wondered whether she was going down to the beach to ride with Blake or whether she was on her way home. Her big Italian car was in the courtyard in front of the hotel, as Lesley had noticed as she came to the front of the New Manor.

Lesley went into the office and sat down at the desk on which her typewriter stood. She seldom wasted any words on Sorrel since that occasion when the girl had left her high and dry in Exeter and had never thought fit to make either an explanation or an apology.

'Jennifer and I were just talking about you,' Sorrel said in an insolent voice.

Lesley did not raise her head. 'Really?' she said indifferently.

'Yes, we were discussing what we both believe is Blake's plan for you.'

That did rouse Lesley. She swung round in her typing chair, and tension tightened her throat. 'Blake's plan for *me*? What plan?'

'We've both got the idea, Jennie and I, that he has it in mind that you and Dominic might make a match. That would unite the two branches of the family and make everything neat and tidy about your claim to the estate.'

'The claim isn't mine. It's Rick's,' Lesley said stonily.

'Oh, anybody can see Rick isn't interested either in the estate or in the hotel and Rita will go back to Australia as soon as she can. So that leaves you.'

Does it indeed? thought Lesley grimly. What a shock Blake Defontaine would get when he knew the real truth—that she had no business here at all since she wasn't a Trevendone. Though oddly enough, she had always feared that he'd half suspected it right from the beginning. But evidently not, if what Sorrel was suggesting was true. So much for his wanting to make everything 'neat and tidy.'

But the last person with whom she was going to discuss this or anything else was Mrs Sorrel Lang.

'You and Jennifer must have been enjoying yourselves,' she said contemptuously as she swung back to her typewriter. 'Was Dominic in at the discussion too?'

Sorrel smiled, reminding Lesley, as she so often did, of a handsome black cat. 'Dominic! Well, of course, *he* hasn't a clue. Naturally.'

Her black eyes flashed as she repeated the word, 'Naturally!'

Lesley thought; she isn't in love with Dominic, but she won't let him go to anybody else. In so many words she's warning me off.

She got up and went to the window. There had been a mist far back in the sea for most of the morning. Then it had seemed to clear, but now it had thickened and the wind had brought it swirling inland. It seemed to press silently against the office window, almost menacingly, just like this woman who stood by the door, menacing too in her own way.

Lesley said, 'Frankly I don't know what all this is about.'

'You like Dominic, you like him a lot?' Sorrel questioned. Lesley shrugged and went back to her desk. 'Of course I like Dominic a lot. He has been nicer to me than anyone else here. Also he's very good-looking and very good fun—a dreamboat. So of course I like him.'

And Sorrel could make what she could of that.

Sorrel's black eyes blazed. 'Well, take it from me. It just isn't on!' she almost spat.

Lesley sat down in the swivel chair and inserted some paper into the typewriter. 'Isn't that a matter between Dominic and myself?' she asked provocatively.

'No, it isn't. It concerns all of us—all the Trevendones, that is. When we had that first conference you announced loudly enough that you were going back to Australia to get married. Rita says your young man is coming over here for the summer. So don't get involved with Dominic or it might be . . . awkward.'

'When you've quite finished dissecting my love life, perhaps you'll let me get on,' Lesley said in a voice of ice. 'And if it's of any interest to you or to . . . anyone else, I'm not contemplating marrying anybody at the moment.'

'Don't throw your Australian boy-friend to the winds in the hope of getting a better catch,' Sorrel said, her eyes still blazing vindictively. 'A bird in the hand, you know. . . .'

She sauntered out, leaving Lesley staring after her with sick distaste on her face. Sorrel Lang was quite impossible . . . a fit match for the revolting man she was going to marry.

Her thoughts went back to Jennifer. So she had heard of the unpleasantness this morning and was evidently intent on making amends. Lesley hoped to goodness she would leave well alone. It was over now, and it was a mistake she wasn't likely to repeat.

The affair had arisen from the fact that a client had rung up on Tuesday morning to say that he would not be taking up his reservation that night but would be arriving after lunch on Wednesday. Later a couple had phoned asking for accommodation for one night—the Tuesday—and Jennifer had happened to answer the call. She had turned to Lesley suggesting that as Mr Forsyth's room was vacant they should accept this booking.

Jennifer was a much keener business woman than Dominic, anxious, as she had said bitterly more than once to Lesley, to free Trevendone from debt so that she could live a life of her own.

Lesley was dubious. Mr Forsyth, it seemed, was an old and valued client, a wealthy man, and there was no question of his not paying for the reservation.

She had shaken her head, well aware by now how Blake Defontaine liked the hotel to be run, but Jennifer with a very set face had reminded her in icy terms that in theory at least, Dominic and she were the owners of Trevendone Manor.

Lesley could do no more than accede and offer the room for the night. That might have been the end of it, but unfortunately this morning when it came to paying, the couple had quibbled over the bill. They had arrived rather late in the evening, had not asked for any refreshments nor for the hotel terms, and Lesley, largely through inexperience, had not mentioned them.

This morning when she had presented them with their bill there was a certain amount of unpleasantness into which unfortunately Blake had appeared. Lesley was fairly confident that she could have coped with the situation, but Blake immediately took over in an icily correct manner, found out that the couple hadn't been quoted terms, asked what they had expected to pay, and still icily correct, had ordered Lesley to accept that amount.

The affair was over in a few minutes and the couple departed, not at all sure that they had come off best. But then, so far as Lesley was concerned, had come the deluge. She was determined not to involve Jennifer, so she had said nothing to justify herself and that had enraged him even more.

'I gave you credit at least for being able to carry out orders,' he said sweepingly. 'What would you have done had Mr Forsyth changed his plans and turned up unexpectedly last night—as was well within his rights? He hadn't cancelled his reservation. He had merely had the courtesy to let us know that he couldn't arrive until today.'

Lesley stared down unhappily at her fingers and found nothing to say.

When on the following morning Blake came to where she

was sitting at the reception desk, Lesley scarcely raised her eyes. She had spent a disturbed night, and felt weary and unrefreshed. Before she had finally gone to bed, she had stood for a long time by the window looking at a star-spangled sky which seemed to mock her mood of burning anger and resentment by its very remoteness.

Remote as *he* was. It had satisfied some dark devil in him to hold her in his arms till her bones melted, kiss her once, and leave her to feel like this, unsettled and bereft and with a knowledge that for her life would never be quite the same.

And more or less at the same time, he had been discussing with his girl-friend and Jennifer the pros and cons of her marrying another man, deciding whether he would approve or disapprove, give his consent or withhold it.

At the moment Lesley felt that she hated everybody here at the Manor. What a fool she was to stay—to become, as they thought, a pawn in their schemes.

'I'd like a word with you, Miss Trevendone, in private,' Blake said above her head.

That constricted feeling was in her throat again. If he referred to that kiss; if he *dared* to apologise, she would walk out even if it meant leaving Rick and Rita here.

She said, in a muffled voice, 'I'm very busy. These accounts have to be checked.' It was Dominic's work, but as usual he had left it to her.

'I won't keep you for more than a few minutes,' he said, and it sounded to her as if there was half the Arctic Ocean in his voice. He walked behind her chair to the small office and after a moment she followed him.

'Sit down,' he said, and when she had sat in front of the typewriter he closed the door and leaned his broad shoulders against it. 'Why didn't you tell me the real facts about the Forsyth booking yesterday?' he questioned, his eyes bleak.

Lesley was so relieved that this was the subject he wanted to see her about that she almost sighed with relief. The unexpectedness of the question left her unprepared and in an off-hand manner she said, 'Why should I?'

It wasn't really what she would have answered, given time, but at the moment there was little room in her mind to think of anything else except his intolerably insulting behaviour yesterday afternoon beside which his sarcasm of the morning paled into insignificance.

His face went darker than ever. 'Doesn't it matter that you were blamed for something that wasn't your fault?'

She gave him a quick look and saw that his black brows were drawn in a forbidding bar across his face. With a sudden spurt of anger she stood up. 'Where *you* are concerned, Mr Defontaine,' she said, 'it doesn't matter in the slightest.'

He moved from the door so that she could pass, and it was surely just a trick of the light that on his face was an expression of hurt bewilderment. Which was, as Lesley told herself when she sat down at the reception desk, about as wild a flight as her imagination had ever taken her.

CHAPTER VIII

Now it was early May and in the hedgerows of the Cornish lanes the primroses had faded to give place to a wealth of spring flowers whose names Lesley did not know, while the cliff sides and edges were bright with sea pinks and yellow vetches.

Lesley glanced through her last sheet of typing, flicked it out of the machine into the wire basket and flexed her fingers. If she was going for a stroll on the cliffs before dinner she'd better start now, she told herself apathetically. She didn't expect Blake to come in with more work for her tonight, but as she was typing in the little office off his lab next to the Lodge, it wasn't beyond the bounds of possibility.

It was still lovely and sunny outside and Cornwall in May was out of this world, but tonight for some reason Lesley could feel no thrill. Why did life seem so empty just now? she wondered. Was it just the *malaise* of spring when most people became restless or was she homesick for Australia . . . and Steve?

Since she had arrived in England, Steve had written to her every week, short scrawled air mail letters with no more than a sentence or two. Now he was coming to England with the surfing and life-saving demonstration group who were giving displays up and down the coast during the summer. Steve wasn't an actual member of the group, but somehow he had got himself attached to them and since his father was a wealthy pastoralist, Lesley suspected he might be helping to finance the party.

Lesley recalled the time she had been the Wentworths' guest at the Royal Show in Sydney and how proud she had been of Steve dressed in what was practically the uniform of the rich pastoralists' sons—cavalry twill and a wide-brimmed hat. It had been gay and exciting and she had known that Steve's parents liked and approved of her. They would have welcomed an engagement, and then had come the message from Lactatoo that Margaret Trevendone was ill.

In the end she had quarrelled with Steve about the twins. He had poured scorn on Lesley's promise to Margaret Trevendone to bring her children to Cornwall to claim their father's inheritance and in a temper Lesley had handed him back her eternity ring—the one he had given her as a ' friendship ' ring when they had first met while she was still at school.

Steve had recovered his temper before they sailed and had come to Melbourne to see them off. He had looked at Lesley with upraised brows and a quizzical expression when both Rita and Rick had declared gloomily that they didn't want to go.

Well, they had come, and now Lesley never heard either of them speak of returning. In the past weeks they had been making lives for themselves quite apart from her, simply because she had been so busy adjusting herself to the strenuous tasks that had been piled upon her. Yet could she have done anything else in view of the fact that she had to earn not only her own keep but theirs in addition to doing an infinitesimal amount to paying off the Trevendone debt to the slave-master?

Lesley's brow creased. That was Rita's phrase these days rather than anyone else's. She just hadn't reconciled herself to life at the Manor in the way Rick had. At one time she had spoken a great deal about Steve's forthcoming visit because in Melbourne she had obviously had a schoolgirl crush on him, but now his name was never mentioned.

It all seemed to stem, Lesley thought, biting her lips, from that night of the family discussion when she had said rashly that she was returning to Australia to marry.

Rita had uttered that one cry of outrage, Lesley recalled, and never once since had she referred to the subject again.

What had possessed her to say that about marrying? In a way it had just come into her mind when she had wanted to make it clear to the Trevendones that they need feel no responsibility for *her*—that it was the twins who must be considered.

That surely had been her motive. Or had there been another one? A desire to show that arrogant, impassive man who had sat at the head of the table that though he might despise her as an awkward, red-haired, green-eyed young woman from over the sea, there were men, and one man in particular, who admired and loved her sufficiently to want to marry her.

Lesley brushed her thoughts away impatiently, put the cover

on her typewriter and picked up her yellow sweater. There had been a high wind all day, and though it was very sunny, it might be a bit chilly on the cliffs.

'Lesley.' Blake Defontaine stood in the doorway, looking across at her with those cold repellent handsome eyes of his. Lesley's own eyes widened slightly. Odd for him to use her Christian name. Usually he was formality itself. Always 'Miss . . . Trevendone' with that hesitation between the two words that even now left her feeling uneasy. As if he knew she had no claim to the name, and was mentally accusing her.

'Yes, Mr Defontaine.' Formality there too. She might think of him as Blake and sometimes as 'the slave-master', but to his face it was always formality.

'You have a visitor,' he said coolly, and stood aside to let a squarely built fair young man follow him into the room.

'Steve!'

'Lesley!'

They moved instinctively towards each other, met in the middle of the room where Steve's arms went round her in a bearlike hug.

'Les, it's seemed like years,' he said, kissing her again and again.

Lesley managed to release herself. 'Steve, it must be telepathy! I've been thinking about you tonight, and now here you are, though I didn't expect you for weeks. Surely the party isn't coming till June?'

'I decided I couldn't wait any longer,' he grinned. 'Oh, Les, I've missed you.' He would have begun to kiss her again, but Lesley drew back.

'Steve, this is Mr Defontaine. I told you in my letters that I'm working as his secretary.'

'It's a bit on the late side to be still working, isn't it?' Steve's blue eyes were faintly hostile as he turned to nod to Blake. Lesley had always thought of Steve as tall and broad, but beside Blake he looked almost a boy.

'We work all hours here,' Defontaine returned, giving Steve an assessing stare. 'Actually I think Miss Trevondone has just finished work now. Where are you staying, Mr . . . er . . . Wentworth, isn't it?'

He was being, as Steve was to remark later, a Limey at his worst.

'Les said there was a hotel set-up here,' Steve said bluntly. 'I'd thought of getting a room here.'

'I'm afraid the hotel is completely booked, isn't it, Miss Trevendone?' Blake said, with no regret whatever in his voice.

'Yes, Steve, I'm afraid it is.' Lesley looked rather embarrassed, for Steve was staring at her in a puzzled fashion. This wasn't Australian hospitality. She could read the expression in his eyes and knew what he was thinking.

And now it was Blake Defontaine's turn to be blunt. 'Mrs Trevendone is very old and though she had extended her hospitality to Miss Trevendone and the twins in the old Manor, I don't think Miss Trevendone would care to impose on her further.'

'No, no,' Lesley said hastily, her face flaming. How could she think of asking the Trevendones to entertain one of her friends when she herself was an impostor? Oh, why hadn't Steve written to say he was arriving earlier than the other life guards?

'We'll get you a room at the King's Arms in St Benga Town, Steve. It's only three miles away and Mr and Mrs Cleaver who run it are very pleasant people.'

'Quite a good idea,' said Defontaine blandly. 'I suggest you ring the Cleavers up, Miss Trevendone, and then you'll be able to run your friend down in your car.'

He went out and Steve opened his mouth to say something uncomplimentary, but Lesley put a slender hand up to his lips to restrain him. 'Wait till we get up to my car, Steve, and I'll explain,' she said hurriedly. 'There was a lot I couldn't write.'

And indeed why should she? It was Steve who had broken with her in his first anger at her leaving Australia with the twins, and the distance and the weeks of separation and all that had happened had created a gulf which couldn't be bridged in five minutes.

Mrs Cleaver had a vacant room and she would reserve a table for dinner for two. Lesley suggested that Steve should leave his bags in the porch of the Lodge where they could pick them up when she drove down. Then she took him up the drive across the garden and into the courtyard. He stood staring at the pseudo-Elizabethan front of the new Manor and shrugged. 'Quite a place, isn't it, Les? But no room for a visitor from Down Under!'

'Steve, it's terrifically popular. People come year after year, and there just isn't one vacant room. After all, I'm the receptionist, so I really do know.'

'You seem to be running the place, if you ask me. . . .' His voice changed. 'Why, if it isn't Rick! Say, old chum, I'm real glad to see you, too right I am!'

It was Rick, with Dingo on the lead, who had just walked round into the courtyard. The puppy, of course, set up his usual chorus of excited welcome and in desperation Lesley drew Steve away from the front of the hotel and round to the old Manor in the stable yard of which her Mini was parked.

Rick followed, declaring as soon as he heard that Steve was booked in at the King's Arms that he was coming too.

'Where's Rita?' Lesley asked, once they were out of earshot of the new Manor.

'She's rushed to do her face and hair,' Rick said laconically. 'The slave-master phoned up to say Steve had arrived and that Les was taking him down to St Benga Town in the Mini. It seems the limit that we can't put Steve up here in our own place, Les,' he finished in some disgust.

Lesley was busy trying to puzzle out why Blake should have bothered to phone up to the twins of Steve's arrival. It almost seemed as if he was ensuring that they should accompany her when she drove Steve down to the King's Arms.

She said almost absently, 'Rick darling, it's still old Mrs Trevendone's house in theory at least, and she *is* very old. We can't expect her to entertain any more strangers . . . and the hotel *is* full.'

Ricky frowned. 'I suppose you're right, but I don't like it. Steve coming all this way and our not offering him hospitality. We're still Aussies and always will be.'

'Never mind about that,' Steve smiled, putting a careless arm round the boy's shoulder. 'But what's this slave-master caper? Some ye olde English custom?'

Ricky rushed in with full explanations of their arrival in England, their two unfortunate encounters with Blake, their final coming to the Manor and eventually what they had found out as to the true situation.

'What a load of old rubbish!' ejaculated Steve indignantly.

'He can't be the owner of all this. And if he is, why should you three stay slaving for him?'

Ricky gave a little grimace. 'Well, actually Rita and I don't do much slaving. It's Les who does that. She says she's paying for our keep while we're here. As it happens,' he finished with elaborate carelessness, 'it suits us to stay here, at least for the rest of the summer.'

'Why?' Steve asked bluntly, and his eyes were on Lesley. Was it just while *he* was here? they seemed to be asking.

Ricky was only too anxious to explain. 'I've become a member of a group—guitarist and vocalist, just at week-ends. Dominic told me yesterday that he hadn't any idea we were so good. . . .'

'Dominic?' Lesley's eyebrows rose. 'Has he heard you?'

Rick nodded. 'Yes, he and Sorrel were at the discothèque on Sunday night, and he says they're coming again this weekend. Dominic says he's going to recommend it to some of the hotel visitors.

'Oh, I know,' he added hastily as he saw Lesley was going to speak, 'that most of the people here are fuddy-duddies who come down here to get away from it all, but we *do* get the odd young person or so who could be interested. Not that we need to do anything to pull in the crowds. They're there, especially at the weekends.'

'He has a good line in sales talk, hasn't he, Steve?' Lesley laughed, but she was thinking, Sorrel and Dominic! What exactly was the dark girl up to now? She had never brought up again the subject she had once mentioned to Lesley—that Blake might have in mind a match between herself and Dominic. She had warned Lesley off, and she was perhaps now consolidating her own position with Dominic. Though why she should do that when she was going to marry Blake wasn't very clear to Lesley. Was she the sort of girl who must have more than one man in her life? If so, it occurred to Lesley that she had chosen one of them badly. Blake Defontaine wasn't the sort to stand for that. Unless he too. . . . But Lesley closed her mind to that memory as she always did when it came to her. He had never referred to that kiss, probably had never given it a second thought, and that was how she too should treat it.

'Les, you and I must go and investigate this night spot,'

Steve was saying. ' I'd begun to wonder what sort of dump I'd arrived in.' And he made a disparaging gesture at the old Manor lying sleepily in the evening sunshine.

' Rick, if Rita is going to be much longer, we can't wait. Mrs Cleaver will want to serve dinner spot on.'

Fortunately the girl came running out of the front door just then. She had changed into a pale pink trouser suit with a Victorian type blouse in white and though she was rather overdressed for the occasion, she certainly looked very pretty and ' with it '.

Steve smiled broadly. ' Why, if it isn't my favourite girl-friend all growing up!' he exclaimed.

She rushed towards him, putting her arms round his neck and kissing him. Steve released himself. ' Give me time,' he ejaculated in mock terror. ' I haven't got used to the permissive society yet.'

Rita blushed. ' I'm sorry, but oh, Steve, I'm so glad to see you, to hear an Aussie voice. These Limeys. . . .' and she began one of her clever imitations, this time of Blake, who was frequently the target of her venom.

' Oh, that's the guy who owns the stately home,' Steve guessed. ' The slave-master, Rick called him. Not been try-ing any of his tricks on you, has he, Rita?'

She shook her dark head. ' No, on the whole he leaves me alone. " You're your sister's responsibility," he said to me once, " and God help her." No, it's Les he tries his tricks on. I believe she's frightened of him. She jumps to it when he cracks his whip. Even Sorrel says so.'

' Rita, you're just being silly,' Lesley put in, her face dis-turbed. ' Get in if you're coming with us.' The girl did so, and Lesley switched on, crashing the gears as she raced down the drive. She hoped to goodness there would be no sign of Blake when they stopped to pick up Steve's bags, and luckily there wasn't.

She could hear the twins telling Steve about the Lodge, and the laboratory beside it, both of which he had already seen. At least they were saving her a great deal of explanation to Steve. Although when she came to think about it, what was there to explain except to say that she was doing a job while she waited for the twins to settle down in their new life with their family in Cornwall?

They were now back to the all-absorbing subject of the discothèque at Penpethic Harbour and already they had arranged to have dinner at the King's Arms as quickly as possible and then run down to the old cinema to have coffee or drinks.

'Officially we're closed tonight, but some of the boys will be around practising,' Ricky promised.

Steve managed to say to Lesley, 'I'd rather have had you to myself tonight, but as the twins are with us and look like staying, we may as well go down to this disco place.'

Lesley agreed, and if the truth be told was grateful that the twins had decided to stay. 'I've only been twice myself. Both times it was packed out. They really are good—no getting away from it. But I just don't know. . . .'

Once again, it was a wakeful night for Lesley. The lovely evening had lengthened into the blue and amethyst shadows of a tranquil twilight, and even now it was not really dark.

It was a night to be thinking of love, but her thoughts were not really on Steve, although his manner of saying goodnight to her had made it only too clear that he had come to Cornwall with the intention of asking her to go back with him to Australia as his wife, at the end of the summer. There had been messages from 'Mum' and 'Dad' and. . . .

Lesley pushed away that problem. It was Rick's which was worrying her. During the past few weeks she had tried to put it aside, hoping against hope that the craze would subside. She had already met Tim Drage, the man who was running the discothèque, a young Cornishman who had agreeably surprised her by his steadiness and good sense. But tonight he had buttonholed her, asking her bluntly whether she was 'for' or 'against'.

Lesley, taken unawares, had pretended that she didn't know what he meant. He had said, staring at her gravely, 'I'm absolutely convinced that Ricky has a big future as a pop singer. He's the best thing that's happened to me since I went into management. He's very young, of course, and he has a long way to go. He's told me a bit about this Trevendone inheritance. Is that what you have in mind for him, running that hotel, getting him trained in hotel management, I mean?'

That was the last thing, to be truthful, that Lesley had ever contemplated. She had come to Cornwall, starry-eyed, wanting nothing more than to see Ricky claim his romantic inheritance. But the truth was that there *was* no inheritance as she had imagined it . . . and if there had been she very much feared Ricky wouldn't have been very interested. He was staying down here because he had been made the vocalist in Tim Drage's group at Penpethic Harbour. He had told Steve that, and Lesley was sadly aware that it was true.

Rita! Lesley was worrying about Rita too, though she didn't know why. Sometimes the girl defied Blake and there was a row, but for the most part she kept out of his way, attended her commercial course at the technical institute and did a minimum amount of homework. Only with Sorrel Lang and the horses did she show any enthusiasm.

Tonight she had been more like her old self. That was probably because Steve had arrived, bringing with him a breath of the old life and of their own country. Rita, thought Lesley, would go back to Australia tomorrow without the slightest sigh of regret. But would she leave if Ricky stayed on in England? And what about Lesley herself?

The scents of the sweet early summer night drifted into the room as Lesley turned back to her bed. What indeed was *she* going to do?

Those lovely days of May wore on and sea pinks and yellow vetches on the cliffs blazed with colour and faded. In the hedgerows campion, white and pink valerian, Queen Anne's lace and a host of wild flowers whose names Lesley never knew bloomed in colour and delicate beauty.

The changing sea, sometimes turquoise, sometimes heavenly blue, sometimes, though rarely during this lovely month, a dull pewter, but always with its heavy white embroidery of surf and spray.

The hotel was completely booked, its elegant and unhurried service moving smoothly from day to day. Lesley's work at the reception desk and in the little accounts office, relieved from time to time by Dominic and more often by Jennifer, was pleasant and far from onerous. But it seemed that Blake Defontaine's demands on her time could never be satisfied. It was as if he was unwilling to allow her ever to leave the little office off his research lab where she worked for him.

Steve, with time on his hands before his party arrived from Australia, waxed angry and indignant with what he, imitating the twins, called the slave-master's slave-driving.

Lesley placated him as best she could and gave him every moment of her spare time. They swam and surfed together, sunbathed among the rocks on the private beach below the hotel, strolled on the soft springy turf of the downs, danced at the disco at Penpethic Harbour, sometimes drove further afield to dine at one or other of the famous eating places on the coast or drove in the Mini to some of the legendary beauty spots of Cornwall which Lesley herself had not seen till now. By tacit agreement between them, the twins were almost always excluded from their meetings, and while Steve looked very very happy, Lesley became more fine-drawn and tense as the month came to its close.

She knew quite well that so far as she was concerned the breaking point was very near and she couldn't keep up the pace much longer. But of course the one person at Trevendone who never missed anything was all too well aware of the situation.

'When does that Australian start the demonstrations of surfing and life-saving he's supposed to be here for?' Blake enquired one evening as Lesley covered her machine in the little office next to his lab.

Lesley swallowed, tense as ever whenever he addressed her directly on something unconnected with work. There was a a dark look on his face, but as usual since that episode under the Kissing Trees she avoided his glance though she was all too conscious of it.

'The group arrive next week,' she said briefly.

'And what are you doing tonight?' he asked, and it seemed to her that half the Arctic Ocean was in his voice.

'I'm going to the reception desk to take over from Jennifer,' she said quietly. Her brow was pleated slightly. She had had a headache most of the day and it had gradually become worse.

'You're doing nothing of the sort,' he said grimly. 'How much longer do you think you can go on like this, burning the candle at both ends? You didn't come in till three o'clock this morning and you were on duty again at the desk at eight o'clock.'

The scowl on his face made her wince, and she was very near to tears, but she struggled to hold them back. 'What I do in my spare time is no concern of yours, Mr Defontaine,' she told him defiantly.

'True enough,' he conceded. 'But what *does* concern me is your undertaking to do the job you took on here efficiently till the beginning of October. I had your promise, remember. And at the time I thought you were a woman of your word.'

She shot him a quick glance. How brutal he was, and his expression seemed to suggest that he could think up much crueller things than those he had already said.

'I have asked for no time off, Mr Defontaine, and I believed I was doing my work to your satisfaction. Will you tell me now what I've done wrong? What you're complaining of?'

She looked at him again, and then turned away quickly. There was something dangerous in his eyes, and also something else . . . she must be mad to imagine it . . . something tender. In Blake Defontaine's eyes!

'I'm complaining of nothing—except that headache of yours. And I'm prescribing for it—a couple of aspirin, a cup of tea, and an early night. I'm coming over with you to the old Manor to see that Mrs Piper gives you that cup of tea.'

Lesley got up and walked over to the door. 'You're very kind, Mr Defontaine,' she said with a touch of irony, 'but I'm already due at the reception desk. I can't let Jennifer down. She's got a date down at the Drews' farm. Please excuse me.'

'You needn't worry about Jennifer. I'll take over tonight,' he said. 'Now for once in a while just stop being so damned independent, get off your high horse and accept a bit of help from someone else.'

Lesley was so taken aback by these remarks that she could think of nothing further to say. In silence, she walked with him up the drive to the Manor, but hesitated in front of the big doors leading to the great hall.

'I ought to explain to Jennifer,' she faltered.

'I'm quite capable of doing that,' he responded grimly. 'Have I your promise that you'll go straight upstairs to bed once you've had that cup of tea, or shall I come to see that you do?'

Hastily and with a heightened colour she said, 'I promise.'

'Good.' He nodded. 'And don't be afraid the hotel will fall down just because you're not on duty. It won't, you know.'

'No,' Lesley agreed meekly.

Jennifer came upstairs a few minutes later with the tea that Lesley hadn't had the energy to ask for in the kitchen. 'I promised his lordship I'd see you had it and a couple of aspirin. It's not often he notices anybody is off colour. You're honoured.'

If this was sarcasm Lesley felt quite unable to cope. 'I've got the worst headache I've ever had,' she admitted. 'Sorry about it, Jennifer. But Blake did say he'd take over. I didn't suggest it.'

'Blake!' commented Jennifer, but again Lesley couldn't or wouldn't take up the challenge.

'I'll be all right in the morning,' she promised. 'You dash off now, Jennifer. I'm sorry if you're rather late.'

'You do look a bit off colour,' the other girl said. 'Sure you'll be all right?' Jennifer never ailed anything, so she wasn't given much to sympathy, and this suited Lesley, who hated fuss. 'I'll be fine,' she assured her.

'Funny his being so considerate,' Jennifer mused now. 'I wouldn't have believed it.'

Lesley kept her eyes tightly closed. If Jennifer went on much longer she would scream, she told herself, but fortunately the other girl suddenly noticed the time and with a careless wave she rushed out of the room.

Lesley turned her face into the pillow and wondered through had said with unwonted modesty. 'After all, I don't pretend in her life.

The following week brought a relief of tension and Lesley began to feel as if she could breathe again. The Australian Life-Saving and Surfing Association team arrived and almost immediately began their demonstrations not only in St Benga Town but at other places on the coast. Though not actually a member of the team, Steve was helping out with administration and there was no doubt too that he welcomed his sessions with 'the boys' so that he was making less demand on Lesley's spare time.

On an evening during that week she hurried over to the old Manor so that she could have her evening meal with the twins, whom she was guiltily conscious of neglecting during the past few weeks. She found Ricky in his room changing from the more conventional clothes he wore at the Technical Institute to what he called his 'gear'.

'Lend me the Mini, Les,' he said, pulling on a gaily coloured shirt. 'I'm off down to Penpethic Harbour for a practice and the bus was so late I've no time to eat here. I'll get a bite at the disco if you can let me have a sub.'

'Sorry, darling.' Lesley shook her head. 'I've had no time to go to the bank this week so far, and I'm short myself. If you're going to eat tonight, you'll have to eat here. How's it going at college?'

'Oh, so-so. They've just started a record club, and I'm joining. That will mean staying to the last bus, though. What about letting me use the Mini? Working all the hours you do, you scarcely ever use it.'

'Don't be an ass, Rick,' Lesley said warningly. 'You haven't got a licence, and I still think that Blake knew you were driving that night we came down from London.'

'Oh, that's ages ago, and what does it matter if he does know? We're the family now and he wouldn't do anything to get us into trouble. You've got to hand it to him, he does think a lot of the family and he's accepted us all right now. In a way, I'm quite sold on him these days. You know he's been down to the disco with Sorrel several times, don't you? He and Tim Drage had a long natter last time he was there.'

Lesley turned away. She was crying softly inside—like a fool. After all, she had Steve, so why should she be so sad to think she had lost Rita to Sorrel, and now she was losing Ricky to Blake?

'Where's Rita?' she asked abruptly now.

'She got into her riding gear and dashed off. I expect she's somewhere around the stables,' the boy said carelessly. 'Come on, Les, if I've got to eat here, let's have it. Rita can have hers later.'

Lesley hadn't much appetite for the cold meal which Mrs Piper had set out in the dining room, but Rick did it full justice and then rushed off, confident that he would be able to cadge a lift down to Penpethic Harbour.

When he had gone, Lesley went up to the bedroom she shared with Rita. The clothes Rita had flung off were strewn round the room. Lesley picked them up, a frown on her face. No doubt of it, just now Rita was something of a headache to everybody. Why had she put on riding clothes at this time of night, especially as she had no horse of her own? Sometimes now Sorrel allowed her to ride one of her horses, and sometimes she rode Dominic's. But Sorrel wasn't at Trevendone tonight and Dominic had not yet come in.

Still feeling worried, Lesley went downstairs deciding to go into the stable yard to find Rita, but in the hall a member of the hotel staff came to query a booking and she went back to the reception desk where in any case she was on duty for the rest of the evening.

It was later than her usual time for leaving when she eventually went back to the old Manor and it must have been only a few minutes afterwards that the phone call came through, taken by the night porter.

Lesley was sitting in the lounge glancing through a letter which she had received that morning from a friend in Australia and had not till then had time to read when Dominic came in. She wasn't sure where he had spent the evening, but he had been drinking, though he wasn't completely intoxicated. He declared that he was ravenous, so she went into the kitchen, made him a couple of sandwiches and was preparing to take the plate with a pot of black coffee into the dining room and leave him there when he followed her into the kitchen, evidently in an amorous mood. Lesley felt quite capable of dealing with Dominic. Even when he had been drinking he was a gentleman, and she was just eluding an affectionate arm, declaring that she was tired and intended having an early night, when Blake Defontaine strode in to interrupt what he evidently thought was a love scene.

'Do you happen to know where your young sister is?' he asked in a blistering voice.

Lesley stared, and bit her lip. Engrossed in the work she had been doing at the reception desk, she had quite forgotten that she had intended going to the stables to have a word with Rita. But that was three hours ago.

'I expect she's in bed,' she replied, looking at him with eyes that were suddenly anxious. 'Why?'

The explanation was forthcoming, still in that blistering voice. Blake had been in Plymouth all the evening and had arrived back at the Lodge a few minutes ago to have a phone call from the night porter at the new Manor, who it appeared could get in touch with no one else. A neighbouring farmer had seen a young girl riding Mr Defontaine's black mare on the cliffs. He had ridden out to find out what was happening and she'd urged the mare on at a breakneck speed and had been thrown. She didn't appear to be badly hurt, but the farmer had had her carried to his own nearby farmhouse and called a doctor. The doctor had said she was suffering only from shock, had given her a sedative and the farmer's wife had put her to bed. The mare hadn't got off so lightly. She seemed to be lame, but the farmer had stabled her and asked the vet to come round when he was free.

He had, it seemed, been ringing the Lodge for quite a long time, but finally had decided to ring the hotel.

This was from Blake, so quietly furious that he was terrifying, standing tall and distinguished in evening dress and just back, as he said, from a dinner in Plymouth. Lesley could see from his expression that he thought she had spent the evening in a flirtation with Dominic.

'I'll get the car and bring her back,' Lesley said in a trembling voice. 'Oh, I hope she's all right. I shall never forgive myself if she's badly hurt. I knew she'd put on riding clothes, but I never imagined she'd take one of the horses out.'

'A pity you didn't keep a closer watch on her. Where were you when she went out?'

'I hadn't come off duty. Rick said she had changed into riding clothes, but I thought she'd just gone to the stables to pet the horses as she so often does. Then I was called back to the reception desk and . . . and. . . .' Her voice faded away. No point in telling him that she had stayed there a long time, sorting out some accounts which Dominic was supposed to have made up but which were hopelessly wrong. No doubt Blake thought she'd been here most of the time, flirting and perhaps drinking with Dominic.

'You don't seem to have much control over either of the twins,' he commented now, still white with temper and rubbing salt into the rawness of her wound—that she had lost both of them since they came to Trevendone. And she brought them here with such high hopes. 'You were—are—much too young to have had the responsibility of them heaped on you.'

For a moment unutterable weariness washed over Lesley and then her green eyes flashed. 'I seem to have heard *that* before, and I seem to have reminded you that you too had plenty of responsibility when you were younger than I am now!'

They had both forgotten Dominic, who was sitting on the edge of the kitchen table finishing his sandwiches. 'My darling little Yseult,' he drawled now, 'Blake is a very different proposition from you.'

Blake ignored that. 'What possessed Rita to take the mare of all the mounts she could have chosen?' he demanded. 'Not only is she the most valuable but she's as tricky as a wild thing. Somebody must have helped the girl to mount. You're sure. . . .'

'I'm not sure of anything,' Lesley interrupted him stormily. At one time when she was having a blazing row with Blake, it had seemed to make her more angry than ever, and perhaps irritated if she hadn't come off best, which was seldom. But now it always left her feeling wretchedly miserable with the tears that ached in her throat almost ready to fall.

'If you think *I* encouraged her to go off on your beastly mare,' she went on wildly, 'you must be mad. I'm sorry if Sheba is hurt, but it's Rita I'm worried about. I'll get the car and fetch her back.'

Blake didn't move from the doorway by which he was standing, and Dominic, still sitting on the corner of the table, glanced from one to the other, amusement in his sea-blue eyes.

'You can't do that, Lesley,' Blake said now, and she noticed that once again he was being less than his usual formal self. 'Rita has been put to bed and is under sedation. She'll be all right till tomorrow when *I* shall fetch her back and demand an explanation.'

'You mean you'll bully her until she doesn't know what she's saying,' Lesley flamed. 'All you care about is Sheba. Rita has done wrong, I admit that, but please don't say anything to her until I've talked to her. Something has upset her, and I've got to find out what's wrong.'

Dominic got up. 'Dear little cousin Yseult,' he said mockingly. 'Don't you *really* know?'

Lesley transferred her wide green gaze from Blake to the young man standing unsteadily by the table. 'What do you mean, Dominic?' she asked distrustfully.

'Don't you know she's quite crazy about that husky young Aussie you spend all your spare time with and whom you said you were going to marry when we had that family conference?'

'Steve? You must be crazy!' Oh, that stupid, stupid boast of hers that night of the family gathering. As to Rita. . . . Lesley stared at Dominic, frank disbelief in her green eyes. 'Rita is only a child. She's only sixteen and she hardly knows Steve.'

Dominic took her by the shoulder and looked intently into her face. 'She really believes it,' he marvelled. 'Young Rita may be only sixteen, little cousin Yseult, but she's as old as Eve in the ways of men. Young Rita and I have something in common. We're as jealous as hell, she about you and I about . . . well, perhaps about Steve. And you, you poor blindfolded infant, don't see it.'

'You're drunk, Dominic,' Blake said harshly. 'You'd better get to bed.'

'I've certainly had more than enough,' agreed Dominic portentously. 'That's why I'm so truthful tonight. I know exactly what young Rita is going through.'

Without looking at either of them, he went lurching out of the door and a moment later they heard him stumbling upstairs. Lesley's stricken gaze went to Blake, but he seemed to be staring at some distant object, well over her head.

Lesley took a deep breath. 'Mr Defontaine, I've got to go to Rita. I can't leave her alone tonight.'

'You couldn't do the slightest good if you went to her,' he said brutally. 'I've already told you she's in bed under sedation. Farmers keep early hours and nobody would thank you for barging into a sleeping household. Just have a bit of consideration for the people who've taken so much trouble with her already.'

No doubt it was a salutary speech, but Lesley hated him for it, hated him also for his next remarks. 'As I've told you before, you worry too much about the twins. You're not old nor wise enough to be the mother and father to them that you're trying to be. Actually they're well able to take care

139

of themselves. They're both completely self-centred—they're true Trevendones.'

'It *looks* as if they can take care of themselves with Rita in this predicament and Rick down at the disco till all hours,' Lesley responded in bitter weariness.

He took her shoulder in a grip that hurt. 'You've had enough for one night. The best thing you can do is to go to bed and sleep on it. We'll work something out tomorrow.'

'Promise you'll let me fetch Rita back and talk to her first.' She raised her eyes to his hard face—the first time she had ever asked him a favour.

His hand on her shoulder tightened even more so that she almost winced. There was something in his eyes she had seen there once before—the dull pewter glowing like molten metal and behind it a tenderness about which she must be completely mistaken.

And then the tension had gone. He gave her a little push. 'All right. Fetch her back yourself . . . but she's still got to have a reckoning with me. You understand that?'

She clenched her hands, feeling more unhappy than she had ever felt in her life, the pain in her heart a physical thing. 'If only we'd never come here!' she cried. 'If only we'd stayed in Australia. We were happy there.'

She stumbled out of the kitchen and up the oak staircase which it was said had been put in at the time of the first Queen Elizabeth. Blake Defontaine watched her go.

Lesley stood in her room shaking with nerves and anger and with shocked disbelief. It couldn't be true that the twins were capable of running their own lives.

It was fantastic and horrible to suggest that Rita was jealous of her because of Steve. Lesley flung herself on her bed. Jealous! That was Dominic . . . translating his own pain to that of someone else. And his suggestion that his jealousy too was against Steve. That was no truer than what he'd said about Rita. Poor Dominic! He had been drinking too much and didn't know what he was saying.

CHAPTER IX

Rita was obviously not hurt but rather pale and subdued when Lesley fetched her home in her lunch hour on the following day. Lesley had been on duty at the reception desk all morning and Blake Defontaine hadn't suggested she could take any time off—indeed she hadn't seen him at all this morning. Earlier she had spoken to Rita briefly on the telephone, telling her she would pick her up in the lunch hour. Rita had accepted this with a better grace than Lesley had expected, but now they were together in the Mini, at first the younger girl just refused to say anything at all.

Then all at once in a sullen, monotonous voice she said, ' I'd got my riding things on, but I was only going to the stables to be with the horses. And then it was Sorrel . . . what she said. . . .'

'Sorrel?' Lesley raised her eyebrows. 'But she was going to Plymouth to dinner with Mr Defontaine.'

'I don't know anything about that.' Rita's eyes were suddenly furtive, and she gave a silly little snigger and wouldn't look at Lesley.

The older girl's glance was dubious. Rita was often devious, but there seemed no point in lying just now. 'What *did* Sorrel say?' she enquired.

Rita shrugged pettishly. 'She often asks me why I dress up for riding and she says as I'm supposed to be one of the owners of the Trevendone estate why don't I take out one of the horses whenever I feel like it. Well, I told her that Dominic's belonged to us just as much as they did to him. So she said they didn't really belong to Dominic any more than anything else did around here. It was all the slave-master's property and if I was set on riding one of the horses why didn't I take the mare out.' Rita shivered. 'I don't think she meant it, but then she laughed and said I was chicken. That we were all scared of Blake and he had us all where he wanted us—under his thumb. So I said yes, the slave-master, and she said she'd tell him we called him that and I said, " While you're about it, let him know I've gone out riding Sheba."

'Then she said, "Why, you daren't even mount her. Come on, I'll help you up." And she got her saddled and held her till I mounted. So if anybody is going to be blamed, Sorrel will have to take her share.'

Lesley stared at her in a horrified manner. 'She couldn't have been so wicked,' she protested.

Then Rita burst into hysterical laughter. 'Lesley, you'll believe anything,' she giggled.

To Lesley's relief there was no sign of Blake or Dominic when they arrived at the old Manor. She quickly got a tray ready and took it up to their bedroom, where Rita was lying lethargically on her own bed. She persuaded the girl to have coffee and a sandwich and quickly ate a sandwich herself as it was almost time for her to go back to the reception desk.

'Better stay here for the rest of the afternoon, darling,' she advised. The girl still looked very pale and shaken and Lesley was determined to ring the doctor and ask him to call again. She was worried about Rita's hysterical account of what was supposed to have happened last night. Was she perhaps suffering from concussion?

'I'll go down to the beach and sunbathe a bit later on,' Rita yawned. 'Don't fuss, Les, for pete's sake. I just want to keep out of the way for a bit.'

'You'll have to see Mr Defontaine pretty soon and apologise,' Lesley said in a worried manner. 'You'd better tell him the truth—about Sorrel, I mean—if it *is* the truth.'

'I'm not going around telling tales just to get myself out of trouble,' Rita flared, ' and don't you mention Sorrel either.' Her voice changed. 'Les, I do hope the mare isn't badly hurt. She's marvellous to ride and I felt I was part of her, even though I was secretly terrified. The slave-master must be pretty terrific as a rider. He always takes her so easily. I wish she hadn't caught her foot in that hole. I don't think I should have come off if that hadn't happened, though she was trying to throw me all the time.'

'You must have been pretty good yourself to stay on so long. Thank goodness you weren't killed when she did throw you. But how crazy could you get, to take Mr Defontaine's mare? Why not one of the other horses? Even though as Sorrel says he really owns the lot.'

'Even us,' muttered Rita. 'Body and soul. The slave-

142

master—I never thought of a better name for him.'

'Rita!' Lesley started nervously and almost looked over her shoulder. The younger girl saw her flinch and jeered, 'You'll be crossing your fingers soon, every time his name is mentioned. Even Sorrel says you're terrified of him.'

Lesley went very white. 'Sorrel seems to say a lot of things she'd be better not to say. But I must go now. Don't go on to the beach. Stay here and rest and I'll try to slip up to see you later in the afternoon.'

'Oh, I'm all right. Don't fuss,' Rita entreated her again.

Lesley went back to the office, a crease between her fine dark brows. She didn't really know how to tackle Rita now. She was ill at ease and awkward with her, feeling she must choose her words after what Dominic had said last night.

Had Sorrel really been there, helping Rita to saddle the mare? If so it was completely criminal. Rita might have been killed.

Lesley rang the doctor and he was reassuring. There was nothing wrong with the young lady, he assured her, and later, when Lesley managed to slip away from the reception desk for a few minutes, she found no sign of Rita in her room.

'I seed her talking to Mr Defontaine in the stable yard half an hour ago,' Mrs Piper told her, and when Lesley looked apprehensive the housekeeper went on comfortably, 'Now, m'dear, don't you be fretting. They seemed to be talking quiet-like, and Mr Defontaine didn't look as if un was taking on as you might say. Quiet, both of un were.'

It had been too much to hope that he would leave Rita alone for this first day and let her recover from the shock of her fall, thought Lesley indignantly. She didn't see him herself until just before dinner when he came into the hotel office to look through some accounts.

Lesley gave him a glance from under her sweeping lashes. He didn't seem in a good mood and she moistened her dry lips. There was that constricted feeling in her throat that was always there these days when she had to speak to him, but it was cowardly to evade the issue that he was evidently not going to bring up first.

'I . . . I . . . fetched Rita back from Trenewick Farm at lunch time, Mr Defontaine. The farmer, Mr Price, told me you'd already been and collected the mare in a horse box.

Has the vet seen her yet? Will she be all right?'

She was talking rapidly and nervously, giving him no opportunity to comment on her remarks or answer her questions. He swivelled round in his chair. 'Shall we take things just a bit more steadily?' he suggested, irony in his pewter-dark eyes. 'In answer to your last two questions, yes, the vet has seen Sheba and he thinks she'll be all right if the leg is rested for a day or two.'

'Oh, thank goodness for that,' Lesley replied, her face clearing. 'Mr Defontaine, Rita is really very sorry for her prank. I think she has had her lesson and she won't do anything of the sort again.'

'I'm quite certain she won't,' he replied, a hard gleam in his eyes. 'I've told her she's to come straight back from college for the next fortnight and she's not allowed out once she's back at Trevendone—not for any reason, or with anybody.'

'Oh, but you can't insist on that,' Lesley protested. 'She's started going down to Penpethic Harbour most evenings with Ricky and when they're down there together, I feel so much happier.'

'I *can* insist on it . . . and I *have*,' he replied deliberately. '*I've* had a talk with her this afternoon and she had the grace to apologise and accept her punishment. I hope you'll do the same.'

'My punishment?' Lesley's green eyes blazed, wilfully misinterpreting his remark. 'Am I too confined to the slave quarters for the next fortnight?'

'My dear girl, heroics are very boring,' he said with a lash of mockery in his voice. 'You seem rather prone to them, and someone should have told you so back in Australia long ago.'

She struggled for some remark equally devastating as he sat watching her with his cold, pewter-coloured eyes, but found nothing to say and he went on, 'Naturally in your free time you can come and go as you wish. You, after all, are of age, if we agree that eighteen makes one an adult. But Rita, as you said last night, is still a child—at least in law.'

Lesley breathed in deeply. 'I'm sorry she apologised,' she said recklessly. 'She wasn't really to blame so far as I can discover. It was . . .' She paused in some confusion. Rita had begged her not to mention Sorrel and Lesley herself could scarcely believe that the Cornish girl had been anywhere near the stables last night. But she had gone too far now to draw back, especially with that horrid sarcastic expression on his face and his next hateful words. 'So she wasn't to blame! It was . . . who, may I ask? One of our famous Cornish piskies, perhaps?'

He obviously wasn't expecting the name she blurted out, for he looked completely taken aback. 'Mrs Lang . . . Sorrel, you mean? But, my dear girl, what could Sorrel have to do with it? We were both in Plymouth at the time.'

Lesley's heart sank when she heard his positive statement. She had been hoping that by some chance Sorrel hadn't gone to Plymouth last night, but that was too much to expect. When would *she* ever cut a date with Blake Defontaine?

He sat quite still and his stony silence was nerve-racking. How bitterly he resented even the slightest criticism of his girl-friend.

Now very deliberately he got up and went out of the office. 'Sorrel,' he called, 'will you spare me a minute?' Lesley had no idea Sorrel was anywhere around, but she might have guessed. They were so seldom apart. She must have been in the great hall waiting for her fiancé. She never let him out of her sight if she could help it.

Sorrel, in riding breeches and a white blouse, strolled after him into the office. 'Hello,' she said, 'want any help?'

'Just for you to assure Miss Trevendone (not 'Lesley' to-night) that you were in Plymouth yesterday evening when Sheba was hi-jacked.'

Lesley was watching the girl carefully and she saw a peculiar expression, almost one of embarrassment, cross her vivid face. Then she was laughing up into Blake Defontaine's grim countenance. 'What's all this about, Blake darling? Surely you've not forgotten last night already, my sweet.'

There was a soft intimacy and a wealth of implication in her voice and something almost unbearable pierced Lesley's heart with a pain that for a moment stopped her breath. With an effort she fought it and put it aside. Her eyes glinted green as she stared accusingly at the other girl.

'Mrs Lang, if you weren't in the stables last night, have you at any time been encouraging, *daring* Rita to ride Mr

Defontaine's mare?'

'Have I what? You crazy imbecile!' Sorrel's voice rose stridently. 'Are you out of your tiny mind? As if I'd *dream* of doing any such thing!'

'Sorrel, keep your voice down,' Blake warned her quietly, and then turned to Lesley. 'I think that's enough, Miss Trevendone. I've told Rita what she's to do. Let's leave it at that, shall we? Sorrel, I'm ready now.'

He held open the door for her to pass through, but as she did so she sent a vindictive barb at Lesley. 'If this is Australian sportsmanship, please deliver me from it!'

Lesley closed her lips sharply. She didn't intend indulging in a slanging match, but she was pretty sure there was something in Rita's accusations. Perhaps Sorrel hadn't been there last night, but there had been some previous occasion when she had dared Rita to take out the mare. Was there anything she wouldn't do to injure the Trevendones from over the sea and deprive them of their inheritance?

And what an inheritance, thought Lesley drearily. But she wasn't going to leave the matter there. Sooner or later she would get the truth from Rita and then she would have it out with Sorrel.

Actually it was Sorrel herself who was not content to let the matter rest. She sauntered into Blake's office next to his lab on the following afternoon where Lesley was working.

She said, 'You're not being stupid enough to try to get Rita off the hook as far as Blake is concerned, are you? If you are, you're just wasting your time. He never goes back on his word.'

'He'd do so if he found out that Rita wasn't really to blame,' Lesley said bluntly. 'But I haven't time to talk about that now. I've some work to finish that has to go by tonight's post.'

She looked rather pointedly at the door and Sorrel strolled over to it. 'By the way, why don't you make up your mind about your Australian boy-friend? If you don't want him yourself, give your young sister a chance. She's crazy about him, you know.'

Lesley's eyes were a hostile green. So this was the source of Dominic's remarks the night before last! She had suspected as much. 'How do you know?' she challenged. 'Has she confided in you?'

'Of course not, and heaven forbid.' Sorrel gave a theatrical little shudder. 'Anybody with half an eye can see it, though.'

Lesley's temper continued to rise, though she told herself that she was a fool to take any notice of this hateful girl. 'Why can't you mind your own business?' she asked angrily.

Sorrel gave another theatrical shudder. 'You're so charmingly direct, aren't you, all you cousins from a new country. Do the words politeness and courtesy figure in anyone's vocabulary down under?'

'They don't seem to figure in yours to any noticeable extent,' Lesley snapped. 'I'm all for plain speaking myself and that's why I'm telling you to mind your own business and keep out of our affairs—Rita's, Ricky's and mine. We're no concern of yours.'

'But, darling, you *made* yourselves our concern when you blew in from God knows where claiming to be our family. That's still to be proved, and as soon as we find you aren't Trevendones—and I for one suspect you aren't—out you'll all go, and it can't be too soon for me.'

Lesley started up. 'As soon as you find out we aren't Trevendones? What do you mean?' There was a horrified expression on her face and the other girl eyed her closely.

'You look as guilty as hell,' she said viciously. 'I told Blake right from the beginning that you were impostors.'

'Of course we aren't,' Lesley said, but Sorrel was staring intently at the hand holding the ballpoint pen. It was shaking perceptibly.

'We'll see about that,' she murmured, an odd expression in her black eyes. 'But to get back to the point we were discussing . . .'

'I don't want any further discussion,' Lesley flashed back. 'I'm busy. Just let me get on with my work, will you?'

'Work or no work, there's still this matter of your marriage.' Sorrel was pretending to walk through the door, but she threw this over her shoulder. As she probably guessed it would, it brought Lesley to her feet again.

'What has my marriage to do with you or anyone else here?' she asked fiercely.

Again Sorrel flung one of her inscrutable smiles over her

shoulder. 'Darling, you may remember that some time ago. I got the idea that Blake was cottoning on to this Tristan and Yseult game you and Dominic play. He has quite a conscience about the family, you know, and I suppose he thinks if you two made a match of it, it would solve the problem of the Trevendone inheritance. Actually, you know, once Blake gets an idea it's the very devil to shake him out of it, so my advice to you is to latch on to that strong-armed surfing young man of yours and get cracking. Naturally we'd see you had a marvellous wedding, and I might be able to persuade Blake to give you away.'

Lesley gasped out her indignant repugnance. 'I can't think of anything more revolting!' she said.

Sorrel came back into the room, her black eyes narrowed to slits in her gypsyish face. 'Revolting! That's quite a strong term, isn't it? Well, if you're off the young man from down under, would you settle for Dominic? He's very handsome, as you must admit, and really rather sweet. I should know.' And she showed her teeth in a smile that was no smile at all.

Lesley looked at her with something like horror in her big green eyes, reflecting that she had never come up against anyone quite so cold-hearted as Sorrel Lang. She must know how Dominic felt about her and indeed she gave him plenty of encouragement, especially when Blake Defontaine was away.

'Last time you brought that subject up you said it wasn't on,' Lesley remarked contemptuously.

'Oh, I can always change my mind when it suits me,' Sorrel replied smoothly. 'I take it you wouldn't find marriage to Dominic revolting.'

Actually the word had come scaldingly to Lesley's lips at the thought of Blake Defontaine's giving her in marriage. Blake . . . to give her to someone else! The thought came unbidden and was stamped on in passionate anger.

'It's revolting to speak of people marrying when they aren't in love,' she said tensely.

'My goodness, you *are* looking fierce!' Sorrel's black eyes seemed to be dancing in amusement, but in their depths was something hard and watchful. 'You can't be such a little puritan as to be shocked. Surely even in your part of the world there are arranged marriages. Some sheep farmer's daughter marrying another rich farmer's son in order to unite two estates, or stations or whatever you call them out there. Mergers are the fashion these days.'

'In the part of the world from which I come,' Lesley said, gasping out her indignant disgust, 'a man and a girl marry for just one reason—that they happen to be in love.'

'And how long does that last?' Sorrel asked in a bored voice. 'Who would have thought you were as romantic as that? Actually I thought that sort of thing went out with crinolines and the Blue Danube. Anyway in families like the Trevendones arranged marriages have always been the rule. So if I were you I'd get cracking with your Australian. Then Blake's mind will be set at rest about you lot when we go away.'

'When you go away?' Lesley faltered, and something inside her seemed to turn like a fierce wounding blade.

'You don't suppose Blake and I are going to stay here when we're married, do you? Once his book is finished, he'll take another University appointment, abroad, of course, and I'm all for it. I want to see a bit of the world.'

'He'll leave Dominic and Jennifer in charge here . . . of the hotel and the Home Farm?'

'That's the idea, darling.'

'And what about my . . . my . . . Ricky? What of *his* claim?'

'A lot of boloney, if you ask me,' retorted Mrs Lang vulgarly. 'Not that you need to worry about him. He'll be all right. He plays and sings too well not to make a hit sooner or later. As to Rita—well, as I've warned you, watch your step there. She's a sexy little piece if ever there was one. I understand Rita a lot better than you do. We've a lot in common. She's like me. What she wants she goes all out for, and she'll have your precious Steve unless you keep your wits about you. And there's another one you've got to watch too—Blake. I've got the feeling that he thinks you'll just be right to help Jennifer and Dominic to make a go of this place. And when he gets an idea into his head . . .'

Lesley had a sudden uncomfortable memory of old Mrs Trevendone saying, 'What Blake Defontaine wants, he usually gets.'

Lesley's hands clenched and her face went very tense. They were all so sure, weren't they? But this time it was going to be different, Mr Blake Defontaine was just not going to get what he wanted.

She flicked the sheet of paper out of the typewriter. She hadn't checked it and now she wasn't going to. She was covering the machine when she heard him come in. 'Have you finished that last sheet, Miss Trevendone?' he demanded.

'Yes, it's here,' she said.

He looked at her downbent face and then at Sorrel who was standing by the window, a smile still on her lips. 'You two haven't been on about the mare again, have you?' he asked in a bored voice.

With a start, Lesley remembered that that was what the conversation had been about in the first place—that and her determination to clear Rita. But instead it had resolved into . . .

'The mare?' Sorrel raised her black brows. 'Indeed no,' she drawled. 'Lesley has merely been telling me about love, Australian style.' She turned to the girl. 'All the same, Lesley darling, I don't believe it will be love in a cottage, or a log cabin or whatever is the equivalent in Australia. Rita tells me that your young man's father is a wealthy pastoralist, so I expect life will be pretty good for you when you get back there.'

Blake almost jerked the papers out of Lesley's hand. 'I didn't want you to stay overtime,' he snapped. 'You should have gone half an hour ago. I'll see to the post.'

'I'm going now,' Lesley replied in a stifled voice, and brushed past him and ran out into the blinding sunshine.

Even Jennifer, who usually refused to listen to criticism or complaints, had to admit they couldn't go on much longer at this pace when the high season in a summer of unusual heat was upon them.

Blake was on the go from dawn till dark and though he worked all the staff hard, and especially the Trevendones, it seemed as if he drove himself even harder. His dark face had grown rather thin and gaunt and there were shadows of sleeplessness under his eyes. His only relaxation just now was an early morning swim and an occasional ride on the beach on Sheba.

One day when she and Dominic were off duty together and

had come for a quick swim and then half an hour's sunbathing, Dominic said abruptly, 'You don't know what it's all about, do you, young Lesley?'

Lesley had been idly watching the sea creaming round the great whale-like rocks and deciding that it would soon be time to move. Now she raised up on one elbow and looked at the young man lying beside her. He would be most girls' dream-boat, she thought with a smile. Gay and laughter-loving, so easy to live with.

'All about what?' she queried.

'It's not supposed to be talked about,' he went on, 'but it's something like this.'

In a conspiratorial whisper he started to tell her that this was the crucial year so far as the hotel went. For some time a group of business men had been interested in taking over the New Manor and also developing the old manor into a similar annexe of old world charm but of superlative comfort.

'It's practically on,' Dominic said confidently. 'We're doing so well this year that we shall break far more than even. But not a word. It's still a state secret.'

Lesley stared at him in an appalled silence. To some extent Sorrel's remarks had revealed that Blake and she were pulling out, and going abroad when they married, but she had implied that the Trevendones would be left in possession and she hadn't said anything about the old Manor being drawn into the orbit of the hotel.

'But what about the family?' Lesley asked now in a small voice.

True to type, Dominic began to tell her about his own prospects. 'The Home Farm will do me fine,' he said cheerfully. 'The Treswins who have managed it since my father's time haven't any children and they want to retire at Christmas. That's why I've spent so much of my time these past few years getting the know-how there.

'From the Home Farm we can supply the hotel with fresh produce. Blake is going to build a whole series of glass-houses for lettuce, tomatoes and early vegetables, and with poultry, meat and milk we should do fine.'

Lesley wasn't quite sure who he meant by 'we' and did not enquire, though she imagined he was including Jennifer in his ambitious plans.

'Jennifer is going to hate leaving the old Manor. She's much more attached to it than you are,' she commented dryly.

'But surely you know about Jen and Rodney Drew. She's down at their farm whenever she's free, and don't you remember she rode one of their horses in the Cumballick point-to-point? She and Rod Drew have been sweethearts since they were at school. He took a course in hotel management in Plymouth, then he was at a West End hotel for a year and he's in Switzerland now. He's the likely one to take over as manager when Blake gives up, especially married to someone with Jen's experience. There's to be a flat in the old Manor for Great-grandma while she lives and I expect Jen and Rod will eventually take it over.'

'All very nicely cut and dried,' Lesley said now, her green eyes glinting, her lips tight. 'And where do the Australian Trevendones come into Mr Defontaine's arrangements?'

Dominic, as usual, retreated as soon as he came up against any unpleasantness. He put his hands up in mock surrender and begged her not to slay him with her beautiful eyes.

'There's that brawny Aussie who seems to be monopolising one of them,' he mocked. 'Don't you know I'm jealous as hell of him, little Yseult. As for Rick, within a few years he'll be able to buy Trevendone up ten times over. If I'm not serious about anything else, darling, I *am* about Rick. He's got what it takes. He'll never need to bother about Trevendone. As to Rita, you've got a problem there, no doubt of that. Get her married off as soon as you can, preferably to someone who'll beat her three times a day. That's my advice about Rita.'

Lesley frowned and refused to take up that challenge. Her lips were compressed. She wasn't going to allow Rick to be cheated of what was due to him at Trevendone, and nobody need think she was.

She got up, dusting the sand from her suntanned body. 'Come on, time's up, Dominic,' she said, flinging her towel round her shoulders. 'I'll race you.'

She left him still sprawling on the sands and began to run towards the steps and the pathway up to the cliffs. Within a few moments he caught her up and held on to one of her hands. 'Les, there's just one more thing. Blake's been making enquiries in Australia. He's found that Ralph Trevendone wasn't killed in a mine disaster in Queensland as the family have believed for years, but there's one thing nobody seems able to trace, and that's the marriage certificate. . . . Ralph Trevendone's marriage certificate to your mother. I thought I ought to tell you,' he went on hastily as he saw the way her face had gone very pale. 'It doesn't matter in the slightest', Les, and I expect it will turn up all in good time, but . . .'

Lesley nodded, her lips very stiff. 'Thanks for telling me, Dominic. I'll be seeing you.'

She raced ahead of him again, into the old Manor and up the Elizabethan staircase to the bathroom on the floor where she and Rita shared a bedroom. She peeled off her bikini, had a cold shower and then with her towel around her ran into the small bedroom. She slid quickly into her scanty underwear and the plain blue frock which she wore at the reception desk. There were still a few more minutes before she need take over from Jennifer.

She went over to one of the small windows about which Rita grumbled incessantly, saying she couldn't breathe, though they stood wide every night, allowing the distant roar of the surf to lull them to sleep.

This was it, then, the tightrope she had been walking ever since she had decided to bring the twins from Australia. For among Margaret Trevendone's papers she hadn't been able to find the marriage certificate either. It must be somewhere, or some record of it, but Lesley hadn't known where to enquire. She knew Margaret Trevendone far too well to think there had been no marriage. It was somewhere, that certificate. It would turn up, she was sure. Then they would know she wasn't Lesley Trevendone, but by that time it wouldn't matter. She would have succeeded in what she had set out to do—to bring the twins to their father's home and see them established as the heirs to the Trevendone estate. And then Lesley laughed. An estate that didn't exist . . . an estate that the twins didn't want!

Her thoughts went again to what Dominic had said about Rick a few minutes before. Steve said very much the same thing, and even, to her surprise, Blake Defontaine was of the same opinion.

He had spoken to her about it one morning after he and

Sorrel had been with a party from the hotel to the discotheque down at Penpethic Harbour.

'I might not have all that faith in my own judgment,' he had said with unwanted modesty. 'After all, I don't pretend to be an authority on that sort of thing, but I talked to Tim Drage and he's more sure of Rick's ability to succeed than he's ever been sure of anything in his life. I know Drage. He's straight. He'll give Rick a square deal. Frankly, I've got complete faith in both of them.'

Lesley looked at her watch. She hadn't time to stand brooding here. She ought to be at the reception desk . . . now.

The summer days wore on with no let-up, for Lesley at least. It was as if Blake was determined to get the last ounce of energy from her once her work in the hotel was finished.

She realised sadly that he was working against time himself too, wanting to get the affairs of the hotel settled and his book finished before he and Sorrel were married at the end of the season.

The twins were now on holiday and Rick was spending all his time practising with the groups down at Penpethic Harbour. Lesley lay awake some nights. It was not what she had wanted for Rick, but how could she possibly stand in his way when everybody about her predicted phenomenal success for him?

'Not that you'll be able to even if you tried.' That was from Blake, as always, grim and direct. 'Rick is an artist and nothing and nobody will prevent him fulfilling himself in his own way.'

Rita was around rather more than the boy. Sulkily she gave Mrs Piper the minimum of assistance in making her own bed, tidying their bedroom and Ricky's and helping with the washing up. The rest of the time she spent surfing and sunbathing when the weather was kind either on the hotel beach, but more often at Penpethic Harbour with Ricky or on the St Benga Town surfing beach where the Australian rangers gave most of their demonstrations.

Lesley had tried without success to find out Rita's motive in taking Sheba out on that early summer evening. Sorrel had not spoken of it again and Rita always shrugged the subject off. One strange change had come out of the episode. Her animosity against Blake appeared to have vanished, either because his discipline had tamed her—and that seemed an unlikely conclusion to Lesley—or that she had come to admire him for some quality of his own.

But so far as Lesley was concerned, one thing she was determined to do and that was to ignore the suggestion from Dominic and Sorrel that Rita was infatuated with Steve. She might have a schoolgirlish crush on him—in a way it had started in Melbourne before they sailed, but there was nothing more to it than that. Down at Penpethic Harbour at the discothèque she danced with boys of her own age and seemed to enjoy their company.

The golden weeks worn on. In the sheltered parts of the hotel garden the palm trees rustled in the soft westerly sea-scented wind. Magnificent hydrangeas in deep pinks and blues and dark wine colour gave dramatic foregrounds to the wide windows and terraces which led down from the back of the new Manor.

In the flower beds of the Elizabethan courtyard, Mrs Sinkins pinks scented the air with idyllic fragrance and petunias, mesembryanthemums and a host of other flowers added colour and glamour to the lovely Manor House basking in the golden summer.

Occasionally in her brief moments of leisure, instead of going on to the cliffs or the beach, now full of hotel visitors, Lesley would wander up the narrow winding lane which led from the Manor to the village, free of the traffic of the busy coast road. Now its high banks and hedges were dotted with wild roses and the sweet-smelling honeysuckle.

The village itself was small, a huddle of cottages of grey Cornish stone, but the church was by contrast large and Lesley had once or twice looked round at the plaques inside, placed in memory of long-dead Trevendones, buried not in the big vault in the churchyard but at sea in naval battles, one killed by pirates on the coast of China and others lying at rest on the American continent.

It seemed a far cry from the peace and old-fashioned atmosphere of the village and the old Manor House to the quiet comfort yet sophistication of the new Manor. One of her pleasures was to sit occasionally over a cup of tea in the kitchen and hear Mrs Piper talk about the old Cornwall—the superstitions that were still part of village life, the whisper of witchcraft and of course the piskies.

'And now we're just praying for the good weather to hold over for the Revel,' Mrs Piper remarked. Lesley had already discovered that this was the patronal festival of the village church, dedicated to a Cornish St Freda.

Even Blake Defontaine couldn't ignore the Revel, it seemed. 'We are all expected to put in an appearance at some of the events,' he told Lesley. 'It's one of the things expected of the Trevendones, who were once the feudal lords of the district. There's the church service in the morning, the children's service in the afternoon and then on Monday a jamboree of sorts in the field next to the church and a supper and dance in the evening. We shall just have to split up as to when we go. A pity it comes at the beginning of August just when none of us has time for fun and games. You'd better settle for the dance. Jennifer says she'll do reception desk duty on Monday night as she's helping at one of the stalls in the afternoon.'

As usual he was settling things in his own lordly manner, thought Lesley. He might say none of them had time for fun and games just now, but Sorrel was always hanging around the Manor. Of course they were engaged, if not yet officially, and you couldn't blame her for wanting to be with the man she loved.

Blake's housekeeper had brought Lesley a tray of tea, for she was going to work on late into the evening. As she poured herself a cup she saw Blake and Sorrel walking across the lawn from the Lodge. A wind had risen this afternoon, driving away the sea mist which earlier had come creeping inland, pressing up against the windows of the little office like spirits trying to get in. Now the wind sent Sorrel's black hair flying as she raised a laughing face to Blake's.

It was the mist earlier on that had made her feel so depressed, Lesley told herself drearily. The sooner she came to terms with herself, the better. She had just got to get her stupid emotions under control.

CHAPTER X

The weekend of the Revel didn't prove particularly kind. There was a thunderstorm on the Sunday and then it settled down to steady rain for most of the night and the next morning. But later it began to clear and in the late afternoon the sun came out, the raindrops glistening on the flowers and leaves.

Lesley had suggested that Steve accompany her to the dance and he had said cheerfully that it sounded as if it would be fun. Then nearly at the last minute he had phoned from some place miles down the coast saying there had been trouble over the demonstration and he would have to stay down there and sort it out.

Rita had turned up her nose at the idea of a village dance and gone off with Rick to the discothèque. However, Mrs Piper had come back from her duties at her stall in the afternoon in order to give her son Jeff his tea.

Lesley had been lending Steve the Mini as she herself was using it so seldom. Jeff had a motorbike and would have given Lesley a lift up to the village hall, but there was Mrs Piper, so the three walked along the narrow high-banked lane, the flower scents rising like incense after the day's rain.

Lesley was wearing a sleeveless white dress, a stunning contrast to her lovely honey tan. She was carrying her green sandals and wearing a necklace of flat green stones that matched her eyes.

The gates which broke the banks and the high hedge showed the ripened barley with scarlet poppies and pimpernels at the edges of the fields. In the cottage gardens bushes of buddleia and lavender and large white arum lilies with other colourful flowers gave off their evening scent all the sweeter after the rain.

In the village hall long tables were spread and people were already sitting down to plates of luscious ham and tongue, salads, sandwiches, sausage rolls, Cornish pasties, trifles, bowls of fruit, jugs of Cornish cream and delicious cakes.

Lesley sat between Jeff and Lennie who ran the village store and ate a larger meal than she had ever eaten in her life. ' I shan't be able to dance a step!' she gasped.

At the farther end of the table she could see Dominic, gay and laughing with Sorrel beside him, vivid and beautiful in a scarlet dress of wild silk. Dominic waved to Lesley, but Sorrel, though she looked her up and down with an insolent dark glance, did not appear to recognise her. Lesley searched in vain for one more figure, but he turned up only just before supper was finishing. She was amused by the way so many women jumped up to ply him with refreshments. The Trevendones, he had said, were expected to attend. It went back to the time when they were the feudal lords. And it was so very obvious who was the feudal lord here tonight.

The tables were cleared and pushed aside and a three-piece band began to play, sometimes modern, sometimes old-time, for many of the dancers were middle-aged or even elderly.

Lesley danced with one or two young men whom she didn't know and Dominic, pausing with his partner, one of the hotel guests, enquired about Steve. He didn't ask Lesley for a dance, for he was obviously expecting to claim Sorrel again. She was now dancing with Blake. When her dance was finished, Lesley went back to Mrs Piper, but as the band struck up again, she saw Blake walking across the floor in her direction. Something like panic seized her by the throat, but before he reached her, Sorrel was at his side, her hand on his arm.

'I did think maister were coming to ask fer yew, m'dear,' said Mrs Piper comfortably, ' but Mrs Lang now, she don't like to see his arm round another maid.'

Lesley had a partner the next moment, but it wasn't so very long afterwards that she realised neither Blake nor Sorrel were there any longer. Dominic stayed on dancing with girl after girl, drinking just a little bit too much but always gay and courteous. Finally he settled for Lesley, for as he said, she was the prettiest girl in the room, and their steps fitted perfectly. He assured Mrs Piper and Jeff that he would see her home and later, in his expensive sports car, they roared down the lane to the main road.

'What about Plymouth?' he asked, as they reached the corner. 'What about making a night of it?'

Lesley shook her head. She knew how he felt, and she felt rather like it herself, but he had had too much to drink to be safe driving any further. And as far as she was concerned, there was tomorrow morning when she was on duty at eight o'clock.

They sat for a little while longer in his car at the front of the old Manor. It was very warm, with more thunder in the air and a feeling of waiting for a storm to break.

'Look, little Yseult,' Dominic said suddenly, 'if you don't want to go back to Australia and this hotel deal goes through, there'll always be a place for you at the Home Farm. You and Ricky and Rita.'

Lesley wasn't sure whether it was meant as a proposal or not. He had made laughing ones to her more than once before. He had been drinking since Sorrel left the dance and now he was making light-hearted love to her.

'I'll bear that in mind, Tristan darling,' she said gently, with tears for both of them aching in her throat. 'But now I must go in. It's been a lovely evening.'

She let him kiss her, then extricated herself and got out of the car. 'It's been a lovely evening,' he echoed. Lesley willed herself to disregard her own heartache. At least they had consoled each other.

Before she reached her own room, she heard his car start up and roar away. She sighed, and went to stand by the open window. Rita was fast asleep in the bed at the other side of the room.

Lesley stared at the darkling sky, where now and then a flash of lightning made all the world bright. She was thinking of Dominic, so gay and laughter-loving, so gentle. The temptation to accept that proposal was very great. She loved this magnificent cruel coast, the changing sea, the beautiful setting of the Manor—loved it all as neither of the twins did. But she had no place here. She wasn't a Trevendone.

The morning started badly. Lesley had been sleepless for a long time because—or that was the excuse she made to herself —the night had been so sultry one could scarcely breathe, let alone sleep.

Blake had been at the reception desk when she eventually arrived there, ten minutes late, the first time it had ever happened, and it *would* just be the morning when two clients were leaving early.

His face was like granite, but he made no comment and she got down to her own work conscious that she had a slight headache, possibly from over-sleeping, possibly from over-eating last night. Three or four of the accounts on which she was working were incorrect and not sure of her own accuracy with this headachy feeling she had to go through them again. They were Dominic's responsibility, but his methods were slapdash and there *were* inaccuracies. Then, what seemed the last straw over a long and intricate letter right near the bottom of the page, she got her fingers on the wrong keys for the whole of a line. She couldn't possibly erase all that, so the only thing was to retype the page. For the rest of the morning she was working against time and she realised she would have to come in tonight to finish.

The afternoon was to be devoted to Blake's own work in the little office next to his lab. He seemed more impatient than ever about it, and of course one could guess the reason. It was August now and within the next eight weeks there was so much for him to do. Naturally he was under strain too, with his marriage presumably approaching, and Sorrel demanding so much of his company.

Lesley decided to forgo her lunch break. The thought of food anyway made her feel sick. So she went straight from the hotel across the gardens to the office by the lab.

It was unbearably hot, though there had been only a few glimpses of the sun during the morning. If only the storm would come, she thought. Through the inverted vee opening of the Kissing Trees she could see the sea, smooth and oily and pewter-coloured with practically no swell. An ugly sea today, she thought, and a matching leaden sky.

It certainly wasn't her day. She had managed to get three pages typed before she heard Blake's step in the lab. This part of the work was particularly urgent and he had been taking each page as she finished it and reviewing it. Usually it was passed without comment. Well, he had the three pages to occupy himself with, so she wouldn't see him for a while, she reflected. She had put the finished work on his desk, but after the briefest interval he came storming into the office, his face like thunder.

' I suppose it would be superfluous to ask what's wrong with you today, Miss Trevendone,' he said grimly. ' Late this morning, and now . . . this!'

He flung one of the pages she had just typed in front of her and she stared down at it, at first uncomprehendingly, while the pain in her throat threatened to choke her.

'What . . . what . . . ?' she stammered, and her eyes blurred so that she could scarcely see.

'You've missed a whole paragraph out just here,' he said, and came behind her, his arm inadvertently brushing against her bare shoulder. She was all too conscious of the faint scent of good soap and an after-shave lotion, as his finger pointed to the paragraph in his original manuscript.

'I'm sorry. I'll do it again,' she said in a low voice.

'Yes, do that,' he rasped, 'and remember I want it in the post by tonight.'

He paused for a moment and she waited for him to move from behind her. Suddenly he said, 'What happened to your Australian friend last night?'

'He couldn't make it,' she said mechanically.

He moved now and stood in front of her, and though she didn't raise her eyes, she knew he was standing giving her a long, considering survey.

'What time did you get to bed last night, or should I say this morning, Miss Trevendone?'

The remark was so unexpected that Lesley's first reaction was one merely of surprise. 'I didn't stay to the end of the Revel dance. I don't know what time it finished.'

'That wasn't the question I asked you,' he said grimly. 'I asked you what time you got to bed.'

And now Lesley's eyes had frozen to the green of an icy glacier. 'I really don't see what that has to do with you, Mr Defontaine,' she said in a voice that matched her eyes.

'Naturally it has nothing to do with me,' he almost shouted. 'But what *is* important is that people who work for me should be fit for the jobs they're doing. Not able to concentrate and looking half dead in the middle of the afternoon.'

'I'm quite able to concentrate, and as to my appearance, I'm sorry if it displeases you. Perhaps if you left me I could get on and repeat this work.'

He mouthed something unprintable and smothered it almost before it was uttered. The thundery weather was evidently having an effect on Mr Blake Defontaine as well as on other people.

'All right, do it again, and then for God's sake take the rest of the afternoon off. Go on to the beach and see if you can get some fresh air there before the storm breaks. Have you any tablets for your headache?'

Lesley sat for a moment after he had gone, needles pricking the back of her eyes. So he thought she looked half dead, did he—which in a man's language meant singularly unattractive. She fumbled in her handbag for a mirror and grimaced at her pale face and the violet shadows under her eyes. Well, perhaps he was right. But what sort of tablets did one take when the pain was not so much in one's head as in one's heart?

There were roars of thunder and flashes of lightning as she ran from the Lodge towards the hotel later that afternoon. Heavy black clouds were piling up in the sky, and as she reached the old Manor, the storm broke with a howling wind and a roaring hungry sea.

'I hope to my dear goodness,' said Mrs Piper, 'that young Mr Dominic bain't out in this in that car of his'n. Un shouldn't have gone out again, and so I telled him. Un never come in this morning till five o'clock and oh, my dear life, un was in a way when un got up.'

Lesley said nothing... So Dominic had been living it up last night after he had left her, and Blake Defontaine suspected *she* had been his companion.

The storm was succeeded by a patch of bad weather, and Lesley, feeling unutterably depressed, was convinced that the short English summer was over. Very soon now she must make up her mind what she was going to do next. For her, as well as the summer, this Cornish idyll was nearly over.

'The summer over? Not a bit of it, m' dear soul,' said Mrs Piper comfortably. 'We'll have weeks of it yet down here right into September. And then we'll be having our Harvest Home Supper Dance just like we had at the Revel. You enjoyed that, didn't you, m'dear? I'll never forget you and Mr Dominic—the handsomest couple in the room, you were, and we all said it.

'And then we always get a spell of lovely weather in October—an Indian summer, they dew call it.'

But so far as the Australian team of surfing and life-saving was concerned, their summer in England was over and by the end of August they were packing up and preparing to fly home.

Steve rang Lesley one afternoon early in September and she took his call in the office next to the lab. He knew she was free that evening and they had already arranged to meet in St Benga Town.

'Darling,' he said exuberantly, 'I've had a brainwave. As I'm off to Scotland tomorrow, let's make it a celebration tonight. I've already been honoured by being offered a table at your so-so exclusive establishment. So is it on? Will you dine with me there?'

'But, Steve. . . .' Lesley was stammering slightly because Blake Defontaine was in the doorway between the office and the lab . . . 'was there a vacant table . . . and who took the booking?'

'I rang this morning, and the slave-master himself answered and was graciously pleased to allow us to dine together in the sacred precincts. So make yourself extra beautiful, my sweet. See you.'

With that he rang off, leaving Lesley staring at Defontaine and hating him for the sardonic gleam in his eyes. 'Don't look so embarrassed,' he said unkindly. 'I take it that was a personal call from your Australian admirer. I didn't hear a thing. Have fun tonight.'

In spite of a certain disquiet, Lesley couldn't help feeling excited at the thought of dressing up and dining in the hotel. It was something she hadn't done before and lately she hadn't been out much in the evening.

So she was humming gaily as she went up to her room, peeled off her dress and underwear and settled for a really luxurious bath, revelling in the ravishing perfume of the bath crystals she had sprinkled so lavishly in the bath water.

Quickly she dried herself and stepped into another set of flimsies and then a dress of brocaded silk in jade green—the colour of her eyes. Shoes to match and a long gold chain which had been her mother's—the only valuable piece of jewellery she possessed.

She left her make-up light, merely emphasising the darkness of her brows and lashes and shadowing the greenness of her eyes.

Steve was waiting for her in the great hall of the new Manor. She looked at him as he came to meet her and all at once a sense of panic shook her. Steve—Steve of all people who had been her boy-friend in Melbourne—seemed like a handsome bronzed young stranger with whom she was reluctant to dine *tête-à-tête*.

The panic died when she saw the old familiar grin and heard his Aussie voice. They had a drink and then went into the dining room. The meal was excellent, but neither of them really noticed. Steve was talking a lot about his forthcoming visit to Scotland where he was visiting some of his father's relatives and Lesley was watching Blake Defontaine who was entertaining two business acquaintances in a far corner of the room.

She was half glad, half apprehensive when Steve suggested they went for a walk in the garden and towards the cliffs—glad to avoid having to speak to Defontaine and meet the mockery on his face, yet fearful of what Steve might want to say to her. Already the shadows were gathering in the garden, and in the green of the sky over the sea one star was faintly shining.

Lesley knew it was something she couldn't put off any longer. It was time to call a halt now to this thing that had started when she was at school.

Steve's hand closed down hard on hers as they walked towards the cliffs. ' After Scotland, what I do next depends on *you*, Les. No, don't say anything. Just listen.

' Les, when I go back to Australia I want to take you with me. I can't get you out of my system. No girl has ever meant as much to me as you do. Is it on?'

Lesley shook her chestnut head rather sadly and her green eyes were troubled. ' No, Steve, I'm sorry, but it isn't. Since you came here in May, I've asked myself often why it didn't seem the same, and all I can think is that . . . well, we aren't like those.' She pointed to the Kissing Trees which they were just passing. ' See, they've bent towards each other as time has passed, but it hasn't been the same with us. Since those Melbourne days we've grown apart.'

She clenched her hands, willing herself not to think of that time she had been kissed under these very trees, willing herself to forget for ever the moment when Blake's face had bent over to her upturned one, his eyes dilated, brilliant, his lips hard upon her own. It had been a moment of madness—perhaps for him a desire to punish her for her defiance of him. She was out of her mind to be thinking of it now.

Steve kicked moodily at the turf over which they were walking. '*I* haven't grown away from you, *I* haven't changed. It's you, Les, who's different. You're in love with someone else, aren't you? Is it Dominic? He's madly handsome, I give you that.'

'No . . . no . . . I'm not in love with anyone,' Lesley gasped quickly, and even to herself the words sounded incredibly forced.

For another half hour, Steve pleaded and cajoled while they walked the cliffs seeing nothing of the magic beauty of the summer sea stretched in a silken sheet of turquoise and emerald, nor the black cruelty of the rocks below them.

The long twilight began to fade and over the hill the moon lifted its shining apricot globe. In the end Steve said sullenly, 'I shall go to Scotland tomorrow. After that, I don't know . . . I may come down here again, I may not. It depends. Will you think it over, Les, and perhaps give me another answer when I come again?'

'Steve, I'm sorry, but my answer won't be different either tomorrow or next week . . . or ever.

'Well, what am I going to do about young Rita, then?' he asked deliberately.

Lesley stared at him, her eyes anxious as she remembered Sorrel's innuendoes, remembered too how different Rita's attitude to her had been since that night she had announced that she was going back to Australia to be married.

'Rita?' she echoed. 'What should you be doing about her, Steve?'

He said glumly, 'I've promised she can come back to Sydney with me. She's mad keen to get into the Outback again and I said I'd write to Mum asking her to invite her to stay.'

'Oh, Steve!' Lesley looked at him despairingly. 'That isn't on. It isn't on at all, and you must have known it. Her place is here at Trevendone until some other arrangements can be made. You'll have to tell her. . . .'

'It's all on the level, Les, I assure you,' he protested.

'I wouldn't have promised if I hadn't hoped things were going to work out for you and me. Rita tells me this Defontaine bloke is going to pay her fare back. She's changed her attitude to him completely, you know. He's just great, according to her. It seems he's going to put some of the Trevendone money in trust for her and Rick . . . or so she says.'

Lesley's green eyes widened. 'All this is news to me,' she said faintly. 'I'm half afraid Rita has been pulling your leg, Steve . . . just making it sound easy for her to come as your parents' guest. But it isn't on, Steve, not like that. It just isn't on.'

'No,' he agreed uneasily, 'I realise I got carried away. What's to do, Les?'

Lesley said quietly, 'My job here will have finished at the beginning of October and I shall be returning to Australia. I don't think Rick will. His future seems pretty well planned, but if Rita wants to come back with me we'll probably be in Melbourne by Christmas. After that, it's up to you. If Rita meets your parents and they invite her to your home in the Outback it will be all right so far as I'm concerned.'

His face had brightened at the thought of her return. 'No hard feelings about Rita, Les?' he questioned. 'I haven't been playing around with her, I promise you.'

'No hard feelings, Steve,' Lesley assured him, but her face was still troubled.

They parted, he optimistic that they would meet in Melbourne, but Lesley's mood was one of deepest depression. She was bewildered by the turmoil in her own heart.

Mrs Piper came out of the kitchen of the old Manor as the girl began to mount wearily the polished oak stairs. Worked too hard, she did, Miss Lesley, and worried too much about those twin scallywags.

As the girl turned, she said admiringly, 'Oh, but you look real bonny in that dress, Miss Lesley. Not but what I liked you fine in that white one you wore to the Revel dance.'

Lesley smiled. 'I hear more jollifications are in the wind.'

'Yes, 'tis Harvest Festival come Sunday week. Yonder out there 'tis the harvest moon, as no doubt you've been looking at un,' and she smiled slyly.

'Yes, there's a lovely moon,' Lesley agreed.

'That Harvest Thanksgiving is a service I dew like, and started first round about these parts, or so they dew say. Then come Monday, t'will be Harvest supper and dance. Perhaps you'll bring that young man o' yourn this time.'

Lesley shook her head. 'He isn't my young man, Mrs Piper. He's just an old friend. He's going up to Scotland to see some of his relatives and then he's off back to Australia.'

'Well, better chanst for them as *is* down here,' remarked Mrs Piper obscurely.

As had become customary Lesley spent a sleepless night, her thoughts very much on Steve's revelations of Blake's plans for the twins. So far as Ricky was concerned, they caused her no surprise. The group with Tim Drage in charge were moving to London in October and Lesley had already sadly accepted the fact that Rick would go with them.

And as to Rita and herself, Blake had evidently decided they were to go back over the sea. He had informed Rita, but as yet, no word to her. It was as if these days they were unable to communicate at all.

He was still working himself and her at a savage pace. Bookings at the hotel continued high and true to Mrs Piper's forecast the autumn weather was perfect. Misty mornings sometimes, but followed by days as warm as in July.

Blake spent very little time in recreation. Once or twice when she got up early because she couldn't sleep, Lesley would see him riding on the beach, deserted at that hour. It was too early for Sorrel to be with him, and Lesley would stand well hidden at the top of the cliffs watching the raking stride of the mare and the man who sat her so perfectly.

He had not mentioned again that night of the Revel dance and she concluded that he still believed she had returned with Dominic at dawn. On the day after she had dined with Steve he had come to the Reception Desk and said, 'I hope everything was satisfactory last night, Miss Trevendone.' She had met for a moment his ironic glance and then her attention had seemed fixed on something far above his head.

'It was a lovely meal and the service was excellent,' she said in a colourless voice.

'And now the surfing and life-saving is over!' It was a

comment rather than a question, and more irony, she thought, but again her voice was colourless.

'Steve leaves for Scotland today. His father's people came from there and he has several relatives to look up.'

'Romantic, isn't it,' he smiled, ' to come from over the sea to look up one's own people. To find . . . who knows what?' One dark eyebrow was raised and his mouth was curved in mockery. Did he guess that one girl who had come over the sea had found only . . . heartbreak?

There was that constricted feeling in her throat again and she was conscious as so often these days of the unending battle between herself and Blake.

The Harvest Festival weekend came and went, with a misty Sunday morning but brilliant sunshine by the time she and Mrs Piper and Ricky and Rita drove in her Mini to the morning service. The lovely little church was beautifully decorated with flower arrangements of sophisticated design and the simpler tributes of fruit and vegetables.

Second from the front were the Trevendone pews, one on either side of the aisle. The twins and Mrs Piper and Lesley sat on one side, while on the other were old Mrs Trevendone and her companion, Dominic and Sorrel. Jennifer, glowing like a rose, sat with Rod Drew and his family just behind. And then at the last minute, Blake Defontaine himself came in, sliding into the end of the pew next to Lesley.

She kept her eyes averted, trying to still her stupidly racing heart. How he would laugh if he knew that she couldn't sing the beautiful hymns herself because she was listening to him.

So far as the Harvest supper dance was concerned, Lesley hadn't the slightest intention of repeating her experience of the Revel dance, and it was with heartfelt relief that she found Rod was staying over Monday and Jennifer was anxious to go to the dance with him.

'Of course I'll do the reception desk duty, Jen,' Lesley said warmly. 'Go and have a lovely time.' She saw Jen and Dominic and this time even Rita set off. Mrs Piper was sad about her not coming but promised to return home with a full account of all the happenings—something Lesley wasn't at all anxious to hear. To her surprise, however, she saw Blake come out of the dining room with the two men who she suspected were interested in taking over the hotel. He would

be seeing them on their way, she supposed, and then joining
Sorrell at the dance. Once again, poor Dominic would be left
in the lurch, and this time no little Yseult to play second
fiddle.

Mrs Piper had returned home early and was waiting to ask
Lesley to have a cup of tea with her in the kitchen when she
came off duty.

'Too crowded,' was her verdict. Harvest supper was
always popular, and with the good weather there were still a
lot of visitors crowding in too.

Miss Rita seemed to have had a good time, but she had come
home earlyish too and had already gone to bed. Lesley raised
her eyebrows at that news. Mr Dominic and Mrs Lang had
danced together a lot, and then gone on somewhere else. Mr
Defontaine? Well, that was an odd thing, but Mrs Piper had
never seen a sign of him tonight.

Lesley was wondering about that as she went upstairs. Rita
seemed to be already asleep, so the older girl got undressed
quietly and crept into bed, but not to sleep. Blake must have
taken those men down to the Lodge to go talking business.
How furious Sorrel would be! She had had to make do with
Dominic all the evening—poor Dominic.

Lesley thought rebelliously, Blake has made his plans, it
seems, to send me back to Australia. Sorrel wants to keep
Dominic as a second string. Suppose I confound them both?
I could do it if I wanted. I could take Dominic and hold
him. I could make him love me. In his own way, he is so
lovable . . . my dear, dear Tristan.

Life with Dominic would always be gay. One would never
need to plumb the depths, but then you would never reach
the heights. You could always mould him to your own way of
thinking. Her gallant Tristan. In a way even, they could
have a romantic love life.

How different would life be with a man whose harsh corners
could wound a woman to the very heart of her. There would
be no moulding *him* to any woman's will. He would always
be dominant, ruthless even perhaps, though he loved her.

Lesley turned restlessly. How soon would it be morning?

This particular morning she was working in Blake's office—
still working against time. She hadn't seen him as yet and

thought he must be over at the hotel. That was why it was a surprise to see Sorrel. The dark girl's face had a particularly vindictive look.

'You impudent impostor! I suspected it right from the beginning,' she burst out. 'If it's left to me you'll be put in charge for false pretences!'

Lesley gave her a quick look from her long dark lashes and then bent again to the page she was checking. 'I'm very busy, Mrs Lang. If you're looking for Mr Delfontaine, I think he's probably over at the new Manor.'

'Don't try to talk yourself out of it, you impudent slut! Young Rita let the cat out of the bag last night. She didn't mean to—it was just a slip, but I noticed it, though luckily for you no one else did.'

'Mrs Lang,' Lesley said deliberately, 'I think you know as well as I do that Mr Defontaine is determined that this work shall be finished by the beginning of October. It won't be if I'm taken off it . . . or if I'm continually interrupted.'

'Blackmail! It's just what I might have expected of you.' Sorrel's dark face was still furious, but there was a calculating look in her eyes. It was obvious that Lesley had struck the right chord.

'All right,' she said, pacing about the office, one clenched fist beating into the other open palm. 'I'll keep quiet about it and not mention it to Blake, but on one condition—that you leave here the day the hotel closes. Blake isn't the sort to stand for the deception you've practised on all of us. He'll be out for your blood once he knows, so for your own sake pack up and don't let either Blake or Dominic know you're going. Understand?'

'I don't suppose Dominic would mind. He'd only laugh.' Lesley couldn't resist the thrust.

'Don't dare to inveigle Dominic. I've told you before that Tristan and Yseult caper isn't on. Get back to Australia to your precious Steve. Blake is sending Rita back so you can go together.'

'How kind of him,' drawled Lesley tantalisingly, 'but *I* might want to stay.'

'If you attempt to stay I'll see you go to jail,' Sorrel threatened wildly, and rushed out of the room. Something *had* upset her, and Lesley didn't really think it was because

170

she had discovered that Lesley Trevendone was really Lesley Arden.

'Les, I didn't mean to tell her,' Rita was sobbing stormily. 'It just sort of slipped out, and she latched on to it and got me into a corner. I wouldn't say any more, but she said she could guess. Don't tell Rick, will you? He'll never forgive me.'

Lesley shook her head and Rita went on, 'Sorrel and Dominic were quarrelling. I think she was upset because Blake didn't come to the dance and because he sat next to you in church on Sunday. Dominic said he wished you *had* come because you'd both had a smashing time at the Revel dance. But they made it up afterwards.'

'Yes,' said Lesley thoughtfully. 'They always do.'

'Les, they won't put you in prison or anything, will they, like she said? She won't tell Blake, she promised, as long as you leave the very day the hotel closes.'

'Well, why not?' Lesley asked calmly. 'There'll be no need for us to stay any longer. We want to go to London and see Ricky settled there. Then we can go back to Australia, you and I. I hear Blake has made arrangements to cover your passage back.'

Rita shifted from one foot to the other uneasily. 'I feel awful about that too, Les, but he told Ricky and me not to mention it to you. He said you'd enough on your mind with all this work you're doing for the hotel and for him. He said he'd got arrangements lined up for you too. But,' she added doubtfully, 'that was because he thought you too were a Trevendone. If Sorrel splits, it may be different.'

Lesley's green eyes were brilliant. 'It won't be in the least different, darling. Blake Defontaine will be making no arrangements for me once I've finished working here. He won't be my slave-master any longer.'

'Don't call him that, Les,' Rita pleaded. 'I'm ashamed I ever thought of the name. Rick and I have both realised how mistaken we were about him. We both wish you could alter your mind too.'

Lesley smiled rather oddly. How long ago was it that she had realised that the first look he had taken at her on a February night of snow and sleet had dealt a glancing blow at her heart—a blow from which she had never recovered. 'No, I haven't altered my mind, and I don't suppose I ever shall ... now.'

CHAPTER XI

Only a day or two now. Lesley relaxed in a warm bath and then with her thin dressing gown slung around her she went into the bedroom. As she was having an early night would it be a good idea to do some packing? Rita was down at Penpethic Harbour with Ricky, so she had the room to herself.

Downstairs, she had just had a cup of tea with Mrs Piper who had been telling her about the fairy ring on the downs opposite the Kissing Seat. Jennifer, drinking tea too, had laughed, 'You and your Cornish superstitions, Mrs Piper! You'll make Lesley think we're still living in the Middle Ages.' She'd turned to Lesley. 'It's just a dark green fungus growing in a circle round an area of grass. Don't believe a word about the piskies dancing round it.'

But when she had gone, Mrs Piper had shaken her head. 'She can say what she likes, Miss Lesley, but them circles is made by the piskies—fairies you call un—dancing round. And they dew say if you'm be foolish enough to go out in the moonlight and see un, they'll dance you away wi' un and you'll not be seen for a hundred years.'

Lesley laughed. 'Moral is to keep away from the fairy ring, especially in the moonlight.'

No, she was too tired to do any packing. She slid into bed and almost immediately she was asleep. Too good to last! Lesley hadn't slept well for a long time. Perhaps that was why those violet shadows were always under her heavy eyes.

What had wakened her? Rita creeping in quietly. But Rita didn't usually creep anywhere. She blew in like one of the gales that sprang up over the turquoise seas here, lashing them into pewter cauldrons.

Lesley had been heavy with sleep an hour ago, but now she felt wide awake. She slid out of bed and went to the small window on her side of the room, its casement flung wide to get as much air as possible. The low roar of the surf came into the room like the giant breathing of a huge sea monster.

As she turned her head slightly, Lesley gave a little gasp. The moon was coming up over the garden. It must be almost full.

It was pale orange in colour and so very, very large. She gave a nervous little laugh. Her first crazy idea was that something had gone wrong with the moon, as if it had moved much too close to earth. But it was because it was only just above the horizon that it seemed so big. Mrs Piper had said this was called the hunter's moon, and now Lesley remembered that she had heard Dominic making an appointment with someone to go shooting next week.

The hunter's moon—a full moon or near enough—and there was that fairy ring on the downs. If you were ever likely to see the fairies dancing it would be at the time of the full moon.

The idea was too much for Lesley to stay any longer in this stuffy little room. Even if she saw no fairies, at least she could breathe some sea air and walk in the moonlight. A sense of the ridiculous shook her for a moment. If you were a fool—and where could you find a bigger one than Lesley Arden—then you might as well go the whole hog and be a real fool. Go out alone in the moonlight and dance round the fairy ring, and if by chance the piskies came and stole you away for the next hundred years, then so much the better. After a hundred years surely this bitter pain in her heart would have vanished completely.

Of course she ought to have known that she was asking for more heartbreak. After all, it was a night for lovers.

The house was very quiet. Jennifer was in her own room asleep, no doubt dreaming of her wedding at Christmas when Rod came home from Switzerland for good. Dominic, Rita and Rick were still out because it was not very late.

She pulled on jeans and a thin sweater, stepped into her walking sandals and went quietly downstairs and out of the front door. She went quickly across the garden, paused for a moment by the Kissing Trees, and then when the pain in her heart was more than seemed humanly possible to bear she went through the gate.

The fairy ring was there, but no piskies, and it was doubtful if Lesley would have seen them had they been there. She was walking blindly, quickly, running away from herself and from her memories . . . memory of a kiss under those trees, memory that tonight she had typed the last of Blake's manuscript. Her work for the slave-master was finished.

Tomorrow all she need do was to go into the little office and tidy up the desk. At the end of the week the last guests would be leaving and the hotel would be closed. And the girl from over the sea could go back from whence she had come.

Blake had been away all day. Dominic had whispered to her that he was sure he was making the final arrangements for the transfer of the two Manors to a hotel consortium in which the Trevendones would have shares, but no one else spoke of it.

Lesley had walked—run, rather—so swiftly in her efforts to escape her own thoughts that she had come to where the downs overhung the little harbour of St Benga Town. The tide was low and the beach stretched away in lonely moonlit beauty—the beach where he had reined in the runaway Sheba and told her at their second meeting that she was a menace that he hoped never to see again.

And now she was near to the cliff road above which the lovely houses stood, one with a blue door and shutters. For a moment Lesley stood in the shadows, and then she saw them—two lovers, closely locked.

Sorrel's voice ripped through the moonlight. 'Come, my love. It's time we went in.'

Lesley did not wait to see or hear more. On silent footsteps she fled back along the downs, not pausing for breath until she came abreast of the Kissing Trees. No piskies dancing round the Fairy Ring, and no truth either in Mrs Piper's other story that when a man and a girl kissed for the first time beneath the Kissing Trees they would be true lovers, for ever and a day.

There were no tears in Lesley's green eyes. Only in her heart.

Lesley whistled to Dingo. He, like the twins, had gone over to the side of the enemy, but this afternoon he was at a loose end, and he responded ecstatically to the suggestion of a walk. Not that she intended to walk, at least not on the Trevendone estate. She felt if she stayed anywhere in the vicinity she would disgrace herself by lying down and giving way to the misery which was tearing out her heart.

She hadn't seen Blake this morning. Probably he was still in the white house on the cliff above St Benga Town. But she had gone into the little office, left it tidy, moving out all her own possessions, leaving the typewriter covered.

This afternoon she was free, but she wasn't going to bother about lunch. Food would choke her, she thought. This afternoon, she would go off on her own and say a final farewell to her dreams of the lovely land of Lyonesse, of Camelot and the legends of chivalry. It had turned sour on her, this lovely cruel coast. Farewell now to all that. Tonight she would pack and begin to prepare for the vigorous reality of life in Australia.

She ran the Mini out of the garage, opened the door for Dingo to jump in beside her and set off much too fast down the drive and along the main road. Weeks ago she had promised herself that she would explore a little ruined church on a steep cliff point about five miles north of St Benga Town.

She parked just outside the farm which advertised cream teas, though now there was the word 'Closed' across the notice. They must regret it, she supposed, in this glorious autumn weather with plenty of tourists still around. No doubt if the new Manor House was remaining open there would still be visitors. But she didn't want to think about Trevendone or anyone who lived there this afternoon. She just wanted to breathe the air, find a warm sheltered spot on the cliffs and indulge her own misery and then brace herself for the future.

She took only a cursory glance at the ruined church and the old gravestones. They slept quietly enough in this peaceful spot, those who had been laid to rest here.

She shivered and hurried through the lych-gate into the meadow that led on to the cliff. Her mood was sombre enough without such thoughts. She held Dingo tightly on the lead when she saw some young heifers grazing nearby. *His* mood was far from sombre and he began to pull away and bark. Fortunately the animals were distant enough to take no notice and his attention was soon distracted by a late butterfly fluttering ahead of them.

It was a windless day, but as Lesley reached the cliff path she could hear the surf thundering below her. Even on a day like this, a throwback to midsummer with the grass green and scabious and harebells still studding the hedgerow which marched right up to the cliff edge, when she peered over she could see the surf breaking in white foam against the black teeth which like a great monster's fangs opened a giant maw to the waves. Yet beyond the breakers, the sea, summerlike, stretched in a band of dark blue silk to the horizon, cloudless too, and only a few shades lighter than the sea below.

At first she sauntered along the cliff edge, watching the meadow grasses shiver and sway in a tiny breeze that was imperceptible at her height. Then the ground dropped suddenly and she was looking down into a steep combe. It was as if some giant hand had cut a perfect vee into the landscape. Beyond on the other side was the rich deep colour of purple heather.

Lesley turned back and began to descend a steep path which led down to a tiny cove. There was some shingle and just at this state of the tide, a bit of sand. She would throw pebbles into the water for Dingo to retrieve. He never made any real attempt to get them, but he enjoyed dashing to the edge of the water and barking enthusiastically. In this lonely spot his vocal efforts would be of annoyance to no one.

Then she had a slight qualm. Under Blake's firm handling Dingo was losing some of his more offensive mannerisms. Perhaps it would be wiser not to encourage him in this barking session.

She shrugged. Who wanted to be wise? Not she just now. After all, if she was thinking in terms of wisdom, then what *she* should have done was to have stayed in Australia and never come searching for the fairy gold of romance that didn't exist.

She had lost not only her own peace of mind in coming here but her close contact with the twins. They had their own thoughts now, their own dreams, and in a way were indifferent to hers. There was nothing more cruel than indifference. All at once her throat was aching and her thoughts now on someone else. Oh, what was the use!

She began to plunge down the narrow cliff path, Dingo rushing in front of her in the headlong manner with which he did everything. He was at the bottom long before her, his tongue lolling out expectantly.

It was hotter down here than she had imagined, for in the shelter of the cove the cliffs gave off a stifling heat on this day of midsummer-like languor.

For a while she found bits of driftwood to fling into the lapping tide for him to retrieve. The water was very calm down here, but further out on the rocks, jutting cruelly out on either side of the cove, the surf was breaking with its usual angry roar. You never got far away from the cruelty of this coast, Lesley reflected with a shiver. Any more than she could get away from the stabbing cruelty of the knowledge that had come to her last night. Probably they were married already. It was a permissive society, but Blake Defontaine and Sorrel Lang . . . no. It would be marriage for them.

Dingo kept reminding her that they were supposed to be having a game, but in the end, even he grew tired of it. His barks grew less raucous and his chasing to the edge of the sea more languid.

The tide had now turned, and whistling the dog, Lesley began the steep upward climb. She was sticky with perspiration when she reached the top. The afternoon seemed hotter than ever and the climb had left her completely exhausted—or was it last night when she had not slept at all?

' Dingo, I'm all in, and so are you by the look of you, poor old thing. Come and lie down.' She patted the sward on to which she had thrown herself and he came and put his chin on her knee and looked up at her with the adoring expression he knew so well how to assume.

' You're a fraud,' she told him dreamily. ' You look like that for lots of us, but there's only one person you really go for now, isn't there? The slave-master. But I mustn't call him that now. Even the twins object.'

She sighed. She was back to the same theme and that tightness in her chest and throat was getting worse. She turned and lay quite flat on the grassy down, pressing hard against the soft turf as if she could still the pain in her body by the pressure, her arms stretched out on either side of her as she dug her fingers into the grass.

Around her was the low murmur of insects rejoicing in this golden day. A brown and yellow butterfly fluttered near and then sailed gently away. Muted by the height of the cliffs and her nearness to the turf, the roar of the breakers was like a dying symphony. All at once, the heat and exhaustion and that sleeplessness of last night took possession of her senses. The sweet smell of the turf was heady. Her right hand came up to her cheek. She turned slightly so that she was lying on her side . . . and then came oblivion.

Some noise had awakened her. Lesley blinked, sat up and rubbed the arm on which she had been lying. It wasn't so warm now and the sun had moved down well towards the sea, sending a golden pathway over the water towards the creaming surf.

She got up, looking around for the dog, whistling and calling him. There was no answering scuffle and Lesley's anxious eyes turned towards the meadow near the church where the young heifers had been grazing, but they were still standing around placidly, so he hadn't gone in that direction. She peered over the cliff, but the cove where they had played earlier was covered with waves which splashed over all the rocks.

She whistled again and this time there was a yelp of distress. Alarm tightened around her chest as she went towards the deep vee of the combe. Was he stuck down there in a rabbit hole? She peered cautiously over the edge where it was beginning to get very shadowy. When she whistled again she realised his yelp was coming not from below, but somewhere on her left nearer the cliff edge. Now she called, 'Dingo, don't be silly. Come, boy, come!' His answering yelp convinced her that he was trapped somewhere or he would have been here by now.

She began to speak quietly and reassuringly, though her heart was beating very fast and she felt sick with worry. 'I'm coming and I'll soon have you free. Just another little bark to say where you are.'

As she spoke she was edging to where the combe met the cliffs facing seawards. When she had been in the cove below she had noticed that just here the cliffs fell precipitously and at the top there was a dangerous overhang of soft shale and turf. It was too risky to go near and peer over; she'd have to go a little way down the combe and look upwards from there.

It was very steep, but the grass and shrubs gave her footholds and handholds as she edged seaward towards the cliffs, her legs and arms getting scraped and scratched.

Now she saw Dingo, crouching on a ledge just a little way under the overhanging piece of cliff. She didn't know whether he was hurt or suffering from dizziness. Perhaps he had looked down, realised how precarious his position was and had taken fright.

At first she could not see how he had got on to the ledge and then decided he must have jumped from the nearest rock. In which case he should be able to jump back. She edged to it as near as she dared, pointing to it. 'Come on, old boy, jump, then on to this one nearer me and you're home. At least near enough for me to grab your collar and haul you up. Come on, pet.'

The puppy gave an answering yelp and a feeble wag of his tail, but remained where he was. Lesley felt sure he wasn't hurt and she said sharply, 'Dingo, jump!'

She went on talking and whistling. Dingo just stared with those adoring brown eyes. 'You do something, chum,' he seemed to be saying. 'You've always got me out of scrapes before.'

Lesley moved away with the idea of going back to the farm to ask for help, but he howled so heartbreakingly that she had to turn back to the place where he could see her. He had stood up, but as soon as he caught sight of her he settled whimperingly on the ledge again.

As she lay uncomfortably on the steep edge of the combe the vee of its entrance to the sea was suffused with crimson as though caught in a finely styled glass window. Then it faded finally to the dull grey of the oncoming night.

She could scarcely see Dingo now, but very soon the moon would be up and then she would try again to persuade him to jump. Occasionally she spoke to him to reassure him she was still there. She didn't know what they would be thinking of her absence at Trevendone Manor—perhaps she wouldn't even be missed. She didn't think she could have dozed, but suddenly she heard Blake Defontaine's voice.

'Lesley, are you there? Answer me!' To imagine that there was anything like desperation in his voice was rank foolishness. She was dreaming, and you could put all sorts of wishful thinking into dreams. If by chance someone had traced her here, it wouldn't be the slave-master pacing up and down on a cliff, a note of desperation in his voice.

But she wasn't dreaming and she *had* come himself. For that was his voice again: 'Lesley, for God's sake, answer me!'

Dingo had perhaps been asleep too on his precarious perch. But now he too was alert and had recognised the voice. He began to yelp excitedly.

'Dingo,' Blake shouted, 'where is she? Find her, old fellow. Find her!'

And then to Lesley's petrified astonishment there was a rattle of stones, a swift leap and the dog was bounding at her as she lay precariously on the slope, wedged between a bush and a big rock.

'Dingo, you wicked, wicked fraud!' she gasped, and burst into tears.

Dingo yapped excitedly at his own cleverness and then went pounding up the side of the combe. Lesley managed to stagger to her feet, feeling cold and cramped. Tears were pouring down her cheeks and she wasn't sure whether she was laughing or crying.

She called out, 'I'm here a little way down the combe. Will you shine your torch? Unlike Dingo, I can't see in the dark.' The moon hadn't risen yet.

'Lesley!' There was something odd about his voice. 'You're hurt. Stay where you are. I'll come down and carry you up.'

'No, I'm not hurt, and now I'm beginning to see better. I can manage.' Everything in the world suddenly seemed all right, gay and bright and glistening though the hunter's moon was still behind the hill.

She began to pull herself up the slope, then a pencil of light caught her. A moment later, strong hands clutched hers and dragged her over the edge.

'You're not hurt?' he demanded, putting his hands possessively on her shoulders and bringing them down her arms as if he was testing whether anything was broken.

'No, I . . . I'm all right,' Lesley began, feeling shy and yet elated by that possessive touch. And then all at once her flesh crawled and all the gaiety and brightness ebbed away, leaving only a cold flood of despair.

For Sorrel's voice demanded raspingly, 'Then why this vigil on the cliffs? You aren't hurt, the dog isn't hurt, so what does it add up to? Have you taken to bird-watching, or is it just another dramatic episode from down under?'

Dominic was there too. He gave Lesley a quick hug. 'Glad you're all right, little Yseult. We were worried.'

Lesley swallowed. She had thought this afternoon alone would enable her to recapture her composure. But the sight of one man and the sound of his voice had left her in the same abject state, and as usual in her misery she said the wrong thing.

'There's quite a search party out. Why the panic?'

Sorrel could be sarcastic and there was no reply; but mockery from *her*, and here he was gripping her arm so fiercely that it hurt and saying gratingly, 'Lesley, stop acting the fool. Somebody at the farm who knew you lived at Trevendone phoned to say your Mini had been parked there for hours. What happened?'

Again she forced herself to flippancy. Nobody must guess at this awful pain in her throat that was threatening to choke her. 'Dingo, the silly old thing, got stuck on a ledge on the cliffs and I couldn't persuade him to jump. I couldn't leave him, so . . .' Her voice almost broke there.

'A likely story,' Sorrel's voice rasped. 'The yellow pest is here, not on a cliff ledge, and you'd better get hold of him or Boris will nip his throat out.'

'What a pity you brought him if you were really looking for Dingo and me,' Lesley flashed back. 'Dingo hates the sight of him.'

Again it was an unfortunate remark. Blake said grimly, 'Sorrel brought Boris along because he might have been able to find you if you hadn't been able to speak.' Once again, Lesley's flesh crawled in abject misery.

They found it hard to understand that according to her Dingo had been trapped and yet he had come bounding up the moment Blake had called his name. How could she explain that they were both in the same boat, she and Dingo? The slave-master called, and they were there . . . to heel.

The thought made her start to giggle uncontrollably and a moment later there were tears. 'Hysteria now,' said Sorrel in disgust. 'Let's get back to the cars.'

'Lesley.' This was Blake's voice again with that odd note in it. 'It doesn't matter now. You're both safe. Come along, put my coat round you. It isn't exactly cold, but you're shivering.' As he spoke he shrugged out of his thin tweed coat and pressed it around her shoulders.

She tried to protest, but he kept it around her by the pressure of one arm. 'Get going, Dominic,' he said curtly. 'Take Sorrel and Boris ahead. Lesley, where's the lead for this ridiculous hound of yours?'

'It's in my pocket,' she said, getting it out. Her voice was faint and the giggles and the tears had gone. She was cold and hungry and never before had she felt quite so defeated as she did now.

He took it and called to Dingo, who immediately stopped his snapping and snarling at Boris and came to heel. Still with an arm round Lesley, Blake said again, 'Sorrel, go ahead. Do you mind?'

Sorrel obviously did mind. She shook off Dominic's arm, but then as lights appeared near the lych gate of the church, she said pettishly, 'It looks as if half the village has turned out. Well, it will be something else to tell your cobbers when you arrive in the Outback, Lesley Arden!'

'Australian jargon always sounds so elegant on Limey lips,' returned Lesley with a venom worthy of Rita, and immediately felt ashamed. Had Blake noticed the name Arden? Well, he would have to know either tonight or tomorrow.

'I'm sorry you all bothered to come rushing out here,' she said now to Blake as they walked across the meadow. 'I'd have managed.'

'It looks like it,' he jeered. 'Your precious pet stayed put till I came along. Then he jumped.'

'His Master's Voice,' quoted Lesley ironically. 'I suggest you take him off our hands at the end of this week when we leave Trevendone.'

'I might do just that,' he drawled. 'With a name like his he may feel that he's going home. Not exactly to the Outback, of course. Did you know I'd accepted a chair at Melbourne University?'

'Melbourne!' Lesley's voice was almost a soundless whisper. 'I knew you were taking a university appointment, but not in Melbourne.'

'Any objections?' Lesley's heart had almost stopped beating. It couldn't be true. Sorrel and he . . . in Melbourne! It was more than she could bear. She held her head down and let the tears fall silently, not daring to search for her handkerchief, while his arm was closely around her, holding his coat in place, about her shoulders.

Now they were through the lych-gate and the moon was coming up, big as last night. Last night! Lesley gave a little gasp, pulled away from Blake's hold and ran to the Mini, fumbling in her pocket for her keys. If only she could get away, right away, without saying anything more to any of them.

They had evidently all come out here in Blake's big green Leopardia which was standing next to her tiny car. Sorrel had already pushed Boris into the back seat. 'You'd better drive back with Lesley, Dominic,' she ordered. 'Blake, I promised the Radleys we'd call in there for drinks tonight. Come along, darling.'

'Sorrel!' It was just the one word, but on a note that Lesley and perhaps the others had never heard before. It came from Dominic. 'Sorrel, don't you think this is a good time to tell Blake what we decided last night—that we're going to be married—that we got engaged last night?'

'Dominic, you've been drinking.' Sorrel's voice was lightly contemptuous, but there was an undercurrent of alarm in it. If she had intended saying any more, Blake didn't give her the chance.

'That's wonderful—the news I've been waiting for for a long time,' he said heartily. 'My congratulations to you both. Well, that seems to settle it. Dominic, you take my car and I'll follow on with Lesley in the Mini.'

Even in the half-light Lesley could see the angry indecision on the Cornish girl's face. 'I want to get Boris home, so we'll do as you suggest. You know, by the way, that you'll be bringing back a lying little impostor, don't you, Blake? Her name is Arden and she's no relation to the twins.'

'So I've always guessed,' Blake said gently. 'Now, Dominic, go easy on my car.'

'I'll drive,' snapped Sorrel. 'He's drunk, or he wouldn't have said that crazy thing about our engagement.'

'I don't mind which of you drives as long as you don't put her in dock for a week. I'm going to need her a lot.'

He needn't have been so offensive to either of them, thought Lesley, though both were irresponsible behind the wheel of a car. He was unbearably irritated, she supposed, at the thought of letting anyone else drive his precious car. Some men were like that. Not even the woman they loved was as important to them as their cars.

Lesley found her breath. 'Suppose all three of you go in

Blake's car and I come back in my own with Dingo. That's the sensible solution.'

'Indeed it isn't,' Blake drawled. 'You're not fit to drive. You're trembling like a leaf. Your nerves must be all shot to pieces.'

Not my nerves, thought Lesley miserably. Just my heart. Actually she couldn't keep her hands still and in desperation she pushed them behind her. Oh, God, she thought, I can't stand much more of this. I shall break down in a minute and make a complete fool of myself in front of them all. If only they'd all go and leave me here!

Not that she'd dare to stay here, not for very long. In front of her was the sinister outline of the old church and below it the haunted rectory. She couldn't see the gravestones or the prow of a ship that had been wrecked many years ago, but she knew they were there, ghostly and terrifying. Behind her, just as frightening, was the darker outline of the old farm, once a monastery. But she'd say nothing, just give herself time to get over these silly jitters and then drive herself back if she killed herself in the attempt.

But she reckoned without Blake. He opened the passenger door of the Mini, pushed Dingo into the back, and snapped at Lesley, 'Get in.' Then in a leisurely manner he got into the driving seat beside her and waited.

Sorrel took the hint. She flung herself into the Leopardia, hardly waiting for Dominic to do the same, pressed the ignition switch and sent the engine roaring into life. Then she was away, the loose pebbles flying as she drove over the roughest part of the path.

Blake didn't even wince. He sat impassively still till she was out of sight and then started up the Mini. Lesley, who was still shaking, managed to stammer, 'I'm sorry about your car.'

'And so you should be,' he said grimly. 'Leading me this dance. I came back from London with everything settled as regards Trevendone driving hell for leather, and found you'd disappeared and nobody had a clue where you were.'

That silenced her for a while as she battled with her misery. The silver ribbon of the moonlit road spun ahead of them and she watched it until she felt able to force herself into speech again, quavery, yet oddly passionate. 'I wasn't putting on an act trying to dramatise myself by staying out there. Dingo *was* on that ledge. I whistled and called him, but he wouldn't come. Directly I moved away to get help he whined so pitifully I hadn't the heart to leave him.'

'Of course you hadn't,' said Blake unkindly. 'He's got you for a sucker, Lesley, just as the twins have.'

Lesley gritted her teeth. How he loved to bait her, and there was nothing she could do about it. She just rose to it every time, idiot that she was.

They weren't going in the direction of Trevendone. She had noticed that already. Now he turned into a high-banked lane, stopping where a gate led on to the downs. He turned towards her. 'And now may one know your plans for the future? The twins have theirs settled, but what about the girl who came from over the sea with her head full of romantic ideas of Tristan and Yseult, a summer sea of turquoise and emerald and those knightly fellows of Camelot? Reality has been very difficult, hasn't it—a cruel coast and storm-lashed waters and instead of chivalry the hard, hard grind of slavery. How do you feel about it all now, Lesley?'

'I shall always love it—it's like a first love, romantic and starry and unreal,' she flashed back. 'Nothing can spoil *that* for me.'

'And so . . . ?' he asked smoothly.

She swallowed. 'I'm not a Trevendone. I never had any place here.'

'But you made yourself a place here. Gave yourself the job of fighting the slave-master. How much longer is that going on, Lesley?'

'Oh, don't say that,' she begged. 'I'm so ashamed that that name was ever given. As soon as I began to work at Trevendone, I realised the burden you were carrying . . . the way you were neglecting your own work, your own career, just to put Trevendone on its feet.'

'Well, that job's finished,' he admitted with a smothered laugh. 'As to your not being a Trevendone, I knew that almost from the beginning. They're among the world's takers, Lesley—you are a giver. Once I asked you to give yourself to me, and your lips said "yes". How much longer are you going to go on fighting what you know is in your own heart?'

'I . . . I . . . don't understand.' The dull ache of empti-